A Secret Identity

**Center Point
Large Print**

*Also by Gayle Roper and available from
Center Point Large Print:*

A Stranger's Wish

A Secret Identity

GAYLE ROPER

CENTER POINT LARGE PRINT
THORNDIKE, MAINE

This Center Point Large Print edition is
published in the year 2010 by arrangement with
Harvest House Publishers.

The text of this Large Print edition is unabridged.
In other aspects, this book may vary
from the original edition.
Printed in the United States of America.
Set in 16-point Times New Roman type.

ISBN: 978-1-60285-876-3

Library of Congress Cataloging-in-Publication Data

Roper, Gayle G.
  [Document]
A secret identity / Gayle Roper.
    p. cm.
  ISBN 978-1-60285-876-3 (library binding : alk. paper)
1. Amish—Fiction. 2. Adopted children—Fiction.
    3. Manic-depressive persons—Fiction. 4. Pennsylvania—Fiction.
    5. Large type books. I. Title.
PS3568.O68D63 2010b
813′.54—dc22

2010019981

With affection for
Bob and Linda
Rick and Eileen
Barb and Doug
Glenn and Pam
and all the other parents
involved with us in
the adventure of adoption.

God sets the lonely in families . . .
PSALM 68:6

Chapter 1

When I look back on the three-month period that effectively and thoroughly changed the course of my life, I sometimes wonder which event had the greatest impact. Was it the finding of Pop's papers? Perhaps it was the terrible and vengeful things that happened as a result of following to its logical conclusion what I found in those papers? Or was it meeting Todd?

Maybe the best answer is all of the above, though it could be argued that without Pop's papers, without "The Document," nothing of import would have happened.

I sat on my bed in the Horse and Buggy Motel in Bird-in-Hand, Pennsylvania, and stared out the dirty picture window at the real horse and buggy standing on the other side of the street. A woman wearing a white head covering and a light-blue dress that reached halfway to her ankles stood by the chestnut horse, stroking its neck as she talked to some tourists clustered around her. I could tell they were tourists by their shorts and T-shirts and hair. Even someone as ignorant of the subtleties of Lancaster County life as I was knew the purple-and-red hair of one of the grumpy-looking teenage girls wasn't Amish.

My long-haired calico cat, Rainbow, sat beside me as straight as any well-trained poodle waiting for a treat, watching the scene out the window intently. Usually she had all the spine of a noodle, collapsing in a boneless pile wherever she was. Now she blinked thoughtfully as the tourists climbed into the buggy and the woman followed. In a moment the buggy rolled onto Route 340, the horse's front legs prancing high like a trotter pulling a sulky around a racetrack.

Was the driver an Amish lady? Did Amish ladies give buggy rides to tourists? Somehow I doubted it since even I knew that as a people the Amish basically kept to themselves. As I watched the buggy disappear, I thought again about how little I knew about this most interesting and obvious subculture in Pennsylvania.

I reached out and stroked Rainbow on the white spot under her chin. "I guess I need to do some quick research and then some sightseeing if I'm going to be here for a while."

Rainbow responded by yawning, marching across the bed, and curling up on the pillow. She had found today's trip from our home in Silver Spring, Maryland, to be very tiring and unnerving in the extreme, and she'd spent the entire two-and-a-half-hour trip yelling for help. That's exactly what her plaintive cries sounded like: "Elp! Elp!" in high soprano.

I left Rainbow to her dreams and walked to the

motel office. Against one wall was a large rack of tourist brochures. I took one of everything. Several books on Amish life were displayed in a carousel, and I bought four. Hopefully the writers knew what they were talking about, and I'd get legitimate information, not touristy swill.

Back in the room I studied the brochures and found I could do everything from visiting an amusement park to enjoying outlet shopping, from touring a genuine Amish farm to eating seven sweets and seven sours, whatever they were. I could see a play at a Christian theater called Sight and Sound or hear a lecture at a reconstruction of the tabernacle of the Old Testament at the Mennonite Visitors Center. How in the world could I determine what was genuine and what was money-making fluff?

I gave the books I'd bought a more thorough once over and was encouraged by the academic letters after the authors' names. I settled beside Rainbow and read for about an hour, and then I felt too antsy to stay in the room any longer. I left the brochures and books scattered across the bed and took myself for a blessedly silent drive.

I followed twisting, two-lane macadam roads wherever they led me, figuring I could always find my way back to 340 if I got lost. I rolled down the car windows and enjoyed the sweet, heady scent of wild honeysuckle, the clean aroma of newly mown grass, and the distinctive smell of a country staple: cow manure. I eyed the fields of alfalfa, tomatoes, and corn glowing golden in the slanting light of the evening sun. I found myself filled with expectancy and a warm sense of purpose, a somewhat surprising feeling considering the emotional jolt I'd recently received and the changes it had forced on me.

Maybe my inner glow was because I had chosen to make at least some of the changes myself instead of someone imposing them on me. I had resolved to come and search all on my own. Me, Miss Don't-Rock-My-Boat. I'd come in spite of advice to the contrary from everyone, including the almost-family family lawyer and my brother, Ward. I squinted into the setting sun and felt almost happy for the first time in a long time.

I rounded a curve and was forced to slow suddenly and dramatically for a closed buggy, gray and fragile-looking, moving slowly ahead of me. As I inched along in its wake, I stared at the large, red reflective triangle on its lower back and the rectangular red reflectors placed at intervals up the sides and across the top of—what do you call the back end of a buggy? It wasn't a trunk like on a car or a hatch like on a van. It was more like a little wall, but that word seemed too substantial for the gray surface in front of me. Small battery-driven taillights blinked at me but gave no answer.

At the rate we were moving, I'd be back at the Horse and Buggy tomorrow morning. Did I dare take a risk and pass in spite of the solid yellow line and long, slow curve? Or did I have to trail along at one horsepower until the buggy turned into a farm lane somewhere?

As I worried over this quandary with more energy than it was worth, a car zipped up behind me, slowed momentarily, and then sped around both me and the buggy. Question answered. I hit the gas and followed. After all, he had a Pennsylvania license. He must know what he was doing.

I pulled back in my lane and ambled on, each bend in the road opening another vista of patchwork fields, farmhouses, barns, and silos. The overwhelming color was green: emerald, celadon, olive, lime, forest. Fields of burgeoning crops; copses of maples, beeches, and pines; lawns and gardens; and vines. I sighed. I'd never realized before how soothing green was.

I rounded another curve and once again hit the brakes, jarred out of my near stupor by the delightful sight before me. One thing for sure, we never saw anything like this in the congestion and traffic of Silver Spring.

A small Amish girl of eight or ten stood in the middle of the road, her small face screwed-up in concentration as she drove an ungainly herd of Holsteins across the road from the pasture to the barn. She waved a stick to encourage the beasts, but they seemed unaware of the goad or the child as they plodded slowly across the macadam to the safety and release of the barn and its milking machines.

The girl, her hair pulled back in a bun at the base of her neck like a little adult, ignored me and the two cars waiting from the opposite direction. One of the cows stepped out of line and started wandering toward me. The little girl calmly and authoritatively whapped her on the flank. The cow immediately fell back into place.

I looked left and saw for the first time the boy in black breeches and white shirt, his straw hat pushed back on his head, bare feet flying. He was shooing the cows along from behind by waving his arms and shouting at them. As the last milk cow passed out of the pasture and through the gate, he pulled it closed. Climbing the bottom rung, he carefully fastened a rope loop around the top rail of the gate and the adjoining fence. He jumped to the ground, raced into the road after his sister and herd, and turned to grin at me. I grinned back and waggled my fingers. He ducked his head shyly, ran through the gate into the farmyard, and pushed it shut behind him.

That night I dreamed of towheads in straw hats, buggies pulled by graceful horses, and barefoot little girls wielding big sticks. It was the soundest sleep I'd had since I'd found Pop's papers.

I arrived at the office of Todd Reasoner, Esq., at 2:55 the next afternoon. I walked to the receptionist's desk, noted her nameplate, and extended my hand.

"Hello, Mrs. Smiley. I'm Cara Bentley."

I admit I'd gotten used to a certain response to my name. Those who knew Bentley Marts hopped to attention as if I had something to do with the stores' success, and readers of romance novels frequently recognized my name too. Mrs. Smiley, however, turned her dour face toward me, and I felt as though I were not only tardy, which I wasn't, but had brought in a significant helping of manure on my shoe.

"How do you do," she said frostily, letting my hand hang suspended in space while her fingers remained on her computer keyboard. "Mr. Reasoner will be with you shortly. Please have a seat." She tipped her head toward a pair of paisley-upholstered chairs against the far wall.

I took a seat, feeling I should sit at attention and wondering whether everyone who waited under the gimlet eye of Mrs. Smiley reacted the same way. To show she didn't intimidate me— or at least to convince myself she didn't—I boldly crossed one beige linen-clad knee over the other and straightened my beige silk shell.

15

Still, I don't think my shoulders had been thrown back so rigidly since inspection at Camp Sankanac when I was a kid.

Maybe she disapproved of slacks, but certainly mine were loose enough to be modest, and besides everyone wore slacks. Except the Amish. And the Mennonites. I'd seen more dresses in my two days in Bird-in-Hand than I'd seen in years. Then again, maybe Mrs. Smiley's aversion was to beige. Or to me. Or to everyone.

Ignoring me, she bent over her work, her sensible blue dress buttoned to the neck, unrelieved by jewelry or scarf. I could see her low-heeled blue pumps under the desk were pressed neatly side-by-side. Her gray hair was carefully permed and sprayed. Wire-rimmed glasses hung around her neck on a chain. She suddenly grabbed them and pushed them onto her nose. She sniffed, set a folder of papers on her right, and began typing at terrifying speed.

Surprisingly, her fingers were beautifully manicured with hot pink nails. On the third pink fingernail of each hand were little white flowers with jeweled centers that sparkled as her hands danced over the keys, creating a beauty completely at odds with the sterility of the rest of her.

Like the writer I was, I began creating a persona for Mrs. Smiley that explained her hauteur and her nails. Somehow I knew she wouldn't like me giving her a husband who had left her for a younger woman who wore hot-pink, low-necked tops and tight jeans instead of merely pink nails. Nor would she like my imagined pudgy professor who pursued her now, trying without success to find the hot pink part of her that allowed the nails.

She carefully ignored me for an eternity of five minutes, during which I had remade her by dying her hair a soft brown, having her wear lots of corals and roses, and transforming her into a lovely heroine overcoming a lifetime of sorrows and pain. Finally Mrs. Smiley rose, looked suspiciously at me, and beckoned. "Mr. Reasoner will see you now."

I unfolded my legs and followed her to a door, where she paused and knocked softly. When she pushed open the door, she stepped aside for me. "Miss Cara Bentley," she said for all the world as though she were announcing the queen. I tried to look regal.

Todd Reasoner rose, a smile of professional welcome on his handsome face. Maybe it was the last five minutes in Mrs. Smiley's presence or the years of talking to little, brittle Mr. Havens, our family attorney, but I perked up at the sight of my new lawyer.

He glanced quickly at Mrs. Smiley, nodded absently, and said, "Thank you." Her cheeks turned almost as pink as her nails as she bobbed

17

her head in his direction. I watched in fascination.

She's smitten, I thought. Who cares that he's twenty or thirty years her junior. She thinks he's wonderful. The son she never had? Or the man she'd always dreamed of? No wonder my pudgy professor didn't appeal to her.

I looked at Todd Reasoner again and understood why she was so taken with him. It might have been the curly brown hair or the deep-brown eyes or the neatly tailored tan suit over a white shirt and tan tie with incredibly narrow, brown, diagonal stripes. Or it might have been the shoulders, broad enough for one of my heroines to swoon against quite effectively or the jaw so strongly hewn that I could cut my finger on it, were I ever fortunate enough to touch it.

He came from behind his desk as Mrs. Smiley withdrew and indicated a seat in a padded leather chair. "Miss Bentley," he said politely as I took the proffered seat. He then retreated behind his desk to his own padded leather chair.

As he took his seat, I glanced around the room. On the wall were the obligatory diplomas, matted and framed, a BA from Ursinus College, and a JD from Dickinson Law School. I saw he was a member of the Pennsylvania Bar, the frame of this document a magnificent cherry with several gold stripes worked into the wood lest anyone miss its import.

A pair of what appeared to be original watercolors hung on the wall to my right, lovely renditions of Lancaster County without any of the cloying cuteness aimed at the tourist trade. Beneath the paintings were a sofa and two chairs. A beautiful quilt, a kaleidoscope of animals tumbling from an ark marooned on Mount Ararat, hung on the wall behind Mr. Reasoner. A fern, a philodendron, and a hearty croton sat on a credenza under a window.

"How may I help you, Miss Bentley?" Todd Reasoner asked.

I turned my attention to him. Such a hardship. "I'm beginning an adoption search, Mr. Reasoner, and I need clarification on Pennsylvania laws concerning the accessibility of records."

He nodded. "For yourself, I assume?"

"Well, sort of. I'm seeking the information for my curiosity, but the person whose records I'm seeking is my grandfather."

He studied me a moment. "Are you seeking this information for him without his permission? Or can he no longer search himself?"

I felt the weight of missing Pop settle on my chest like a heavy stone, the pressure debilitating. I forced a breath. "He died recently."

The lawyer dipped his head. "I'm sorry for your loss."

"Thank you." I studied my knees for a moment. "He was ninety-three when he died, and I've learned since his death that he was adopted. That we aren't 'blood' Bentleys. That there's a history we know nothing about."

I reached into my purse and pulled out an envelope. I drew from it the Certificate of Adoption and passed it across the desk. I read from memory as Todd read for the first time.

Commonwealth of Pennsylvania

In the Court of Common Pleas, No. 2, of Lancaster County in re: Adoption of Lehman Biemsderfer, June 1919. Be it remembered that I, Herman F. Walton, Prothonotary of the Courts of Common Pleas, No. 2, of Lancaster County, do hereby certify, that the following is the true and correct copy of the decree:

entered by the said court in the above case, to wit:

Now, the 20th day of August A.D. 1919 the court, upon consideration of the foregoing petition, being satisfied that the welfare of the said Lehman Biemsderfer will be promoted by the adoption prayed for in said petition, do upon motion of A.R. Furst, Esq., for petitioners, grant the prayer of said petition, and do order and decree that the said Lehman Biemsderfer shall assume the name of the adopting parents, and be hereafter known and called by the name "John Seward Bentley, Jr." and shall henceforth have all the rights of a child and heir of the said John Seward Bentley and Charlotte Brooks Bentley, equal with any other children they may have, and shall be subject to the duties of such children in accordance with the provisions of the Act of Assembly in such cases made and provided.

In testimony whereof, I have hereto set my hand and affixed the seal of the Court, this 20th day of August in the year of our Lord one thousand nine hundred and nineteen.

The red, raised seal of the Court of Common Pleas of Lancaster County decorated the lower lefthand corner of the paper while the signature of Herman F. Walton, the prothonotary, filled the right.

Todd looked up when he had finished, and I handed him the letter that always made me want to weep.

Chapter 2

I had gotten Todd Reasoner's name from Mr. Havens, our family's business lawyer.

"So you plan to do an adoption search?" Mr. Havens was careful to sound dispassionate. He was a spare little man who somehow commanded great attention and respect. I think it had something to do with the way he carried himself, exactly like the ex-Marine he was, and the absolute authority with which he always spoke. It was like a real-life equivalence of the old ad, "When Dean Havens speaks, everyone listens."

I nodded. "I want to find out what my heritage is—what our heritage is."

"Do you have a medical reason for seeking this information?" He seemed genuinely concerned. "I never heard your grandfather mention any genetic problems, but that doesn't mean there wasn't or isn't one."

I shook my head. "No medical problems that I know of. I just want to know who we are if we aren't Bentleys."

"Cara, my dear, I think a search going back three generations is most likely doomed to failure."

He made his observation gently, but its effect was to stiffen my backbone. When we quiet, go-with-the-flow people actually make a decision, we get very stubborn about it.

I smiled with a sweetness I didn't feel. "I just know I feel compelled to try."

He nodded. "I wish you well. You understand that you'll need a member of the Pennsylvania bar to assist you since state laws differ on adoption and the accessibility of pertinent information and records."

I blinked. Even though I knew the adoption happened in Lancaster County, I hadn't considered the very real need to find a Lancaster area lawyer, but I quickly realized that Mr. Havens was correct. I thought of the Yellow Pages and all those lawyers smiling charmingly out of the full-page ads. The thought of picking one to be my attorney was daunting. "Can you recommend someone in the Lancaster area?"

He spun his chair and stared out his window at the ancient willow tree with its feathery branches touching the ground. I sat and waited while he went through his mental Rolodex. After a minute he turned back to his desk, grabbed the phone, and pushed a couple of buttons.

"Martin, come in here a minute, please." He hung up immediately, the prerogative of the senior partner who assumed—and received—unquestioned compliance.

Immediately there was a knock on the door, and a young man poked his head in. "Yes, Mr. Havens?"

"Come in, Martin."

Martin, wearing bright red suspenders to hold up his navy slacks, smoothed his red-and-blue rep tie as he walked to Mr. Havens' desk.

"Martin, this is Cara Bentley. Cara is in need of legal advice in Lancaster County, Pennsylvania. You graduated from Dickinson Law School . . .

"That's in Carlisle, Pennsylvania, my dear," he said in an aside to me.

He turned back to Martin. "You must know some lawyers who have begun practicing in the Lancaster area."

Martin nodded. "I can think of three who graduated with me who practice either in Lancaster City or close by. Paul Adamson is associated with a large firm in the city. Allison Fleet is the junior partner in a three-partner practice in Manheim, just north of Lancaster, and Todd Reasoner is a sole practitioner in Bird-in-Hand, a small town just east of Lancaster."

"Which one do you recommend most?" Mr. Havens asked.

"What kind of work is needed?"

"Legal advice on an adoption search," I said.

"Paul's firm is located right near the court-house and has the prominence to help someone high profile like you, Miss Bentley."

Martin didn't actually bow as he spoke, but that suggestion of special care because of Bentley Marts and the family money was there too strongly for my taste.

I shook my head. "I don't want anyone to know I have any connection to the family's business. I know it's improbable that someone would try to claim me and my brother as relatives because of our money, but it's possible. I'm making this trip as Cara Bentley, writer. Bentley is a common enough name that it shouldn't be a problem. I don't want flash and prestige in my lawyer. I want competency."

Martin nodded as if he understood, but I didn't think he did.

"Then I recommend Todd Reasoner. He's more than able, has excellent credentials, sailed through the bar exams when the rest of us were sweating bullets, and is conscientious to a fault. He's very religious, but I mean that in the good sense that it makes him want to do everything right."

I nodded. "He sounds like the man for me."

As soon as I got home, I called to make an appointment, hoping I could see him immediately.

"Mr. Reasoner can see you on Friday at three P.M.," I was told.

"Not sooner?" I asked. I was used to Mr. Havens seeing any of us whenever we asked. Not that I'd ever asked much, but I knew Pop and my brother

Ward saw him at their convenience. Of course, Mr. Havens and his considerable staff were on retainer for Bentley Marts and better hop to it when any of us called. Todd Reasoner, Esq., had no reason to revamp his schedule for Cara Bentley, writer.

Now I sat in Todd's office and handed him my second document. Again I read along mentally.

It was a personal letter dated August 1919 to my great-grandmother from Mrs. C.A. Yule, written on the stationary of The Children's Home Society of Lancaster: For the Relief of the Poor and the Care of Destitute Children.

Dear Mrs. Bentley,

I am enclosing herewith the certified copy of the decree of adoption, which finishes up the case.

When visiting with the mother of your dear little boy, she asked me as a last request if you would give me a picture of Lehman for her. She felt that having it would do much to make her live her life as she should. She is doing so well. We are proud of the effort she is making. I shall appreciate it very much if you could send a picture very soon.

I'm glad you were able to get away for a little while. I'm sure John Seward had a lovely time playing in the sand at the shore.

I sincerely hope the dear baby will grow up into the kind of man you will have reason to be proud of. You are doing a very noble thing indeed in taking a baby to raise as you would one of your own. There is no telling what this will mean to his future.

There was also a receipt signed by (Mrs.) C.A. Yule.

Received from Mrs. Bentley, six and 00. dollars: cost of adoption papers.

It broke my heart to think that Pop, who had made millions with his quick mind and canny business sense, cost six dollars.

Todd looked up when he finished reading.

"I'm hoping these documents will help me gain access to the original documents so I can find the names of Pop's birth parents," I said.

He said nothing.

"Can you help me?" I prompted.

Todd shook his head. "Pennsylvania guards its adoption records very carefully. In fact, they are literally locked in a safe for protection. It would be very difficult for you to gain access to your own adoption records without written permission from the birth parents. To gain access to someone else's is virtually impossible."

I frowned. "There must be a way. I see stories on TV all the time about parents and kids finding each other."

He shrugged. "I know there are many adoption advocacy groups that help break the seal of adoption, convinced that knowing is preferable to not knowing."

"Maybe it is," I said, thinking of the yearning in my heart to know something that was three generations removed.

"Maybe. I don't know. I'm not an expert in adoption or adoption law. I haven't thought much about it to be frank. That being the case, I'll have to research this issue before I can give you my final thoughts and recommendations."

"And how long will that take?"

I must have sounded more confrontive than I'd meant to because he sat up straighter and said in a cool voice, "I can have some information for you by mid-week."

I looked at him thoughtfully. Mr. Havens would have had it for me by tonight or tomorrow at the latest—even if tomorrow was Saturday. He'd have underlings like Martin poring through books looking for precedents and loopholes and options. I was missing those perks of power more with each passing minute.

"May I ask why you're conducting this search?" Todd asked. "For medical reasons?"

"Not really," I said. "I think that if there were to be any medical problems, they'd have surfaced in the past ninety-two years, don't you? I just want to know where we come from."

"Three generations is pretty far back to trace."

"My grandparents raised my brother and me," I said. "So three generations doesn't feel that far removed to me."

He nodded, his hands folded on his desk as if he was about to pray. "I still feel compelled to inform you that you may be wasting a lot of time and money on this project, Miss Bentley."

"Mr. Reasoner," I began. My Bentley assertiveness doesn't show often, but when it did, Pop always said everyone should duck, and duck fast. "I'm not asking for your approval of my project. I am merely seeking your legal expertise." I gave him my imitation of Mrs. Smiley's gimlet eye. "Your friend Martin Somebody from the offices of Havens, Smith, and Associates recommended you."

Todd looked surprised. "Martin Stewart?"

I shrugged. "He seemed to feel you were more than competent." I unfortunately made that fact sound somewhat questionable.

He clenched his fine jaw at my lack of conviction but only nodded. "*Res ipsa loquitor,*" he said.

"Yes." I rose. There was no way I was going to ask what in the world he'd just said. With my nose deplorably high in the air I asked, "Shall I make an appointment with Mrs. Smiley or will you call when you are finally prepared?" I emphasized finally just a little bit.

Suddenly one corner of his mouth twitched while he leveled his deep-brown eyes at me. "May I inquire as to your profession, Miss Bentley?"

Nonplussed by the quick change of subject, I replied, "I'm a writer."

"Ah," he said, nodding. "Of course. A word-smith." He raised an eyebrow. "And you use them well."

"*Res ipsa loquitor,*" I said, hoping I wasn't saying that the judge would be back in a minute.

Chapter 3

Saturday morning I sat on my bed at the Horse and Buggy, pillows plumped against the headboard behind me, Lancaster area phone book in my lap. I turned to the B's to look up Biemsderfer.

"Rainbow, I am very nervous." Understatement. "What if there's a bunch of them? What if there are none of them?" A wild thought struck me, and I gave a gurgled laugh. "At least if I'm a Biemsderfer, I won't have to change my monogram."

Unimpressed by the fact that any towels I had wearing B's could remain in use, Rainbow yawned and settled herself more comfortably on the pillow she'd claimed as hers.

I was undeterred by her lack of interest. "This whole situation is making me nuts. I hate surprises. I hate the unexpected."

She probably didn't react because she already knew this fact about me.

My brother, Ward, always told me in great disgust, "You've got no sense of adventure." Ward is six feet tall, handsome in a Christian Bale sort of way, and has enough energy to make me tired just hanging out with him.

"Surprises are what make things fun," he said.

"For you maybe. But I say, 'Remember Disney World.'"

Remember Disney World was my personal battle cry whenever I needed to remind my family that I was different.

Mom and Pop had planned a surprise vacation to that magical place the fall Ward was nine and I was seven. We kids didn't know we were going anywhere until we got up one morning and Pop drove us to the airport instead of school.

I couldn't handle the spontaneity of that move. I became cranky, moody, and an all-around pill, and we hadn't even checked our luggage yet.

"You didn't tell me," I cried to Mom that night as we sat on the bed in our beautiful room at the Grand Floridian. Pop and Ward had gone down to the lobby to listen to the pianist or, more likely, to get away from me. "You've got to tell me! I need to know ahead of time!"

That night as I cried myself to sleep, despairing that no one understood, I heard Pop tell Mom, "We will never surprise her again. Do you understand?"

In spite of his dictum, which, incidentally, neither of them kept, I'd found a surprise like I'd never known two weeks ago. A surprise that sent me reeling.

The day of the surprise, Pop had been dead only two months. He'd been an old man of ninety-two when he died. His spirit and mind remained keen to the end, even though he slowed down physically.

"I hate this," he'd growl when he could no longer lift a box loaded with books or bring in more than two pieces of firewood at a time. He went to the office every day for at least a few hours, just long enough to tell Ward how to run the show. Then Pop had a stroke that incapacitated him. He knew and we knew he'd never recover his speech or his motor skills. He knew and loved God, and I think he asked the Lord to take him. His death was a release and a relief to all three of us—Pop, Ward, and me. Mom had died three years earlier, just before their fifty-ninth anniversary.

I'd never left the home I grew up in, the home made vibrant by Pop's presence. I'd seen no reason to. I was happy there, loved there. Now Pop had left, and the emptiness in my heart and the house yawned before me like a great gray chasm. I knew I had to climb down into that pit of sorrow to be able to climb out the other side to normalcy, whatever that was to be without Pop.

I got through the first weeks after his death by finishing my latest book. I had a deadline looming and I wrote nonstop day and night. I schlepped around in sweats or my nightgown, ate junk food and home-delivered pizzas, and emerged only long enough to go to church on Sunday. My characters lived such full lives that most of the time I was able to ignore the emptiness in mine.

But eventually the book reached its conclusion, I sent it off to my publisher, and I came back from the post office to that empty brick Georgian. In the past, every time I finished a book, Pop and Mom, then just Pop, took me out to a fancy restaurant for a spare-no-expense dinner.

"To Cara, the great American novelist," Pop would always toast me, flashing his warm, magnetic smile. I knew he knew I wasn't that good, but he was acknowledging that I was succeeding in a field where many failed, even if he thought the field I was competing in was effete. I knew he never read my books, but I didn't take it personally. He never read anything but the Bible, the *Wall Street Journal*, and business magazines. It was the dinner and the toast that told me that even though he couldn't comprehend that I actually liked writing romances, he was proud of me.

As I entered that silent, still house after my trip to the post office, it hit me that there would be no dinner and no toast ever again. It was now just me and my microwave.

Pain unfurled in my chest, a black banner expanding, filling my lungs until I could barely breathe. The weight and mass of distress gripped my heart so tightly I felt I had to push on my chest to make certain it continued to beat, sort of self-administered CPR.

I don't know how long I lay on the sofa in the living room trying to survive the pain, but the bright, early June day had become dusky by the time Rainbow climbed on me, her four little feet like four nails being driven into my chest. She stood over my face, staring down at me in her slightly haughty, intimidating way.

"Don't let her push you around, Cara," Pop told me the first time Rainbow stared me down and got an extra serving of Fancy Feast. "She'll be a bully if you let her. Remember, you're bigger. You're the boss."

The problem was that no one had told Rainbow that bigger meant boss. We had to keep reminding her.

That evening I grabbed her and hugged her tightly. Her silky orange, black, and white fur soothed with its touch.

She struggled against my hug, broke free, and waited at a safe distance for me to get up and let her out. When I didn't, she climbed back up on me, and when she reached my face, she put her nose on mine.

I sighed, surrendered, and sat up. She jumped to the floor. She had been Pop's cat, sitting on his lap purring, lying on the back of his chair, one paw on his shoulder, sleeping beside him in the king-sized bed he and Mom had shared. She had only recently stopped her intense grieving for Pop, and I had become the focus of her attention. She didn't love many, but she had apparently decided to love me. I think I alleviated her grief somewhat just because I was present. I know she made me feel better.

I got up from my sofa and let Rainbow out into the backyard. She immediately ducked behind Mom's rose bushes and relieved herself. She was back at the door in less than a minute.

"Life would be easier for all of us if you'd use your litter box," I told her as she sat to clean her paws after her excursion into the dirt. As always, she ignored me. My consolation was that on the litter box issue at least, she'd also ignored Pop. The only time she deigned to use it was if we were gone longer than her kidneys could handle.

Pop was John Seward Bentley, Jr., my grandfather. He and Mom, my grandmother, had raised Ward (John Seward Bentley IV) and me from the time we were quite little. Our parents were killed on an icy road in one of those massive pileups you sometimes hear about in the news. That we called our grandparents Mom and Pop was Pop's little joke. After World War II, he had opened a small store that sold electrical appliances. Though the store had grown into Bentley Marts, a large, privately held chain of 45 stores in the Mid-Atlantic states, he always liked to joke that he and Mom owned a Mom-and-Pop store.

Ward was a lot like Pop. Driven. Type A. Both moved quickly, thought at lightning speed, and had five projects going at any given time. Both would have given the Apostle Peter a run for his choleric money.

"Cara," Pop and Ward would tell me, "you've got to get out of that novel and into real life!" Or away from that computer. Or that movie. Or that how-to-write book.

Sometimes I thought Mom, no slouch in the personality pool herself, almost understood that to me that novel, that movie, that manuscript I was working on—they *were* life. Characters fascinated me. Plotlines struck my imagination. The juxtaposition of purposes, ambitions, and loves filled my mind as I wondered how that character would react if he trusted God instead of himself or how that villain would change if eternal issues ever filled his thinking. Story was all.

So here I was, a thirty-year-old woman who wrote inspirational romances, had a comfortable income from them, shared a home with her grandparents, and lived mostly in her mind. I was happy with myself like that, but no one else seemed to be.

"Cara, baby," Pop would chide me in his booming voice, "you've got to live life large! You're a Bentley!"

I tried for years to follow his advice, but I finally accepted that I'm not the "live life large" type, Bentley or not. I'm more like gentle rain to my family's cyclones. But I enjoyed their whirlwind style because it kept life at 356 Harris Avenue vibrant and interesting, even if it occasionally made me cranky with surprises.

During Mom's illness as her strength ebbed and she neared death, it hurt me to see her once brilliant inner light dim, then flicker, then burn out.

"Cara," she would say as she lay wasting away on her pillows, "come sit by me." And she'd pat the side of her bed with her frail hand. I'd climb onto the great bed and hold her hand.

"Cara, you are beautiful." Her eyes held love and something that seemed like pity.

"Mom, please." It always embarrassed me when she said that because I looked in the mirror every day. I knew what I looked like.

"You are! You have glorious hair."

I had brown hair with a golden sheen to it, but it was just hair that I combed straight back from my forehead. I had little wisps that worked their way free around my face in spite of my best efforts to restrain them with extra heavy-duty hair spray. I dealt with the heavy mass by clasping it out of my way with a barrette at the nape of my neck or twining it into a quick braid.

"And your eyes!"

"Mom, they're just brown eyes like millions of other eyes."

"And your smile! If you'd just smile more, Cara, love. You've always been such a solemn little thing."

"I'm hardly little, Mom," I said, ignoring the smiling bit. I knew I'd never convince her that I was a closet optimist, but I was. I knew the sun was going to come up tomorrow, and I reveled in it. I just didn't want to go out and smile at it. I wanted to write about it. "I'm tall—five eight."

"And all glorious legs," she said.

"I can tell you haven't tried to buy jeans with legs this long."

"Cara, don't do that!"

"What?"

"Mock yourself like that. Just because your heroines all have auburn hair and emerald eyes or raven hair and violet eyes, you think you're plain. Well, you're not!"

"I love you, Mom." And I kissed her and she sighed.

"You need a man, Cara."

"Mom, how politically incorrect! I can manage alone. I'm a big girl now."

"I have never doubted your ability to cope, my dear. I just hate to see you so solitary."

"I'm not alone. I have you and Pop."

As she became desperately ill, she would grasp my hand and murmur, "Cara, love. Please."

She whispered those words to me when I bent to straighten her pillow or brush back her hair and when I gave her medicine or helped her to the commode. In fact, they were the last words she said to me before she died. I knew what she really meant: "Cara, for Pete's sake, get a life! You're a Bentley!"

I loved that she cared. I loved that she and Pop worried, that they despaired of me. It made me feel warm and toasty that though they didn't understand me one bit, they wanted me to be happy. But it didn't make me change my contented bystander life.

After Pop died, Ward took up Pop and Mom's mantle in more ways than the management of Bentley Marts. He was constantly after me.

"I don't care what you do or where you go, Cara. Just *do*! Go! You're a—"

"I know. I'm a Bentley." I put my hand on his shoulder and said as firmly as I could, "But I don't want to go anywhere, Ward, and I'm doing what I love."

"Sitting in one room all day writing?"

I nodded. "I meet the most interesting people that way."

He frowned at me, his choleric nature totally unable to comprehend a phlegmatic, introverted woman like me. But that didn't stop him from trying to make me see the light.

"God doesn't like us to be so introspective,"

he told me one day as he paced in my office. "That's why the Bible is full of 'one another' verses."

I blinked. "What?"

"You know—love one another, encourage one another, do good to one another."

I had to admit I had no answer for that comment, but I gave it my best try. "I regularly attend writers' conferences as well as Romance Writers of America and Christian Booksellers conventions," I said. "I deal with others all the time."

"Right," he said, unimpressed. "And when you go to these places, you hang around all day with other recluses just like you."

I thought of the wild and wonderful personalities of many of the writers and editors I knew. *Recluses* hardly fit the bill. I thought of the panels I sat on and the classes I taught and the fascinating conversations I had at these convocations. In reality I did quite well with people. After all, I'd lived all my life with Pop and Mom and Ward. I knew all about people skills, and I loved my times on the dais or in the spotlight. But I was always happy to come home and be alone again. In fact, I *needed* to come home and be alone.

But Ward never saw me do anything but write, never saw me as anything but alone. He naturally assumed I had serious limitations that were preventing me from enjoying his version of a happy life.

Ward and his wife, Marnie, a delightful, sparkly blonde, lived fifteen minutes away from me in Columbia, in a large and wonderful new house with windows and gables and a stone front and a huge yard for John Seward Bentley V to run around in—as soon as he was old enough to run.

"Cara," Marnie said when they dropped in one day to check on me, "don't stay alone in this huge old house!"

"But I like it here," I said for the hundredth time as I watched my brother begin his now routine tour of the place.

"Just checking," he mumbled as he slid through the doorway to the kitchen.

"It's not going to fall down," I said.

He made a soft grunt, obviously expecting just that now that there wasn't a man living here. As Marnie and I continued to talk, I listened to him go down to the basement to check the furnace. I heard him checking the locks on the back door. I heard him climb to the second and third stories, moving from room to room, methodically going over some mental checklist he'd created.

I felt a bit like Rainbow must when I hugged her too tightly.

Marnie laid her hand on my arm. "This place is too big for you, Cara. There's too much upkeep. We worry about you all alone here."

I smiled and said nothing.

"You need to buy a nice condo near us. Johnny will want Aunt Cara nearby."

I thought that Johnny couldn't care less, but I knew that Marnie, who had all the heart, vitality, and charm of a people person, was as concerned about me as my big brother. I just couldn't imagine why they'd even think I would want to leave the house that had been my home almost all my life. I loved its high-ceilinged rooms, its tall, nearly impossible-to-decorate windows that let the late-spring light stream in, its backyard with Mom's roses and two huge oaks that shaded the patio.

"I think maybe I'll paint the outside," I said to Marnie as I rocked sweet-smelling Johnny softly in my arms. It was my way of saying that I wasn't moving. "You think cream shutters would look good with the brick? Or should I stick with white? Or maybe go to red shutters?"

She didn't say anything as she sank into Mom's favorite chair, but her kind face was full of worry. About me.

"That painting is not a rash decision," I said hastily, acting as if the painting were the main issue that concerned us. "Mom and I were talking about it just before she became ill for the last time, and I've continued to think about it ever since. Four years of thinking means it's not an impulsive decision, doesn't it?" I looked at her with feigned innocence.

"Cara, I don't care if you paint this place purple," she sputtered. She rose and paced, her arms shooting in all directions in her agitation. "It's the place itself that concerns me, and you here in it alone. You're letting life pass you by!"

"Oh, Marnie." I gave her a warm hug. Johnny squeezed between us in a loving nest. She hugged me back, perhaps too ardently because Johnny squirmed. Without thinking, both of us bent and kissed him, me on the top of his bald little head, she on his chubby cheek. One thing in life was certain: Johnny would never lack for love. He was a Bentley.

I smiled at my sister-in-law. "I think you're forgetting one basic thing. I don't like change. No, I *hate* change. I've had too many recently, and I'm not facing another by moving. Let me get used to Pop being gone." I smiled ruefully. "It's going to take a while. I mean, I'm still struggling over Mom's death three years ago."

When Ward, Marnie, and Johnny left, they departed with warm hugs and kisses but no understanding. Bentleys are supposed to be doers in life, not observers!

To some extent Mom and Pop and Ward and Marnie were right about me. I *was* letting life pass me by. I was a recluse. But I was a happy recluse—until that late-May day.

I wandered from room to room, Rainbow trailing behind. As I walked through the dining room,

44

I thought of the time way back near the end of the lean years when Pop had decided he and Mom could afford new wallpaper, though they decided to save money by hanging it themselves.

"Tess, straight! It's got to be straight!"

"Don't you give me straight, John Seward Bentley, until you match that pattern like you're supposed to. And look! You cut that piece too short. We're going to have to buy another roll."

I remembered the fat little paperhanger who had finally been called, a man I had looked upon as a marriage saver. And I remembered Mom and Pop standing in the freshly hung room, arms about each other, smiling in shared pleasure that they could finally afford something as wonderful as new wallpaper and a paperhanger.

In the kitchen I saw the stove Pop had gotten Mom even as she lay too ill to cook on it.

"It's the kind with no burners," he told her as he kissed her pale cheek. "It'll save you clean-up time."

The pain on his face as he leaned over her told me he knew she'd never use it. He just needed to do something concrete for her, something to bring some sort of control to a situation beyond his control.

"John," she whispered, knowing full well that the gift was a Band-Aid on a hemorrhage. "I love you."

I came to Pop's office with its walls of plaques,

commendations, and awards for his years of business achievement and community service. I looked at the neat, cleared desktop holding only his pictures of a young Mom and the last one taken of the whole family before her illness. I knew all the drawers were ordered or empty. Ward and Mr. Havens had taken away everything important and disposed of the rest. I missed Pop's shaggy stacks of magazines, papers, bank statements, investment newsletters, and motivational quotes—the stacks that had driven Mom crazy.

"John," she'd storm, hand on her hip, "you have the most unsightly, packrat habits of anyone I know. One of these days I'm going to clean up this mess, and then you'll be sorry."

"Tess," Pop would answer, "did I ever tell you you're beautiful when you're mad?"

"Don't you beautiful me, John Seward Bentley!" she'd say. "Clean up your room!"

"Or you won't give me my allowance?" he'd reply, walking up behind her and nuzzling her neck.

"John, stop that! The children are watching!" But her frown, never very serious to begin with, would show signs of severe strain.

"Let them," he'd say. "And they'll know what God meant marriage to be." He'd turn her in his arms and kiss her thoroughly, and she'd cuddle against him, smiling happily.

Maybe they were why I write romances. I'd seen what real love was.

Once, about ten years ago, I'd gone to Mom and Pop's bedroom. I needed to talk to Mom about something long forgotten. I knocked on the door and she called, "Come in."

I opened the door to find her and Pop cuddled in the middle of their huge bed, her gray head resting on the grizzled gray hair of his bare chest.

"Oh," I said, blushing. "I'm sorry!" I started to close the door.

"No, no, Cara," Pop called. "Don't go."

I hesitated, feeling I was intruding, knowing I was intruding.

"I called for you to come in, Cara, love," Mom said, "because I want you to know that love, true love, doesn't die with the years. Gray doesn't mean gone." And she rested her hand on Pop's chest. He grinned at me like a young man.

I shook my head in false disdain. "You two are such a bad example to an innocent young woman like me."

"She needs more proof, Tess," Pop said. And he bent over and kissed Mom a great smacker.

"I love you guys so much," I whispered as I closed the door. All day I couldn't stop smiling.

Now I started crying, and the tears spilled over and ran down my cheeks in a rain of loss.

God, how can I survive this aloneness?

47

The thought brought an intense, thrumming anxiety. My heart began to pound and my hands shook as I clasped them to my chest.

Always before I'd been alone by choice, alone yet surrounded by people I loved and who loved me. Now I was alone, period.

I was almost in a panic as I ran to the linen closet and pulled out a new box of tissues. I tore it open, grabbed a fistful, and began mopping my face, but the tears kept coming. I returned to the living room with the tissue box under my arm, Rainbow padding behind me. I sank to the floor and, knees pulled to my chest, laid my head on them. I sobbed and sobbed.

A tentative paw patted my thigh and Rainbow whimpered. I reached out and swept her into my lap. For once, she stayed. "Oh, Baby, what are we going to do?"

She had no answer, but she lay still, letting me stroke her and bury my face in her fur. Finally though, she could bear it no longer, and she hopped down. She stalked under Mom's dropleaf table and began rubbing her head against the box Mom always kept tucked under there.

"So I can enjoy these things anytime I want," she'd say as she reached down and pulled out the generations of photos lying there.

I crawled to the box and tugged it from its hiding place. It suddenly became my life pre-server. I could do better than go to dinner with

Pop and Mom tonight. I could live our lives together all over again.

The first picture I pulled out was a very old sepia photo of Pop's parents, the first John Seward Bentley and his wife, Charlotte, seated in a stiff, formal pose from the early twentieth century. In great contrast, the next photo I pulled out was an informal picture from Ward and Marnie's wedding five years ago. The sun was shining, the warm June breeze was blowing Marnie's veil out behind her, and everyone was smiling. Mom, three months short of beginning her final, fatal struggle, wore a midnight-blue that looked stunning with her white hair. Pop's great chest strained his starched shirt and tux. Marnie was radiant and Ward handsome, though they looked impossibly young.

Even I looked good in the rose gown Marnie made me wear instead of the beige I'd wanted. Marnie had also insisted I "do something with that hair!" The result was an elegant chignon at the base of my neck softened by curls about my face instead of the usual ponytail. The baby's breath and roses tucked in my hair made me look alive in a way my usual slicked-back style never did.

I smiled through the mists blurring my vision.

For two hours I cried as I looked at black-and-white photos of Pop in his World II Army uniform, of Mom, her hair dark, her smile brilliant, holding the young Trey (John Seward Bentley III, my father), of my great-grandparents standing in the front yard of this very house when it was brand-new, the trees and shrubs so small and unformed.

I found a picture of Ward and me standing with Mickey Mouse on that long-ago vacation. Ward was so happy he almost vibrated as he stood tall and proud. I looked furious.

I pulled out a black-and-white of my mother and father who smiled at me from the beach at Ocean City, New Jersey. It had always saddened me that I couldn't remember a single thing about them. In fact, I didn't even think of them as my mother and father. They were Trey and Caroline, the names Mom and Pop always called them when they spoke of them. With a jolt I realized that I was now older than my parents had ever been. They had both been twenty-nine when they died.

I reached blindly into the now almost empty photo box, and my fingers closed over an envelope. I lifted it out. The old-fashioned, Palmer Method handwriting on the front read *John Seward's papers*.

Curious since I thought Ward and Mr. Havens had all Pop's papers, I extracted the contents. I took the topmost page and unfolded it.

Commonwealth of Pennsylvania it read across the top in a swirl of Gothic letters.

Stunned, I read the paper and then the accompanying letter. When I could finally find my voice, I turned to Rainbow.

"Baby!" I said in disbelief. "We're not really Bentleys!"

Chapter 4

There were eleven Biemsderfers listed in the phone book. I took a deep breath and reached for the phone. My heart was thudding faster than Thumper's hind foot.

I hated to admit it, but I'd been disappointed in my meeting with Todd Reasoner. I'd expected him to be clever enough to tell me just how I could get the information about Pop's family in spite of the general consensus about the difficulties—no, the impossibilities involved.

"Go here and ask this question of that person," my fine new attorney was supposed to tell me. Or better yet, "Just give me a minute to tap a couple of computer keys, and I'll have everything you need."

Talk about naïve, but that's what I'd hoped for, expected, wanted so badly I believed sheer desire would make it happen.

Instead he hadn't even offered me hope. I sighed so loudly that Rainbow raised her head from her pillow to check out my level of distress. Apparently it wasn't high enough for concern because she quickly put her head back on the pillow and went back to sleep.

I had to face the fact that Todd was probably

right about finding answers. Probably? He *was* right. He was, after all, the lawyer. And everyone involved in the original adoption was dead by now.

"You've made yourself this sweet, cozy little world, Cara," Ward told me the night we discussed my plans. "Only good things happen where you live. True love always wins there. And if something goes wrong, you just rewrite it."

It was embarrassing to admit even to myself, but I had come to Lancaster with a plotline firmly in place for my adoption search. For me, doors would open. For me, answers would appear. I, in true Bentley fashion, would be in control of the situation. Wasn't that what Marnie had said? I liked to be in control just like Pop and Ward?

"You can control your writing," she told me. "The trouble is, you can't control life."

Of course I knew that on some level. I wasn't stupid. And I had gone online before I came up here, looking up Pennsylvania adoption law. It stated clearly that the adoptee had to approach an uninvolved party like the agency through which the adoption occurred or the state itself with a request to meet the natural parents. Then this impartial party would contact the natural parent or parents on the adoptee's behalf. If there was a reciprocal interest, the plans to meet would be made. If not, that was it. Closed door.

But that law assumed the parties involved were

still living. And because in my case they weren't, I wanted Todd to work miracles to find the answer I sought.

I might as well face it. Neither Todd nor I were going to walk into the Lancaster County Courthouse and be given the information. If it was out there somewhere, I was going to have to search for it in creative ways.

Not that I thought Todd Reasoner was a total washout. Far from it. I smiled softly. I remembered his broad shoulders, his chiseled jaw, his bottomless brown eyes. I actually heard myself sigh again.

I froze, appalled, afraid Rainbow would look at me again, only this time she'd sneer at my adolescent attraction. I sounded just like one of my heroines. I glanced guiltily at Rainbow, but she slept on, deaf to my indiscretion. I sagged in relief and then straightened my spine. Time to take Step One.

Besides, how did I know his eyes were bottomless? I hadn't even been that close to him.

But I knew they were.

Taking a deep breath, I turned to the phone book and the page I'd opened to in the B's. A snippet of a psalm came to mind: *"God sets the lonely in families."*

Father God, I ask that you set me in my family. Help me know where and how to go about this search.

I put my finger under the first Biemsderfer, an Alan with one L and no E, and dialed. As the phone rang, I muttered, "Res ipsa loquitor," using Todd's ridiculous Latin quote as a good-luck talisman, sort of like, "You go, girl." "Res ipsa loquitor."

"Yeah?" demanded a teenage girl with no telephone finesse whatsoever.

"May I speak to Alan Biemsderfer, please?" I asked nicely, just to show her how it was done in polite company.

"Sure," she mumbled around a couple of cracks of her chewing gum. "Hey, Dad!" she screamed, the phone probably mere inches from her mouth. "It's some lady for you."

I shook my head to still the roar careening about my skull. If I were related to this particular set of Biemsderfers, phone etiquette would be among my first efforts at communication, believe me.

In a short time Alan Biemsderfer picked up an extension and asked in a decibel level much more conducive to conversation, "Yes?"

My stomach flip-flopped and my palms became so sweaty I had to grip the phone extra tight lest it slip from my grip. Once again foolish hope ballooned inside, pressing the air from my lungs. Maybe he was a long-lost cousin.

I took a deep breath and launched into my spiel. I was pleased and amazed at how normal my voice sounded. "Mr. Biemsderfer, my name is Cara Bentley, and I'm doing some genealogical research. My grandfather was born Lehman Biemsderfer here in Lancaster, and I'm trying to trace his family. That's L-e-h-m-a-n."

"What is this?" Alan asked. "One of those things where you're supposed to buy your family tree and crest or something?" His voice bore the cynicism of someone barraged by telemarketers. Hadn't he heard of the No Call program?

"No," I said earnestly. "I'm trying to trace my grandfather's origins. Seriously."

There was a small silence. "Well, maybe you are legitimate, maybe you're not, but either way I can't help. I've never heard of anyone in our family with the first name Lehman."

The way he emphasized *first name* ever so slightly made me sit up straight. "How about middle name?" I asked, trying to keep my voice calm. Wouldn't it be a miracle, a true God thing, if he actually knew someone who had both Lehman and Biemsderfer in his name, even if Lehman weren't a first name?

"Nope," he said. "I've only heard of Lehman as a last name. There are lots of Lehmans in this area. Maybe you could try them. Now, I've got to go."

I thanked Alan and hung up. I felt unrealistically disappointed and was mad at myself for it. When would I become realistic about this stuff? I grinned wryly. Not today. I quickly dialed Biemsderfer, Beatrice.

"I don't answer questions on the telephone," a testy voice stated.

"But—" And just that quickly I found myself talking to dead air.

Next was Biemsderfer, Edward.

Mrs. Edward answered. "Sorry, Ed's not here. Can I take a message?"

I explained about tracing Lehman Biemsderfer.

"Gee, I don't know much about the family history. Ed and I've only been married a couple of years, and I'm still learning all the ins and outs, you know? But if you want someone who can help, you ought to talk to Ed's Great-Aunt Lizzie. She's your woman."

I scanned the phone book. "I don't see an Elizabeth in the listings. Or should I be looking for a Mrs. Someone?"

"No, she's not in the book," Mrs. Edward said. "She's in a nursing home someplace. I've never even met her. I just hear them talking about her. And her last name's not Biemsderfer either. I think it's Martin. Her mother was a Biemsderfer though. You could call Ed another time and ask about it if you want."

I thanked her and we disconnected.

Biemsderfer, Gerhard and Biemsderfer, K.M. were not home. Biemsderfer, Marlin, Jr., said, as soon as I mentioned genealogy, "Aunt Lizzie. She knows it all."

"Where do I find her?" I asked.

There was a silence. "I don't think I should tell you. No offense, but I don't think I should." And he quietly hung up.

I tried Biemsderfer, Marlin, Sr., and an elderly woman answered.

"I'm trying to trace my family," I said.

"Isn't that lovely, dear." Her voice was sweet and slightly breathless. "I hope you can. I wouldn't want to be alone. I don't know what I'd do without my boys."

"I'm looking for someone who may be able to give me information about my grandfather, Lehman Biemsderfer."

"I'm afraid I don't know anyone in the family with the first name Lehman." She sounded truly sorry for her lack of information. Again I heard that slight emphasis on *first name*.

"Maybe you know someone where Lehman is the middle name?"

"No, dear. I'm sorry. I only know people with Lehman as the last name. There are lots of Lehmans in this area, you know."

I sighed. The nice thing about Biemsderfer was that it was fairly uncommon, unlike Lehman. I was genuinely thankful for an unusual name simply because the process of elimination wouldn't be so lengthy. "The man I'm trying to trace was born a long time ago. Lehman was born in 1918."

"Nineteen-eighteen? Why that's almost as old as me. I wish there was someone left around here who is as old as me. It gets lonely. Everybody keeps dying or going into one of those awful nursing homes. Retirement homes, they call them nowadays, but they're just death traps, whatever their name. Everyone who goes there dies. I made the boys promise me never, *never!* I've been a widow for almost ten years, you know. Too long. And they made me move to a smaller house. But that's okay because it wasn't a retirement home. I always say I'm not homesick, I'm dog sick. They wouldn't let me bring Bingo with me. We called him Bingo after that song the grandchildren liked to sing." And she began to quaver, "B-I-N-G-O, and Bingo was his name-o."

I stared at the list of Biemsderfers remaining uncalled, and wondered how to get away from this lonely, slightly fey woman without being rude. Then an idea struck.

"Say, Mrs. Biemsderfer, how many sons do you have?"

"Five."

"And do they live locally?"

"Three do. And so do five grandsons."

"Can you give me their names?"

"Alan, Gerhard, Marlin Junior, Link, Edward, Duane, Wesley, and Peter."

I glanced down the list of names again. Alan, Edward, Gerhard, Peter, and Wesley were all there. Duane and Link were not. They were probably younger grandsons who still lived with their parents and didn't have their own landlines.

"Thanks. You've saved me from making some phone calls, I think," I said.

"You know," she said, sounding suddenly very alert and authoritative. "The boys never had any interest in genealogy. They said it was boring. But that Alma is a different story. She's close to obsessed. At least I tease her that she is."

"Alma?"

"My daughter. She's taken courses on genealogy, and she spends hours on that Internet looking for more information. 'I got another leaf,' she'll say, whatever that means. She's done all types of family studies, and she's made this very complicated family tree. Goes way back to William Penn's time, even back to Germany before that. That's when the first settlers came to this area, you know, back in the early seventeen hundreds."

"No, I didn't know." My mouth began watering for a view of that family tree. "Tell me more about Alma and her tree."

But before the next breath was drawn and a sentence spoken, the clouds of mental fog rolled in again, blocking the sweet sun of sanity from Mrs. Biemsderfer. Even the sound of her voice became different, slow and tremulous, breathy.

"When Lizzie was a little girl—she was my favorite cousin—our families were good friends, and she and I used to play together a lot. We'd sneak away and play down by the river on the farm. That's the Conestoga River, you know. We always got into trouble because the adults thought we would fall in and drown. But they didn't tell us that was their reason. They always said, 'You'll get yourselves too muddy down there.' I guess they didn't want to scare us."

Her voice was warm with reminiscence. "Once Lizzie did fall in, but I pulled her out. Then we had to take off her dress and wash it in the river so that she wouldn't go back to the house with a muddy dress. We never thought about the fact that a soaking wet dress might give us away." She laughed like a child might, high and giggly.

Feeling like Alice down the rabbit hole, I said desperately, "But you know of no Lehman Biemsderfer?"

"No, dear."

"And no one in your family gave up a baby for adoption?"

"My grand-niece did about two years ago. I was so sad when she got pregnant, but kids today don't seem to mind, do they? It's not like it used to be, believe me. I didn't even know that men and women did such things when I got married. I thought it was only animals. I'm a farm girl, you know. I didn't know where babies came from, maybe kissing, I suppose. Nice girls never knew in my day." She sighed. "But," and I could hear a smile come into her voice, "Marlin taught me everything I needed to know. He was a very good teacher."

I thought she and Marlin must have enjoyed their marriage quite a bit. Five sons and a daughter were some indication.

"Did you know he's been dead almost ten years now? The boys are so good to me. They made me move, but they didn't make me go to a retirement home. I don't get homesick, I always say. I get dog sick. They wouldn't let me bring him with me, you know. His name was Bingo, after that children's song."

I knew she was going to break into song again any second so I cut in desperately. "Mrs. Biemsderfer, how can I get in touch with Lizzie? Or Alma?"

"Lizzie lives in one of those retirement homes, poor thing," she said.

"Where's that?" I asked.

Mrs. Biemsderfer didn't answer me. Instead she said, "Call Alma. She can help you. Sometimes my mind wanders, I think. But Alma can help."

I scanned the phone book but I already knew there was no Alma Biemsderfer. I took a minute to mourn all the Biemsderfer women who were no longer known by this name and therefore impossible for me to find easily.

"Alma Stoltzfus," Mrs. Marlin, Sr., said.

Stoltzfus. What a unique name. I flipped to the S's and stared in horror at all the Stoltzfus names. Apparently it wasn't so unique after all, at least not in Lancaster. "What's her husband's name?" I asked.

"Arthur—Art. They live in Camp Hill."

"Camp Hill?"

"Yes. It's near Harrisburg, just across the river a bit. That's the Susquehanna, dear, not the Conestoga."

"Do you have her phone number?"

"Of course," she said. "It's here somewhere."

I heard her put the phone down and pictured her wandering about her house, looking for her address/phone book. When the wandering went on for several minutes, I realized that Mrs. Marlin wasn't going to give me Alma's number. She had, in fact, forgotten about me.

Just then the phone was picked up, and I thought for a brief flicker of time that I had misread the genteel woman. A quick click of the receiver as she hung her phone up disabused me of that idea. I smiled sadly but was thankful neither Mom nor Pop had gotten so mentally confused. The physical deterioration had been bad enough to watch. I couldn't imagine witnessing a mental decline that took away the person you had loved for so many years.

I stared at the phone for a few minutes. Should I call Alma Stoltzfus, or was that name and its potential help just the imaginings of a confused mind? But the old lady had seemed very aware during that brief part of our conversation. I shrugged. Why not call? I had spent the morning talking to a bunch of strangers. Why not one more?

I dialed information and wrote down the number of an Arthur Stoltzfus in Camp Hill. I hoped the name wasn't as common over there in Dauphin County as it was here in Lancaster.

In a short time I was connected with Alma Stoltzfus, nee Biemsderfer. Once again I explained what I was looking for.

"Lehman Biemsderfer?" she said. "Never heard of anyone named that. Lehman's usually a last name."

"Yes, so I understand." I found I was gripping the phone again like it was my life line and I was a drowning person. I forced my hand to relax, and it actually did for about five seconds. "Your mother told me you had a family tree. I thought maybe it could give me some help. You know, all the branches of Biemsderfers."

I held my breath. Was this where she told me she couldn't exchange family information over the phone? After all, sensible, middle-aged women were usually cautious.

"You know," she said warily, "I hate to give out private family information on the phone."

I sighed. What a surprise. And I couldn't blame her.

"After all," she said, "how do I know who you are? How do I know you're trustworthy? How do I know you aren't trying to pull some scam?" There was no animosity in her voice, just a reasonable understanding that the world is full of con artists and nasty people.

"I sympathize with your concern," I said. "I know I'm reputable, but how can I convince you?" I thought for a minute. Too bad I couldn't tell her I was a Bentley of Bentley Marts, though come to think of it, why should she believe that? "You could contact my attorney," I suggested.

"Mmm," she said. "That's a possibility. And who might that be?"

I gave her not only Todd's name and number, but I fished Mr. Havens' business card out of my purse and gave her that name too.

"A lawyer in both Pennsylvania and Maryland?" she said.

"I live in Maryland. I'm here seeking this information, and I needed to know Pennsylvania law about adoption and adoption searches."

"This is an adoption thing?" Alma asked, her voice pricking with interest. "I didn't realize that." She was silent for a couple of beats. "Illegitimacy in 1918 was quite a stigma, especially in Lancaster County, steeped as it is in Amish and Mennonite culture."

"I know. I've thought a lot about that and how desperate Pop's mother must have been."

"Anyone who was a mother back then would be long dead," Alma said.

"Yes. Even if I knew her name, I couldn't speak with her. And adoption papers are guarded like the gold at Fort Knox. Getting to them is next to impossible. Otherwise I wouldn't be bothering you like this."

There was a moment of silence during which I could almost hear Alma thinking.

"Look," she finally said, "I'd like to help you if I can. I don't know that our family is who you're looking for, but who knows? Maybe we are. I'm coming to Lancaster next Thursday to get Mom and bring her home for a visit. Why don't you and I meet then? I'll check your references, and I'll bring along the family tree and any other family documents I think might be pertinent."

"And I'll bring along Pop's adoption certificate and the papers I have."

We set noon as our meeting time and the Olive Garden by Park City Mall as our meeting place.

When I hung up, I was restless and excited. *Five days.* I had to wait five whole days. I started to pace. It seemed such a long time, but it looked like I might be on the verge of getting some excellent information. I shivered with anticipation. But five days! I could hardly stand it.

I looked around at the tan walls, the brown-plaid comforters with the orange accent stripes, the brown rug, and the cheap bureau with a portable TV bolted to its surface. I thought of the paper-thin towels hanging on the corroded rack in the dingy bathroom. They couldn't begin to cope with my hair when it was wet. The motel's saving grace was that it took pets. I smiled at Rainbow, who snored back. Her company made the skimpy towels passable—for the moment.

If I had to wait five days until my appointment with Alma, I didn't want to wait in this room. I'd go nuts. In fact, I couldn't stay in it a minute longer. I grabbed my purse and went outside into the humid June noon. The sun was high, the sky a misty-blue wash, and the highway bursting with traffic, mostly tourists if the variety of license plates was any indication.

I looked at all the cars, vans, and tour buses with disfavor, climbed into my car and joined the flow going west toward Lancaster City. I stopped in a little restaurant called T. Burk and Co. and read an inspirational romance by one of my competitors as I ate. I had to admit the book wasn't half bad, but I also had to admit that I thought I did it better. Feeling somewhat smug, I returned to the Horse and Buggy.

I spent a relaxing afternoon at the pool in the front yard of the motel. Granted, in one way it was hard to relax under the scrutiny of all the traffic streaming by only a matter of feet from the fenced area in which I sat on a plastic recliner, but in another, the sheer number of cars made the people in them meaningless.

When I dragged myself back to my room, I was sleepy with sun.

"Just a quick minute," I said to Rainbow as I laid down beside her. "Just a quick minute."

I woke two hours later, rested and restless. I took a shower, pulled my still wet hair back in a tan scrunchie, threw on my new tan jeans and a beige knit top, and went looking for somewhere to eat dinner. This time I turned east and found the Bird-in-Hand Restaurant. The parking lot was full—a good sign. I went in and found a lobby crammed with people waiting for tables. Since I had nothing better to do than wait, I decided I might as well give my name and take a seat. I could people-watch or read the next book on my list. Like many writers I knew, I never went anywhere without a book. When I packed for vacation, I packed my books first and my clothes second. The mere thought of being caught without something to read made me hyperventilate. I patted my purse and the book tucked inside.

On my way to the hostess to put my name on the waiting list, I noticed a circular rack of books and stopped dead in my tracks. Staring at me were several copies of *As the Deer.* I approached the rack, heart pounding in delight. My book! Here in the lobby of a restaurant! For anybody to buy! I glanced at the top of the rack and read *Choice Books.* I looked at the other titles and realized every book was from one Christian publishing house or another. Some titles were fiction, some nonfiction, some were by friends, some by people I'd never heard of. As I circled the rack, I came to *So My Soul.*

Yes! I thought, mentally waving my fists triumphantly in the air and doing a Rocky Balboa trot around the lobby. I hated it when I found *As the Deer* without *So My Soul* since they were written to be a pair. *As the Deer* followed the heroine, one Marci Lerner, to the point of her conversion to Jesus Christ. *So My Soul* examined the ramifications of this decision on her life and the lives of the others she was involved with. Through both books I developed her romance with Scott Henderson.

By the time the books were finished, I wanted to meet my own Scott Henderson. He was tall and handsome, intelligent, and had a heart for God. He also knew how to make a woman happy. He was always there to support Marci through her trials. He held her hand when she was hurt and offered a strong shoulder to cry on. He prayed for her and loved her unreservedly. He accepted her just as she was, encouraging her in the process of becoming God's woman.

Sometimes I was afraid that men like Scott existed only in fiction. I certainly wasn't meeting guys like him. Then I thought of Mom and Pop and Ward and Marnie. They'd found true love . . . real love. And I prayed almost desperately that God would let me find the same.

I rubbed a finger softly over the cover of *So My Soul*. Others wrote trilogies. I wrote series of two. Duologies? Maybe some day I'd think up enough stuff to warrant a trilogy, but for now, two did it. And these two were doing it exceedingly well.

I was standing there grinning to myself when someone bumped my arm. I turned to say I was sorry and found myself face-to-face with the handsomest lawyer in Lancaster County.

"Hey," I said cleverly as I tried not to stare at his magnificent jawline.

"Well, hi," he said, slightly more articulate.

"Here for dinner?" I asked.

He nodded. "I find restaurants good places to come for dinner, don't you?"

I grinned. It was either that or blush a zillion shades of red for my inane remark. "Chitchat's not my strong suit," I said. "Whatever comes to mind comes out, idiotic or not."

He grinned politely back.

"Guess what I did today?" I said.

Of course he hadn't the vaguest idea.

"I called all the Biemsderfers in the phone book."

He nodded as if he were actually interested. "Any of them confess to being long-lost relatives?"

I shook my head.

"I'm glad," he said. "I'd hate to lose a billing before I had a chance to reap all the profits possible."

"Ah," I said. "Res ipsa loquitor."

He shook his head. *"Carpe diem."*

"I know that one," I said. "Seize the day. I also know *et al, ipso facto,* and *et cetera.*"

"I'm impressed," he said. "I've always appreciated multilingual people."

I think that this time I actually did blush at his gentle teasing, but I'm not certain. It could have been the heat from my afternoon sunburn.

A woman's voice said, "Two?" and I realized we were standing before the hostess. She looked at Todd, obviously anticipating that yes, he and I were two and here for dinner together. I definitely flushed now, expecting him to say, "Oh no, I'm not here with her. I'm just making pleasant conversation because she's a client. I'm really here with that beautiful woman over there."

Instead he looked at me and raised an eyebrow in invitation. Surprised and pleased, I gave a small nod.

"Yes, two. Reasoner," he said. Then, in an aside

71

to me, "Thanks for being here. Now I can claim the meal as a business deduction."

Startled, I looked at him and caught a gleam of humor in those brown eyes, those bottomless brown eyes. I'd been right.

"Thirty to forty minutes," the hostess said.

We nodded and moved away. Just then a couple got up from a bench along the wall and we took the deserted seats.

"Tell me about your phone calls," Todd asked. And for the next twenty minutes, I did. He listened attentively, asking questions every so often, laughing at Mrs. Marlin, Sr., hanging up on me.

"So I'm going to have lunch with Alma next Thursday when she comes to get her mother. She's bringing the family tree with her."

When I finished, he just looked at me, a smile on his face. "And you're not the least bit excited about this meeting, are you?"

"It shows?"

"You're positively vibrating."

I stared at him. "Me? Vibrating? I never vibrate. I'm low-key. I'm quiet and laid back."

He looked at me skeptically.

"Truly," I said. "I'm a writer. I lead a quiet life. My brother and sister-in-law say I only live through my characters. Mom and Pop kept at me all the time to get a life."

He shook his head. "I don't know about then,

but this is now and you're having a hard time sitting still."

I grinned. "I am fidgeting a bit, aren't I? But isn't it exciting? I may be meeting my family!"

Todd seemed to just then catch my admission to being a writer. "Did you say you're a writer? What do you write?"

"Okay, don't laugh, but I write inspirational romance novels." I waited for the inevitable incredulous reaction, but Todd only paused a moment, taking in this new information.

"Well, I guess this is where I should be embarassed to say I don't think I've read any of your books," he finally said.

"That's quite okay. I generally give a pass to men when it comes to reading my books."

"Reasoner, party of two," a metallic voice called over a PA system. "Reasoner, party of two."

We followed a young woman with a head covering to a booth along the outside wall of the restaurant. She left us studying two large menus with amazingly inexpensive meals.

"Is she Amish?" I asked Todd.

He glanced at the hostess's retreating back and shook his head. "No, she's Mennonite."

"What's the difference?" I asked. "They both wear those prayer cap thingys."

"They come from the same Anabaptist heritage, but they've diverged through the years."

"How?"

"While the Amish have stayed as separate from the general culture as they can, the Mennonites have accepted change and integrated it into their religious lives. They share the Anabaptist heritage of nonviolence and adult baptism, but they're thoroughly modern."

I laid my menu on the table. "I know Southern Baptist and General Baptist and Regular Baptist and lots of other Baptists. What's Anabaptist?"

He leaned back in his seat and rested a hand on the edge of the table. He lowered his menu so he could see me more easily. "Back in the Protestant Reformation, a group of dissidents decided they didn't agree with the Catholic Church practice of infant baptism. They argued that a person shouldn't be baptized until he was old enough to understand what faith in Christ was all about. So these dissidents rebaptized themselves in the early 1500s. That's what Anabaptist means. Rebaptized or baptized again. One group of the Anabaptists followed a man named Menno Simons and became known as Mennonites. Another group broke from the Mennonites more than a century later and fol- lowed a fiery preacher named Jakob Ammonn. They became known as Amish."

"How did the two groups end up in this area?"

"Religious persecution."

"Pacifists were persecuted? But weren't they gentle people?"

"Yes, in that they wouldn't retaliate. No, in that they stood against the institution of the state church and were considered very dangerous to the political and social order of the day. That was a time when church and state were intricately linked, and those of differing religious views were seen as seditious."

"So they got kicked around?"

"Kicked around nothing. They got drowned and burned and murdered in great numbers. They came here to escape, and by chance they ended up in one of the most fertile areas in the world."

I grinned at the way he emphasized *by chance*. It made me think that he might understand how God can make the evil that people do praise Him in the end. Persecution meant flight, which meant the New World and Lancaster County. Plenty after famine.

Our waitress came for our order. I decided on stuffed chicken breast, baked potato, and a salad. Todd had pork and sauerkraut, mashed potatoes, and cottage cheese with apple butter. We both ordered sweetened iced tea.

She returned in record time with our drinks, my salad, and Todd's cottage cheese, topped with a dark brown substance the consistency of burnt applesauce.

"What's that?" I asked suspiciously.

"Apple butter."

"It's brown."

"Umm."

"You actually eat brown food?"

"With great relish," he said, taking a forkful. "And you eat brown food too. Meat's brown."

"Meat doesn't count. It sort of matches your eyes," I pointed at the apple butter.

He made a choking sound. "What?"

"Well, it does."

"If you say so. No one's ever made that comparison before. Want to try some?" He offered me his dish.

I looked at it dubiously.

"Come on," he said. "When in Rome . . . "

"Res ipsa loquitor," I said.

"Precisely," he said.

I stuck my fork in his dish just enough to get the tines damp.

"Coward," he said.

"Precisely," I said and with great trepidation stuck my fork in my mouth. I was very pleasantly surprised. "It's sweet."

He laughed. "What did you expect?"

"Brown food? Meat. Gravy. They're not sweet." I took a real forkful this time, making certain to get some of the cottage cheese too. "I like it."

"Uh oh," he said and pulled his dish back to the safety of his own placemat. I politely ate my own salad.

"Tell me about your family," I said as we started our main courses.

He shrugged. "Not much to tell. I'm an only child of elderly parents. My mother died when I was five, and my father tried his best, but it was hard."

I could tell by the expression on his face that it was still hard, or at least the memories were.

"How old is elderly?" I asked.

"My father was fifty-five when I was born, my mother forty-three. They had long since given up on the idea of a child."

"So your mother was only forty-eight when she died?"

He nodded.

"Mine was twenty-nine," I said. "I was one."

We looked at each other with sympathy.

"So your father raised you too?" Todd asked.

I shook my head. "My dad died with my mother. Automobile accident. One of those massive pileups where they had the misfortunate of being between two semi trucks."

"Ouch," he said. "My mother died of ovarian cancer."

We were quiet a minute, chewing, contemplating.

"So who raised you?" he asked.

I spent most of the main course telling him about Mom and Pop, laughing, filled with warm memories.

Todd listened, a sad kind of envy just below the surface. "You had a wonderful childhood in spite of everything, didn't you? Just like in books."

I nodded. "Lots of love, lots of laughter, and a real, practical faith modeled rigorously."

Todd sighed. "Well, I had the faith part anyway, and I truly am appreciative of that. My father loved the Lord and saw to it that I had opportunity for real faith too. Church and Bible school every Sunday morning and youth group every Sunday night. Vacation Bible school. Church camp. But the love and laughter parts weren't there." He put his knife and fork on his empty plate and leaned back against his seat, trying to keep his face impassive but not quite succeeding.

"My father is a nice enough man, I guess," he said. "He has a PhD in English literature and taught at Millersville University for years and years. He was there when it was a state teachers college, then a state college, and finally a state university. He is very scholarly, highly respected in academic circles, and very introverted. His life is medieval literature and culture. Samuel Pepys and his diary and John Milton are much more important to him than I've ever been."

I thought of Pop and his great lust for life. I imagined little Todd being read a bedtime story from *Paradise Lost*. I shivered. Certainly one of the rings of Hell.

Todd reached for his iced tea and turned the

glass in circles on the table. He stared at the watermarks as he talked. "I learned as a little boy that my father was happy when I was quiet and invisible, so I became quiet and invisible. He almost smiled when I got good grades, so I got good grades, always hoping. He was almost impressed if I excelled in whatever pursuit I followed, from academic teams to science fairs. I tried everything I could think of to please him, but I don't think I ever got a compliment."

I leaned my elbow on the table and looked at the handsome, competent, well-educated man across the table from me. I concentrated on his words, trying to see the deeper truths behind them, marveling that he was telling me all this information. I was willing to bet he rarely talked about his father and certainly didn't talk about their painful relationship. And certainly not with someone he barely knew. I felt complimented beyond reason. He looked up suddenly and saw my intense look.

He smiled wryly and shook his head. "Sorry. I didn't mean to whine."

"Hey." I reached across the table and put my hand on his arm. "I didn't hear whining. I heard part of a life story. I was just imagining that little boy sitting in an overstuffed chair too big for him, his legs sticking straight out in front of him as he studied the encyclopedia so he could converse with his father."

He nodded thoughtfully. "But it was a sofa with a brown print that was ugly as sin, and it was *Paradise Lost*."

I didn't know whether to laugh or cry as I put my hand back in my lap. "We, on the other hand, saw all the Star Wars and Indiana Jones movies."

"Sounds good to me," he said. "Now what do you want for dessert?" This last was asked as our waitress began clearing the table. He smiled and rubbed his hands, apparently glad for the opportunity to relieve the emotional tenor of our conversation. "How about some shoofly pie?"

"What's shoofly pie? It sounds awful."

"It's a molasses pie," answered the waitress, obviously used to the question.

"A molasses pie?" It still sounded awful. "Filled with flies?"

"It's delicious," Todd assured me.

"I'll take coconut custard," I said emphatically.

"Warm shoofly with whipped cream," Todd said. After the waitress walked away, he looked at me. "You should have trusted me on the pie. You'll be sorry."

When the desserts came, I looked at his. "It's brown! What is it with you Pennsylvania Dutch and brown food?"

"I'm not Pennsylvania Dutch," Todd said. "And what is it with you tourists that you won't try new stuff?"

"Speaking of being a tourist," I said, enjoying

my nice, creamy, familiar coconut custard, "I'd like to find someplace to live besides a motel. Do you know of a boarding house or an apartment or something that might be available and won't require a year's lease be signed?"

He thought for a minute. "You know, I just might."

I looked at him hopefully.

"What would you think about living on an Amish farm?"

I stared at him. "You're kidding."

"I've a friend who used to be Amish before his *rumspringa*."

"His what?"

"His wild-oats sowing. His teenage rebellion."

"Ah."

"Anyway, he was in a motorcycle accident and is now a paraplegic. His parents, who are still Old Order Amish, brought him home to the annex on the house and brought in electricity and a phone for him because they realize he'll never be Amish again. Anyway, he rents the rooms on the second floor of the annex so he can have some income. I happen to know the rooms are newly available because the woman who used to rent them just got married."

"An Amish farm? Cows and horses and buggies?"

"And don't forget the smelly barns," Todd added. "And some of the nicest people you'll ever meet. And Jake put in a bathroom on the second floor after Kristie moved out."

I looked at him, startled. "What did Kristie have to use? An outhouse?"

Todd laughed. "Don't worry. She had indoor plumbing. She just had to share the family bathroom on the first floor. You won't have to do that, but you can eat dinner with them whenever you want. And you'll want to often, believe me. Mary's a great cook."

I stared at my cup of coffee, its steam rising into the air-conditioned air. An Amish farm. I bet even Pop would consider that getting a life. "If I can make arrangements for, say, three months, I'll do it."

Chapter 5

L et me go call Jake," Todd said. "I'll see if he's got a renter lined up already or whether the place is still free."

"You're going to call right *now?*"

"Sure," he said, sliding out of the booth. "It'll only take a minute. Just don't eat my pie while I'm gone."

"Fat chance of that." I eyed the repulsive-looking brown thing.

I took a sip of coffee as I watched Todd walk across the dining room to the lobby and pull out his cell. I noticed a table of women watching him too. I felt a sudden delight that he was eating with me.

I looked at the shoofly pie again. I could see three pieces of it sitting on the table of the four women who had eyed Todd with such interest. I watched as our waitress put two pieces on the table across the aisle from me.

Surely if all these people were eating the disgusting thing, it couldn't be all that bad, could it? I glanced toward the lobby and saw Todd was thoroughly occupied. I looked at Todd's pie again. I looked at the people across the aisle enthusiastically enjoying their desserts.

One tiny taste. Then I'll know what all the fuss is about, and he'll never even notice. Besides, I like whipped cream.

I licked all the coconut custard off my fork and reached across the table. I took a smidgen of crumbs and brown custard. I sniffed it with distrust. I reached back for a bit of whipped cream and stuffed the mess into my mouth. I blinked in surprise.

"Told you you'd like it," Todd said as he slid into his seat. Then he scowled. "But I also told you not to take any."

"What makes you think I took any?" I said as I reached across the table for a decent-sized bite. It was either that or be embarrassed out of my mind.

"Do you steal the food off the plates of all your dates?" he asked.

I blinked. This is a date? "Only the ones I like," I replied placidly.

He pushed the pie to the center of the table, and we took turns taking bites.

"Jake says the rooms are still available, and that if we come out tomorrow afternoon, you can look them over. He says tomorrow is a good day because it's an off Sunday and the family's going to visit Ruth and Isaiah."

I savored the last bite of pie and asked, "What's an off Sunday, and who are Ruth and Isaiah?"

"The Old Order Amish have church every other

Sunday at each other's homes. When there's no church, it's an off Sunday, and they often go visiting. Ruth and Isaiah are the Zooks' daughter and son-in-law."

"They only go to church every other Sunday?" That surprised me for such a religious people.

Todd nodded. "So are you free tomorrow afternoon to go out to the farm? I'll take you if you are."

"Sure. Sounds good." It sounded more than good, but I wasn't going to tell him. "By the way, can you recommend a good church? I'd like to go tomorrow."

"My church. Why don't I pick you up? After service we can grab a bite to eat and then go to the farm."

I shrugged nonchalantly, thinking I should have come to Bird-in-Hand a lot sooner. Silver Spring was never like this. "Sounds like a plan," I said.

The waitress brought the check.

"I want to pay my part of the bill," I said.

We split the cost in half and left the restaurant.

"But you should have paid more," Todd commented as we walked across the parking lot. "After all, you ate half my dinner."

"Only the brown stuff," I said as I looked into his amazing brown eyes. "Only the brown stuff."

We came to my beige Saturn, but instead of saying goodbye, Todd leaned against the fender and asked, "So are you enjoying your time here?"

"I am," I said. "Last night I went for a drive. No matter where I looked, the view was beautiful. I think it's the size of the farms—so compact, the fields all bursting with crops, and the barns and houses so picturesque."

"Is it picturesque?" Todd asked, looking around as if he could see all of Lancaster County from here. "I've never gotten as caught up in the whole Amish thing as lots of people do. Maybe living in the area all my life has made it too common."

I stared at him. "You mean you don't see the beauty of these farms and the fascination of this unique culture?"

He grinned with one corner of his mouth. "I know. I've no depth of soul or appreciation for the finer things. I'm shallow and insensitive. I see the glass half empty instead of half full. But honestly, instead of a sociological paradise, I see a culture that, in order to survive, is fraught with inconsistencies. In fact, there goes one now." And he pointed to the street.

I looked and saw a van full of Amish people driving by.

"An Amish taxi," Todd said. "There are lots of retired men—regular men—who have a nice second career as drivers for Amish folks. The Amish take the taxis places they either want or need to get to quickly. Why, I ask you, is it all right to *ride* in a car but not *drive* one? Or why is it okay to take the bus?"

"The Amish use buses?"

Todd nodded. "I used to think they were almost fraudulent in these inconsistencies, but I've changed my mind since I've come to know the Zooks. I've decided they're just trying to keep their culture alive. My question, I guess, is whether it's worth keeping alive."

"Sure it is," I said, slightly scandalized at his question.

"Yeah? Why?"

"I don't know. I don't know enough about them to know. But it must be."

I watched a pair of Amish boys in straw hats push their way along the road on scooters. How sad it would be to lose something so singular.

"Bikes would be faster," I said.

"But bikes aren't allowed, at least in Lancaster County. Too far too fast."

I looked at him. "I don't understand."

"As far as I can figure it out, anything that pushes the parameters of the culture beyond their concept of what family and church should be is bad. Farms are small and picturesque because they are the size an individual family can handle without the use of mechanized farming equipment. Bikes and cars are forbidden because they would take individuals beyond the boundaries of the group. Electricity off utility poles would bring in the questionable world of TV, radio, and computers. So for the sake of guarding their beliefs, they use 12-volt batteries or kerosene-fueled generators for power. The lack of public utilities, the mode of dress, and the horses and buggies are the outward signs of a very exclusive community."

"Do they proselytize?" I asked, trying to imagine an Amish man on a street corner handing out tracts or standing on a soapbox pleading with a crowd to give up worldliness and come to Jesus.

He shook his head. "They don't seek converts like most religions do, but they are willing to accept them if folks from outside want to join. Not many who seek stay long. The divide between Plain and fancy is too wide."

I watched a buggy roll slowly by, a line of cars stacked up behind it.

"Have you ever ridden in a buggy?" I asked.

Todd looked at me like I'd gone crazy. "Of course not."

"Haven't you ever wondered what it feels like to sit in one of those things, especially when a tour bus zooms past?"

He stuffed his hands in his jeans pockets and said, "I can honestly say I've never pondered that."

"Never?"

"Never."

It was obvious from his tone of voice that he thought the idea ridiculous. It was time to disabuse him of that opinion.

"Then let's go for a buggy ride and find out what it's like," I said.

He stared at me, horrified.

"Oh, come on. Where's your spirit of adventure?"

"Cara, a buggy ride? That's crazy. Besides it's too touristy."

I shrugged. "So what? I'm a tourist."

"Well, I'm not." I watched as he hunkered down, all but attaching himself to my car, a limpet clinging to his rock, a barnacle glued to its piling.

"Todd," I said, smiling as sweetly as I could, "where's your sense of adventure?"

"I don't have one, and I don't want to develop one in an Amish buggy." He clenched his jaw, clearly convinced he'd made his definitive statement on the issue.

I leaned toward him and narrowed my eyes as I stared directly into his. He leaned back instinctively.

"What?" he said.

"Todd," I said softly, my index finger aimed at his chest, "when you grow up, do you want to be like your father or like my pop?"

He blinked. Then he clamped his jaw and glared at me through eyes as narrowed as mine.

The muscles in his cheeks jumped as he clenched and unclenched his teeth.

Finally he spoke, his words clipped and hard. "That is a very nervy question. Do you always play hardball like that?"

It *was* a nervy question, and I couldn't believe I'd voiced it. I usually never ask questions that might make the hearer uncomfortable. I was a peacemaker, a kind and comforting person. But I'd seen Todd's sorrow over dinner and it hurt. I forced my answer around the lump in my throat. "Only when the outcome matters."

He blinked again. We both knew I wasn't talking about any buggy ride. We stood frozen, staring at each other, as all around us life flowed on.

My heart pounded to the point of pain, and ribbons of dread unfurled inside. What if he wanted to be his father? Or what if he couldn't help being his father? I felt like my future was on the line even as I recognized the folly of such a thought. I'd only met the man yesterday.

Dear God, it's the brown eyes, isn't it? And the beautiful curls and that jaw. And he shared his shoofly pie with me. And he found a place for me to live. And he's taking me to church! Oh, Lord, please let him be able to have fun.

Finally Todd broke the tension. He took a deep breath, twitched his shoulders a bit, and said mildly, "I guess we'd better take a buggy ride, hadn't we?"

My breath rushed from my lungs, and I realized for the first time that I'd been holding it. Almost giddy with relief I said, "Abe's Buggy Rides is just down the street."

He looked slightly pained. "I know Abe's Buggy Rides." He peeled himself off my fender and sighed. "Give me your car keys and let's get this over with."

"You're driving my car?"

"Why not? We're standing right beside it."

"But it's my car. I should drive."

"Don't push it, Cara. Let me have some semblance of control."

I understood about control. I gave him the keys and climbed into the passenger side. He backed out of the parking space and pulled onto 340. In a short time we were at Abe's Buggy Rides. We parked and climbed out our respective sides. When we met at the back of the car, he looked at me with an aggrieved expression.

"I've driven past this place for years, always with a great feeling of superiority toward the people who took the rides." He shuddered so intensely that his slicked-down curls almost shook. "Now I'm about to become one of them."

I patted his arm. "I don't know whether it helps or not, but I think you're brave and wonderful."

He snorted. "Don't think I don't recognize sarcasm when I hear it."

I grinned and started for the sidewalk where the buggies stood waiting.

He trailed me, still busy carping. "You eat my food, you don't pay your fair share, you complain when I want to drive your car, and you make me go on a buggy ride." The horror in his voice was comical. "I've never met anyone like you before."

I turned to him, startled, and he added quickly, "And that's *not* a compliment."

Glad for a lifetime of dealing with Pop and Ward, I scowled at him. " 'Fraidy cat."

"What?"

"You heard me. You're afraid to have fun."

"I am not."

"Hah!"

"Hi," announced a happy teenage voice behind us. "My name's Angie, and I'll be your driver for the buggy tour."

We spun to find a grinning Angie wearing a rose T-shirt and jeans with a knee missing.

"Hi, Angie," I said. "I'm Cara. And this scowling hulk is—"

"Yeah, I know who he is. We go to the same church. What are you doing going on a buggy ride, Todd?"

He looked pointedly at me. "I got conned." But I noticed the scowl was gone.

Angie laughed and led the way to a gray buggy with black trim waiting at the edge of the road. She reached in and pulled the front seat aside to give access to the back. Todd stood aside and let me get in first. I put my foot on the round metal step on the side of the buggy and stepped up and in. I sat on a seat covered with burgundy crushed velvet.

Angie pulled the front seat into place and Todd climbed in. He sat on the right of the seat while Angie sat on the left. She took the reins and slapped them gently on the rump of our horse, who knew from frequent practice just what to do. He ambled slowly along the shoulder of 340.

We turned right off 340 and drove down a country road. It pleasured me how quickly the bustle of the major tourist thoroughfare was left behind. Angie kept up a steady patter of information that Todd ignored but I found fascinating. We passed several farms and an Amish school. I thought of the Nickel Mines school shootings that had happened not too far from here. I looked at the little white building and wondered at the despair or illness of a man who would go into such a setting and shoot little girls.

I was shocked when I heard Angie say that Amish kids only went through eighth grade.

"Education takes you from the culture," Todd commented, his arm resting on the open window frame. "It makes you independent, and the Amish prize a cooperative, group mentality."

With the open door and side window and the open front and back windows, there was a soft breeze through the buggy in spite of the warm temperature. I was enjoying my ride and so, I thought, was Todd, who was looking relaxed and handsome.

At least he was enjoying it until the horse did what comes naturally. He raised his tail and Todd reacted.

"Ah, yuck!" he muttered and leaned as far back into the buggy as he could.

Angie and I both laughed at him as the manure fell harmlessly onto the road.

"No one would ever take you for a farmer," Angie said.

When we arrived at our starting place after tracing a two-mile square, we climbed out of the buggy. Todd paid Angie. We both thanked her and walked to the car. Todd went automatically to the driver's side again. I shook my head, amused at his presumption, and climbed into the passenger side.

"So?" I said.

"So what?"

"Did you have fun?"

He snorted and gave me a look of imperious scorn.

"You are such a phony," I said.

"And you're bossy," he said.

"*Quid pro quo*," I said.

"Exactly."

We rode in companionable silence to and past the restaurant.

"Hey, where are we going?" I said, twisting to look back over my shoulder. "Don't you have to get your car? Or do you like mine better, and you're planning to keep it?"

"My car's not there," he said. "I walked."

We turned off 340 and drove for a bit, made another turn, and then pulled into a drive before a brick Cape Cod with white clapboard dormers, a red door, and white shutters. A split rail fence separated a yard about an acre in size from the press of cornfields on three sides.

"You live here?" I asked.

He nodded. "Yep. This is my house."

"I thought you didn't like farms. There's nothing around you but farms."

"I don't like manure, and I'll admit that February and March are a bit fragrant when my neighbors are putting down their homemade fertilizer. But I love the privacy and peace. For them I'll overlook the other."

"Compromise," I said, smiling. "The Amish aren't the only ones."

We sat in the car with the windows down, enjoying the warm magic of dusk. Neither of us seemed to want to move. We listened to the crickets' symphony and watched the lightning bugs flash in the shrubs as sunset faded from lavender and peach to pearl-gray velvet to deep night lit by a full moon.

"Smell the honeysuckle?" I think nothing means peace and summer like that scent.

"Come with me," Todd said.

He got out of the car and walked to the edge of the lawn where a vine grew up a fence post. I followed willingly. He broke off a sprig from the vine and handed it to me. I held it to my nose and inhaled deeply. Sweet, sweet honeysuckle.

"Ever draw the nectar from the flower?" he asked, pulling a blossom free.

"Sure," I said. "We Maryland girls love honeysuckle."

I watched as he pinched the base of the flower and slowly pulled the long stamen free. He put it into his mouth and, closing his lips over most of it, slowly withdrew it, obviously savoring the sweetness.

"That's one way to do it," I said.

"You've got a better way, I suppose."

"Sure." I plucked a blossom and, putting the end in my mouth, bit it off. Then I inhaled the sweet trace of nectar. "Simple, easy, and quick."

We pulled every flower off the sprig and several off the vine on the post, Todd carefully pulling the stamen free, me biting the tip and sucking in the nectar.

Finally we wandered back to my car, and Todd handed me my keys.

"I'll see you tomorrow morning," he said. "How about if I bring us some breakfast? Egg McMuffins?"

"With orange juice and a large coffee. We can eat out by the pool."

I climbed in and Todd shut my door. He leaned in the open window.

"I'm glad we met this evening." Then he grinned. "I had a good time."

I grinned back. "And I'm supposed to believe that?"

He stood up. "Yep. It's the truth."

As I backed out of the driveway, I couldn't wait for tomorrow morning.

"Cara, I'd like you to meet some friends," Todd said after the service Sunday morning. We were standing in the parking lot. "This is Clarke and Kristie Griffin."

I smiled at the couple. He was tall with very dark brows under sandy-colored hair; she was slim and somehow lovely despite being dressed in swirls of ruby, emerald, sapphire, with shiny gold dots all over.

"This is Cara Bentley, a client of mine," Todd said. "I'm taking her out to the Zooks' place to see about her renting your old rooms, Kristie."

Kristie's eyes lit up. "Oh, Cara, you'll love it! I had the most wonderful year there."

"Sure you did." Clarke grinned at her. "You met me."

Kristie leaned into his side and gave him a gentle elbow to the ribs. I remembered Todd saying that the woman who had rented the rooms before me had just gotten married. It showed in the way she looked at Clarke and the way he smiled back.

"You'll love the Zook family," Kristie assured me when she pulled her gaze reluctantly from her husband. "Mary and John are so pleasant and nice and hospitable."

"And Mary is a great cook," Clarke said. "Don't overlook that very important fact."

"And she's an artist." Kristie obviously thought this a great thing. "We've just begun selling some of her landscapes and quilt pictures. In fact, if you're a client of Todd's, you've probably seen one in his office."

I nodded. "There are two beautiful paintings on his wall."

"One of them is Mary's," Kristie said.

"And the other is Kristie's," her proud husband said as he gave her shoulders a squeeze.

Before I had a chance to ooh and aah, Kristie continued talking about Mary. "I still go out to the farm to take Mary on drives so she can pick scenes she wants to paint. Then I take pictures of the scenes with my camera and have them printed for her to paint from."

I was fascinated. Apparently cameras weren't allowed in Amish culture. I couldn't imagine life without pictures, especially now because they served as reminders of the wonderful life Mom and Pop had given Ward and me. But if photos weren't allowed, why were paintings?

I asked that question.

Kristie shrugged. "They're not really. Icons. False representations."

"Then there can't be many Amish artists. At least not the 'good' Amish people, the obedient Amish people."

"You're right, there aren't many. Mary and an artist named Susie Riehl are the only two I know or at least the only two in this area I know who are selling their work to the outside world. Both of them are good Amish women. Of course, there may be others who, like Mary until recently, paint in secret."

"It puts a terrible strain on someone to be gifted in the arts and not be allowed an outlet," Clarke said. "I think that's one reason there are so many beautiful quilts coming out of the Amish community. It's an accepted way to create something of color and beauty."

"But . . . " Kristie raised her finger as she made another point. "If you're gifted, even driven, in a specific area, any old outlet won't do. If you must paint, quilts won't fulfill that need. It'd be like telling a novelist to be happy writing articles. After all, both are words. Or telling a dancer to be satisfied with running. Both are movement."

I understood her point. Telling stories was what I was compelled to do. Even narrower in focus, I was driven to tell stories of romance and faith. Any other kind of writing, no matter how noble, no matter how helpful, wouldn't be as satisfying or wouldn't satisfy at all.

"Cara's a writer," Todd told Kristie and Clarke. He looked at me. "So you'd be okay. If you were Amish, I mean."

"Writing's good," Clarke agreed. "You can make it spiritual, talk about the Lord, discuss the tenets of the church, present ideas on family and child-rearing. But art isn't nearly so practical, so pointed, so didactic."

I had to smile. "I write inspirational romances, about as nondidactic as it gets, so I don't know how they'd look on that."

"A lot of the women read for pleasure," Kristie said. "You might be surprised to find them reading your books."

I tried to picture an Amish woman, a *kapp* over her slicked-back hair, dress and apron pinned neatly together, sitting on the porch reading *As the Deer*. It was a hard image to conjure.

"One thing we need to warn you about, Cara,"

Clarke said. "When you meet Jake, don't let him throw you."

Kristie nodded. "He can a bit touchy at times. In fact, he scared me to death at first. But his social skills are improving daily. Just don't mention Rose Martin to him."

"Who's she?"

"The woman who called 911 the night of his accident and then sat with him until the emergency techs and the ambulance came. She may have saved his life by holding shock at bay."

"So why can't I mention her?"

"She wants to meet Jake—for a long time she thought he had died. He doesn't want to meet her." Kristie shrugged. "Don't try to understand. It's a control thing of some kind. She saw him when he was completely helpless, and it bothers him quite a bit."

I must have looked like I didn't see much sense in Jake's position because she laughed. "I don't understand either. That's just the way it is."

"Jake's really a nice guy," Clarke said. "He and I've been friends for a long time. And getting approval to take those classes at Millersville has been great for him."

"First class tomorrow," Todd said.

"That's all your doing, Todd," Clarke said. "If it weren't for your pushing, I don't think he'd have gotten that high school equivalency degree."

Todd shook his head dismissively. "I'm just concerned he do well in these summer classes. He has to if he wants to gain full admission."

When Clarke and Kristie said goodbye, I watched them walk to their car hand-in-hand. I turned to Todd to make an undoubtedly snide remark about their obvious affection and was surprised by the expression of deep longing on his face.

An unexpected and intense shaft of pain shot through me. I swallowed hard to tamp down the hurt.

"She's very pretty," I said, my eyes again following her. I tried to keep my voice neutral, though I wasn't completely successful. A faint misting of melancholy hung over the words.

He looked at me with one eyebrow raised and said carefully, "Yes, she is."

"Colorful," I said.

He nodded. "Very."

I felt the beginnings of a headache, the special one reserved for sufferers of vain imaginings. It didn't matter that I knew I was foolish; the pain still attacked behind my left eye.

"But then beige is nice too," he added politely, looking me up and down. "Restful."

It was the third day I'd known him and the third beige outfit. Who cared that it was a pricey, raw silk pantsuit? It was beige! Suddenly I felt as boring as Wonder Bread.

"You used to go with her, didn't you?" I asked, my eyes still on the lovely, multi-hued Kristie. I already knew the answer.

"For a couple of years."

"What happened?"

"We broke up."

"Your idea or hers?" I wanted it to be his, but I knew it was hers.

"Hers. She told me I wanted to remake her, and she didn't want to be remade."

I thought about that for a few seconds. "Did you?"

"Want to remake her? Probably. All her quirks that Clarke thinks are enchanting I thought were idiotic."

"Not a good sign for a relationship."

He nodded agreeably.

"Do you miss her?"

He looked at me with a funny half smile. "Do you pick at scabs often?" he asked.

I sighed. I was so obvious, poking where I had no business poking. "Only when the—"

"I know. Only when the outcome matters." He continued to stare at me. "And it matters in this case?"

I blushed and looked at my shoes. They were bone-colored. Boring. "I think I'd like a piece of shoofly pie, wouldn't you?" I managed to raise my gaze to his shirt button, but I couldn't bring myself to meet his gaze. "Where do you think we should eat?"

He put a finger under my chin and lifted, forcing my eyes to his. "I'm over her, Cara," he said softly. "I've been over her for some time. She was right in her analysis of how I felt about her. I liked who I wanted her to be, not who she was."

I refused to be comforted. "Yeah, but you didn't see your face just now. I did."

"My face?" he repeated, looking alarmed and confused.

"Watching her walk away."

He cocked his head. "I'm sorry. I'm not following you."

"You looked like you were dying inside."

He pulled back. "Nuh uh. No way. I don't know what you think you saw, but it wasn't that."

"Deep longing," I said stubbornly. He was right. I did like to pick scabs.

"Not for her," Todd said. Perplexed, he ran his hands through his hair, disturbing his curls. One fell over his forehead just like Superman, and I itched to push it back. I watched him try to figure out what I was talking about and thought he was treating my paranoia more kindly than it deserved.

"Let's forget I said anything," I said, turning toward the car. "I was out of line. What you felt or feel for her is really none of my business, is it? I spoke out of turn."

Todd put a restraining hand on my arm. "Stay here. We need to figure this out."

"No, we don't." But I waited as he stared off into space.

Finally he looked at me. "When I think of Clarke and Kristie, mostly I think of how suited they are for each other and how great it was that the Lord brought them together. That's what accounts for any look of longing you saw on my face. I only hope that someday I'll have what they've found. I haven't seen it all that much in my life, but it's what I want and pray I'll find."

I stared at him, overwhelmed and terrified. I couldn't think of a single thing to say except hallelujah, and I didn't think that was quite appropriate right now.

Dear God, it's too good to be true. He's too good to be true. I'm scared to death! But I'm going to enjoy every moment I get before he disappears.

"Come on," he said, ignoring the sudden onset of my being struck dumb . . . or perhaps he was enjoying it. He guided me toward the car, his hand on the small of my back. "Let's eat so I can get you to the farm."

When Todd drove me back to the Horse and Buggy after I met Jake and saw the farm, I thanked him earnestly for telling me about the rooms.

"It will be so wonderful living there," I said as we pulled up in front of my motel room.

Todd looked at me and grinned. "You're vibrating again."

"I am not."

"Vibrating," he said.

"I do *not* vibrate. I'm quiet and reserved."

"You don't know yourself very well, do you?"

"I *do not* vibrate."

"Just like you don't ask impertinent questions?"

"Oh, I do that. It's a Bentley curse. I just don't vibrate."

I climbed out of the car with great dignity. I took my key from my purse with ladylike grace. I lifted my hand in a slow-motion farewell.

"Phony!" Todd called.

"Critic!" I responded.

He threw his car in reverse. As he looked over his shoulder to back out, I gave in to my excitement about the farm and bounced a couple of times on my toes.

"I saw that!" Todd called out his window as he straightened the car out. "Definitely vibrating."

I was all smiles as I collected my things. I was downright giddy when I turned in my key and left the Horse and Buggy.

"Wait till you see it, Rainbow," I told the unhappy animal as she lay in her travel cage yelling for help. "You'll love it! Lots of yard to romp in, and lots of barn cats to give you a run for your money. In fact, you almost soured the

106

deal, my friend. These farm folk aren't used to house cats. I had to promise that you'd be the best cat in the world, that when you're in our rooms, you'd use the litter box with never an accident."

"Elp!" pleaded Rainbow.

"Yeah," I agreed. "Help is right, given your feelings about a litter box. Just do your best, okay?"

I loved the Zook farmhouse. It was white with green trim and had a great front porch with a blooming wisteria climbing one end, dripping fragrant lavender clusters like soft bunches of grapes among the gray-green leaves. A great maple tree shaded much of the front yard, and the side yard was filled with a large vegetable garden edged with cyclamen petunias.

"Their smell helps keep the rabbits out," Jake explained.

My rooms were on the second floor, and I had to walk through the Zooks' living room to get to the stairs. Jake shared the ability to get to his rooms via the living room, but he also had a separate entrance to his apartment with a ramp for his wheelchair.

My rooms weren't large, but they were airy and open. The living room had a motley collection of secondhand furniture that somehow looked just right. A large blond-colored desk sat by a window. I put my laptop on it, and knew I'd enjoy sitting there to write, provided I didn't keep staring at the pastoral scene before me.

Fields of tilled brown and verdant green swept to the horizon over gentle swells of land. A white farmhouse, barn, and silo lay in the humid-hazy distance to my right. To my left was a farm pond fed by a stream that flowed briskly from a small, dense wood. Around the pond stood several black-and-white speckled cows, but I liked best the one that stood knee deep in the water mooing. If I were a painter like Kristie or the as-yet-unmet Mary, I'd paint her.

The vegetable garden was directly below me with beans and peas scaling stakes, celadon lettuce waving vitamin-laden fronds, and carrots fluttering delicate and ferny leaves.

My bedroom had an ancient sleigh bed with great curved head and foot boards and wore a beautiful handmade quilt in calico prints of royal blue, cream, and crimson. A handmade braided rug covered the floor by the bed. There was no closet in the room, but wall pegs were available for my clothes. I hung my beige silk pantsuit on a peg beside the door to the new bathroom, which was small but complete, every surface in it a blinding white. I put Rainbow's litter box in the space between the pedestal sink and the toilet. I put her in the box several times as I unpacked my meager belongings.

"You get the idea?" I asked as I held her in the

litter, petting her and telling her how wonderful she was. She murped and jumped out, shaking her feet fastidiously to get rid of any granules caught in her pads. She stalked to the bedroom window and, in that marvelous liquid motion cats have, leapt to the windowsill. She settled down to chatter through the screen at the barn swallows that dipped and soared after the late-afternoon insects and at the purple martins that lived in the miniature white apartment on a pole in the middle of the garden.

"I'm going to Silver Spring tomorrow to collect some more clothes," I told Rainbow. "Will you be all right here alone?"

She didn't deign to answer.

I thought of pictures and plants and personal things I'd bring back with me to make these rooms my own. I wondered if the Zooks would mind if I hung some curtains. I'd noticed they didn't have any in their living room. Maybe they thought curtains were too worldly or something, a decoration that defied their definition of simplicity.

"Would they mind?" I asked Jake when I found him out by his van in the drive. "I'll use spring tension rods so I won't make holes in the frames."

"What you do to your rooms is up to you," he hastened to tell me. "They understand that my tenants will be English, and that means things like curtains and TV."

"I'm not English," I said, though come to think of it, how did I know what nationality I was?

"You're English in that you're not Pennsylvania Dutch," Jake explained. "It's a colloquialism. German or English. Plain or Fancy."

"Ah. Interesting."

Jake said, "You'll learn a lot more unusual stuff—at least it'll seem unusual to you—before you're finished. I'm going to go get a hoagie for dinner. Want me to pick up one for you?"

"Sure." I said. I wasn't all that hungry yet, but I knew I would be before the evening was over.

"Oil or mayonnaise?" he asked.

"What?"

"Oil or mayonnaise on your hoagie?"

"You can't put mayonnaise on a hoagie," I said, scandalized at the very idea.

Jake shrugged. "I do."

"Then it's not a hoagie. It's a sandwich on a long roll."

"You sound like Todd. He's an oil man too."

Forty-five minutes later Jake and I sat at his mother's kitchen table and ate our hoagies. Jake was a dark man with heavy shoulders and a strong upper body. He had a powered wheelchair that he handled with great ease. He also had anger leaking from him like air from a latex balloon in spite of his efforts to keep it hidden.

"I met Kristie this morning," I said. "She told me how much she loved it here."

110

"Yes, she did," Jake said. "She did a great watercolor of our barn." He pointed through the window.

I looked at the swaybacked building. "That's one of the pictures Todd has hanging in his office. That means the other one, the one of the quilt with a faceless Amish doll resting against it, is your mother's."

"Mom was so pleased when he bought one of her pictures, and when he showed it to her framed and ready to hang, she actually cried."

I glanced at the walls around me, all empty of any hangings except a calendar with colorful nature pictures and Bible verses and an advertisement for Morton's Funeral Home. What was it like for Mary to have this talent, this drive, this need to paint born in her and yet live in a culture that told her it was wrong? I tried to imagine what it would be like if I were told I couldn't write.

"Old Todd's come a long way," Jake said. "He used to think Kristie's painting was foolish, but he came around when he saw how much Clarke encouraged her and how well she was starting to sell. What he used to see as foolish, he now seems to admire."

"I wonder what he thinks of writing romances."

"Is that what you do?" He looked at me as if he couldn't believe he was having an intelligent conversation with someone who did something so foolish.

I nodded. "It's great fun. I love it."

"Have you been published?"

Since the answer was yes, I loved answering that frequently asked question. "Nine books so far."

"And you can make a living at it?"

"I've been blessed and I can. Most people can't."

"Huh," he said. He looked at me like he couldn't quite believe writing romances was an honorable way to earn a living. He wasn't alone.

"Romances are about people and relationships, love and marriage and family," I said, wanting to convince him how wonderful they could be when they weren't obsessed with the physical side of love. "They're also very big business, and inspirational romances have a strong market niche of their own. Lots of women enjoy reading them, and you can say some pretty important things in fiction."

He still didn't look convinced, but he didn't pick a fight either. Instead he asked, "Why did you decide to move to Bird-in-Hand?"

"I'm looking for my grandfather's family." I picked up the sweet peppers that had fallen out of my hoagie and slid them back into the roll. "He was given up for adoption a long time ago, and I want to find out where he—and the rest of us—came from."

Jake nodded as he wiped a glob of mayonnaise

from the corner of his mouth. I refrained from telling him that if he used oil like he was supposed to, he wouldn't have to worry about neatness. Unless, of course, there was too much oil and the hoagie dripped all over everything like mine was doing.

"I see adopted people on TV who are looking for their parents," he said. "They all sound like such unhappy folks, like there's a big hole or something in their lives. Is that how you feel?"

"No. At least I don't think I do," I said. "If I were adopted, maybe I'd feel that. I don't know. I'm just curious to know where Pop came from. If he wasn't a Bentley, then who was he? Who are we? Do I have family out there? Pop was an only child and so was Trey, so extended family would be nice."

"Trey?"

"My father. And Caroline's family, that's my mother, they live so far away, they might as well not exist. I used to feel that when Caroline died, something in them died. They lost interest in Ward and me. Maybe seeing us was too painful or something. I don't know. I just know they were never there for us. Maybe I can find some people my brother and I can belong to."

"So belonging is why you're doing this?"

"Part of it. There's also tracing blood ties and all that implies."

"DNA, genetics, inherited traits?"

"That's what makes family."

Jake looked thoughtfully at his empty hoagie wrapper. He balled it and one-handed it into the trash basket beside the propane refrigerator. "I don't know about that. Take my family. There are six of us kids. Three of us have chosen to remain Plain and three of us haven't. Sarah's the oldest and she's Plain. Andy's next and he's not. He left over the issue of works versus grace, saying he believed in salvation by grace, not by keeping the *Ordnung*."

"What's the *Ordnung*?"

"The unwritten laws that govern Amish life."

"If they're unwritten, how does everyone know them?"

"We're taught them our whole lives. But some, like Zeke and me, want no part of all those rules. There was nothing religious about our choice to leave the community. We chose not to remain Plain because we wanted freedom and fun and speed."

He bounced his hand on the arm of his chair. "Not that speed did me any good."

We were silent a minute as we contemplated what speed had done for him. Or to him. Then he continued.

"Elam and Ruth, the youngest two, have chosen to remain Amish. Now I ask you, why this diversity of opinion among us when we were all taught with the same intensity and commitment by our parents? Wouldn't DNA and all that stuff tend to make us more similar rather than less, which it seems we are? How come Andy and Zeke and I got independent thinking, even rebellious genes, and Sarah, Ruth, and Elam got good little cooperative Amish ones?"

That was a very interesting question. "Genetics doesn't make family members completely the same. Look at any family and you'll see differences in siblings. It just guarantees that there are various similarities, some unimportant in the larger scheme of life like hair color or a taste for seafood, or some important trait like the need to excel or an ability in mechanical things or art."

"Yeah, maybe, but that's not the part that binds you together." Jake frowned, intent on making his point. "At least I don't think it is. What makes family is like Mom and Father taking me in and willingly dealing with all the fuss my care entails, especially since they don't agree with the choices I made that eventually put me in this chair. That's what makes family. It's caring and loving."

"So you don't think genetics is important?" I gathered my garbage and took it to the trash can.

"Well, yeah, but—"

At this point we were interrupted by the arrival of a horse and buggy in the drive. We both looked out the window as a slim woman in a royal-blue dress and black apron climbed out.

She wore her hair pulled straight back in a knot and her head was covered with a white *kapp*. She stopped and said something to the bearded man holding the reins. He laughed and drove to the barn.

"Mom and Father," Jake said unnecessarily. "No Elam. He's probably gone to a sing somewhere."

So I met John and Mary, and they were every bit as welcoming and delightful as Kristie said they'd be.

Later that evening I was in my room happily arranging and rearranging my few belongings when I realized I didn't know what time Mary served meals. Was breakfast at five to beat the cows or did they eat after milking and I could sleep in until seven? Or should I plan to get up whenever I wanted and pour my own cereal?

I started down the stairs when I heard a murmur of voices.

"*Welcommen*, Martha, Big Nate," Mary's gentle voice said.

Uh oh. Company. I'd ask about breakfast later. I turned to go back to my room when a strident voice echoed through the house.

"I must speak, John. Such disregard for right must be addressed."

I made a face. Just what everyone liked—a guest who came to criticize.

I started back up the stairs when I realized that snarly person was now speaking about me. I sat on the top step to listen, mentally assuring Mom that if the subject matter pertained to me, it didn't count as eavesdropping and bad manners. I swear I heard her snort.

"How could you take in another girl, John? It was bad enough you let the one that painted in. Her and her bright colors." He sniffed in disapproval. "I was thankful when she left, but now you let in another?"

"Big Nate," said a timid, tentative voice.

"Martha, I must speak. You know how I feel."

I just bet she did. She probably heard his opinion 24/7.

"It's all right, Martha," Mary said, more gracious than I would have been.

"Big Nate, I do this for my son." John's voice was amazingly even considering the reaming the unknown Big Nate was giving him. "It's how he—"

"Your son has gotten the punishment of God for his actions. Do not use him as an excuse for your own behavior or God's hand might smite you."

What? Was Big Nate, whoever he was, saying that Jake's accident was punishment meted out by God? And that by letting Jake rent me the apartment, John might have something terrible happen to him? I couldn't believe the man's gall, and I guess John couldn't either because there was a moment of silence below.

"Big Nate, we do not agree here," John finally said. "It would be better if we did not speak of it."

It was as if Big Nate didn't hear John. "It is bad enough that you bring in phone and electricity for him. Do you now bring in women for him?"

My spine snapped straight. Wait one minute! That is my reputation he is impugning!

"Big Nate!" Mary sounded appalled. "You should be ashamed thinking we would allow something like that in our home."

"Mary, be still. Let me." John's voice was gentle.

"Well, who is she?" Big Nate had the grace to sound a little less critical, but the edge was still there. It occurred to me that he was speaking in English instead of Pennsylvania Dutch, and Mary and John were automatically responding in kind. Why English? Did Big Nate hope I heard? Was that why he spoke so loudly?

I heard the front screen door open. "I thank you for your concern for us and our family," John said. "We will see you again soon, I'm sure."

"I am not through here," Big Nate protested.

"Good night, Big Nate. Mary has had a long day and needs to get her rest. She'll be putting up strawberries tomorrow, and you know how tiring that is."

Probably not. I was sure the old Scrooge had never lifted a finger in the kitchen in his life. I could hear his angry footfalls as he stomped across the porch and down the steps.

"I'm sorry." It was such a soft whisper, a mere breath of sound, that I barely heard it.

"Don't be upset, Martha," Mary said. "We understand that Big Nate speaks for himself, not you or the rest of the people."

"I begged him not to come, but he said if your buggy was here, it was God's will he confront you. Still, he knows you aren't doing anything like . . . like—" She didn't seem able to finish the thought.

Thank goodness one of them was sane.

"Shhh," Mary soothed. "You'd better go. He's waiting."

The screen door opened and closed again, and there was silence until the noise of a buggy jingling and hooves clomping indicated Big Nate and Martha had pulled out of the drive.

"Oh, John!" Mary's voice was unsteady.

"Shush, my Mary. We must not let a man like Big Nate upset us. I do not regret that we gave Jake our approval to use his empty second story."

"I'm not worried about having another tenant here. I was thinking about something else. What if Big Nate finds out about my painting? He would love to make trouble for us, and Kristie and my painting would be his opportunity."

"Are you going to tell him you paint and sell pictures?" John asked.

"Never!"

"And neither am I. So there is no way he will find out."

"And I'm not telling him either," came a third voice, Jake's voice, vibrating with intensity. "I ask you, with men like that in the church, why would I ever want to return?"

"Jake." Mary's voice was steeped in sorrow and hurt.

"Don't ask me to be nice about him, Mom. If he somehow learned about what you and Kristie are doing, he'd come down on you like a ton of bricks."

"We will not talk of him," John said. "He's a man who has lost his son, and he cannot forgive us for having ours still."

"He didn't have to lose Davy." Jake's anger reached up the stairs and curled around me where I sat. "He sent him away!"

"Davy had to be shunned, Jake. You know that." John was obviously going over material covered many times before.

"Just because he got pressured into joining the church."

"He races cars!" Mary said, scandalized.

"And I bet it kills Big Nate that he's successful

at it. I saw him in a race on TV last weekend."

"Big Nate doesn't even know, Jake," John said.

"Kristie wants me to be on TV," Mary all but whispered as if saying the thought would earn her the reproach of her people, which it probably would. Certainly Big Nate.

"What do you mean?" Jake asked.

"She said something about a page that showed my work so more people would see than come to the store."

"She wants you to have a Web page, Mom." Jake laughed. "That would be so cool. You should do it."

"But I have to get my picture taken. Kristie says."

"Only if you want. You could put up pictures of your paintings without a photo of you. Come on over to my place, and I'll show you some Web sites."

There was another short silence. I guessed Mary and John were considering stepping over that *Ordnung* line, though probably the rules didn't say you couldn't have a Web page because no one ever thought it would be an issue.

"Do you think Kristie has one?" Mary asked.

"Come on. We'll look."

I stood and went to my rooms. Later, as I lay in bed, I thought about Big Nate's visit and about Mary and John's precarious balance on the edge of obedience to their beliefs. How much could they give in the name of family and in the name of a God-given ability without breaking something?

Family was caring and loving, Jake said. Certainly they were part of family, no one would argue that. But I kept coming back to the psalms that talked about family. It was generation to generation. It was DNA and genes and bone and sinew. It just was.

And that was why I needed answers.

Chapter 6

When I woke up Monday morning, I lay in my sleigh bed and stretched contentedly. If change could bring such wondrous things as Amish farms and families and handsome lawyers into my life, I might have to reassess my life-long aversion to it. I felt myself tense as I thought of actually becoming flexible, but when I remembered I didn't need to achieve that goal today, my shoulders relaxed.

I pushed aside the crispy white sheets that smelled of sunshine from their drying on a clothesline and went into my new little bathroom. I decided that I'd bring some towels from home to add a little color to the utilitarian white, but it was a delight to be the first to shower in the new-smelling stall, the first to steam up the mirror, and the first to drape a damp towel over the rack.

I put on tan shorts and a white T-shirt and brown sandals. I braided my hair loosely so that it might actually dry before I went to bed this evening and tied off the braid with a rubber band. It flopped back to fall below my shoulder blades. Then I went to my laptop on my desk.

I sat down, intending to pull up my Bible program and have my devotions, writing my thoughts in my electronic journal. Instead I became mesmerized by the glorious June day outside my window. I slid the window open. Muzzy pale sky indicated heat and humidity were ahead, but the faint morning coolness made that threat seem toothless at the moment. I stared at the fields of tender corn stalks, golden winter wheat, and tomato shoots, and sniffed in greedily the rich scent of dew-moistened earth.

God, You are so good to me! I typed. *Thank You, thank You!*

I opened to Psalm 78 and read verses 5 through 7 as I hummed "From Generation to Generation" under my breath.

> He decreed statutes for Jacob
>   and established the law in Israel,
> which he commanded our forefathers
>   to teach their children,
> so the next generation would know them,
>   even the children yet to be born,
>   and they in turn would tell their children.
> Then they would put their trust in God
>   and would not forget his deeds
>   but would keep his commands.

I turned to my journal again.

I want to know the missing generations in our family. I want to meet them, to find out things I don't know, to learn family stories that are missing from our heritage. And, Lord, I want to make certain the generations still living know about You.

When I finally came down for breakfast at eight o'clock, Mary insisted on cooking for me even though I knew the family had eaten hours ago. She left a huge pile of cut strawberries sitting on the counter, and in no time two eggs and toast made with her own whole-wheat bread sat before me.

"Are you making strawberry jam?" I asked when she returned from a trip to the basement with her arms full of small Mason jars.

"I am," she said. "I love this job. When I'm done, I have this wonderful feeling that I've done something worthwhile. And next winter when John and Elam enjoy the jam on their potato rusk or oatmeal bread, I'll feel pleased all over again."

I thought about my ignorance of tasks such as making jam and decided that though I thought Mary was clever, conscientious, and to be admired, I had no desire to learn this particular art. I'd rather just eat Mary's . . . or even Smucker's.

Mary put her hand to her mouth, looking distressed. "I hope I didn't sound proud just then. I only meant that I like making jam, though I forget that sometimes in the middle of the job when I'm hot and tired."

"You didn't sound proud," I said, thinking she should meet some writers I knew if she wanted to hear talking proud. "You sounded like a woman who is fortunate enough to do something that gives her satisfaction."

"You don't do things you like?" she asked, looking at me carefully.

"Oh, but I do," I assured her. "I love what I do. But many women don't."

"Many women don't?" Mary was surprised by this statement. "Everyone I know is content with what they do." And she went back down to the basement at a rapid pace.

I thought about Mary's comment. I couldn't say the same thing about many of my friends, even the successful ones. And my friends were women with a wide range of life choices, especially compared to Mary's friends and their limited options. Interesting.

I rose, washed and dried my breakfast dishes, and thought about how much I was going to miss a dishwasher during my stay with the Zooks. Some modern conveniences were required for quality of life, weren't they?

I was looking out the window above the sink when Mary reappeared with another armful of jelly jars.

"There goes Jake," I said. "First day at college. You must be proud of him."

I looked at Mary and found her watching Jake

back the van from the drive. Her face reflected great misgivings and no little sorrow. She felt my glance, gave a small smile, and turned back to sorting her jars.

Mary started to speak at the same time I realized how inappropriate my comment had been, given the family's culture. Eighth grade education, I remembered. College must seem strange and frightening.

"I'm sorry," I said, but she waved me off.

"I guess I'm happy for him in one way." She filled a large pot with water and put it on the stove to boil. "I'm glad he's making a life for himself in spite of his injury, but—" She paused. "Watching him go off to college is hard. It's just another proof that he'll never choose to come back."

I knew she meant back to the Amish community, and while my heart ached for her pain, I knew she was right.

"It's funny," she said. "John and I tried so hard to teach them right. I've never been able to figure out what we did wrong."

"Maybe you did nothing wrong," I said as I opened cupboards, looking for a place for my cleaned dishes. "Children make their own choices."

"I keep telling myself that," Mary said. "But it hurts. And I know some of the people in our district sit in judgment on us. Lots of families have maybe one child who turns from the faith, but we have three of our six who have left." She turned and faced me. "Did you know that most Amish children are baptized and remain in the community? The world doesn't realize that, I don't think. They can't understand why a young person would choose to remain, but I can't understand why anyone would want to leave. Yet half of my children did."

I slipped my silverware into a drawer. "Jake says it's because he's too independent and so are his brothers."

"But how did they get that way?" Mary asked as she scalded the jelly jars with the now boiling water. "We taught them the virtues of obedience and submission. We told them over and over that it wasn't being an individual but being part of the community that's important."

"Have they ever told you why they left?" I leaned against the counter, taking care to be far from the strawberry juice leaking in a glorious shade of red from the pile of cut berries.

"Andy did. He was the first to leave. He became good friends with Clarke Griffin when he lived with his aunt and uncle down the street during high school. Clarke told him all about what Andy calls grace. Andy listened. He wouldn't join the church because he said we were too works-oriented. He used to say things to John that Martin Luther said."

I was surprised she knew of Martin Luther. "You mean like *sola fide* or *sola scriptura*?"

"Maybe. I think. What do they mean?"

"Only faith and only the Scriptures."

"Not the *Ordnung*," Mary said sadly.

"Not the *Ordnung*," I agreed.

Mary was silent for a while, the only sounds the rapid chopping of more strawberries as she cut them in pieces so small they were almost pulp.

"But at least he believes something!" she burst out in what I came to realize was a rare display of emotion. "Zeke and Jake don't believe anything. They just got rebellious. It's like they never got over their *rumspringa*, ain't?"

"I guess it is," I said.

"And Jake's so bitter most of the time. You won't believe it, but he was a happy little boy. He loved to giggle and play jokes on the rest of us. Always a smile." She mixed pectin and sugar and put them to cook, and slowly added the strawberry pieces. "Now I'd give anything for some of that joy."

I was thoughtful as I left later that morning for a brief return home to Silver Spring, my heart aching for Mary but also understanding Jake and his brothers' need for more room to stretch. But the lovely day and the feeling of adventure about my move to Bird-in-Hand soon dispelled any pensiveness. I listened to CDs and sang along at the top of my voice, something I did only in the privacy of my car or shower.

When I got home, it didn't take me long to collect the clothes and items I wanted to take back with me. I carefully packed the car, buckling my printer/fax/copier in the backseat and stacking files and correspondence I thought I might need over the summer in cardboard boxes. I put my dictionary and thesaurus in a box with my printer paper and spare ink cartridges.

I requisitioned the small TV Pop had put in his room so he could face the nights alone after Mom died. I packed three sets of colorful towels, one a soft azure, one a yellow with blue stripes, and one a pretty rose. I also grabbed two sets of floral patterned sheets, one in cream with soft pink flowers growing on deep-green boughs, the other a garden of crimson, gold, and green on bisque. I noticed as I put my shirts, shorts, and slacks in a suitcase that I had an inordinate amount of beige, ecru, and ivory. And the dresses that I draped on top of everything were beige too. Why could I buy colorful towels and sheets but not clothes?

I was definitely in a rut. *You need color, woman! After all, if you vibrate, which of course you don't, you need to wear color.* How sad that I thought even a yellow would be wild on me.

Just before I left, I called Marnie to tell her about my new temporary life.

"Cara! I don't believe you!" She was clearly shocked and delighted.

"Come and visit me," I said. "See where I live. Meet the Zooks. Meet Todd."

"Try to keep us away," she said. "We'll be there in time for dinner Friday."

"Hadn't you better check with Ward? He might be busy."

"If he is, he'll cancel. He'll be so concerned about his little sister and this lawyer who's obviously out for your money that he'll have a hard time waiting until Friday."

"Todd doesn't even know I have money. Tell Ward he worries about me too much."

"Like that would stop him." Her tone of voice was both wry and affectionate.

I laughed. "Poor Marnie. I'll make dinner reservations for four and ask Todd to come along." If I have the nerve to give such an invitation, I thought. Just the idea made me sweat and hyperventilate with all the possibilities.

I arrived back at the Zook farm just before dinner. I was still unpacking the car when Todd arrived. He'd obviously come straight from the office. His suit jacket lay on the backseat, a light loden slash against the gray of the upholstery. His tie, a darker loden with the tiniest gold medallions I'd ever seen, hung loose against his white shirt. His cordovan loafers shone beneath his cuffed slacks.

"Just checking to see how Jake's first day went," he explained, but I noticed he smiled at me as he said it. He also helped me lug everything up to my rooms.

As he set my printer on the big desk next to my laptop, he said, "You take your writing seriously, don't you?" There was a mix of surprise and uneasiness in his voice.

"It's how I make my living," I said. "I have to take it seriously."

"Romances?" He looked dubious.

"Romances. Want to read one or two?"

He looked nonplussed. To give him time to deal with the idea of reading a romance, I fished in one of my boxes and pulled out copies of *As the Deer* and *So My Soul*.

"You don't have to tell anyone," I said as I held them out. "It'll be our little secret."

He took them somewhat reluctantly, which did little for my ego. Then he redeemed himself by suddenly asking, "You'll sign them, won't you?"

I took the books and penned a nice, generic sentiment and signature. He took the books back with a fair amount of aplomb, and I thought there was a chance he might actually read them. I knew that I'd never ask if he did. I didn't want to risk the pain of hearing a negative answer.

We went downstairs, and Mary asked Todd to stay for dinner.

"I was afraid you wouldn't ask," he said and took a seat next to me.

Most of dinner was a discussion of the crops and weather and people I'd never heard of. Near the end the conversation turned to Jake's first day in college.

"I loved it," he said, eyes sparkling. "I was afraid I wouldn't be able to follow the lecture, but I could. Or that I wouldn't know what they were talking about, but I did. And you won't believe the amount of reading I have to do for tomorrow! I've got to get started right after dinner."

I smiled inwardly at his enthusiasm and his naiveté. Big college grad that I was, I knew his workload would only get worse. But I was delighted he was delighted. Next thing we knew, he'd start smiling about life in general.

John looked at his son uncertainly. "They aren't working you too hard, are they, boy? *Himmel*, you don't want to get rundown or nothing."

Jake smiled, at least with his lips. "Don't worry, Father. I'm fine."

Mary served us apple dumplings with real cream for dessert.

"Mom," Jake said, "my favorite. Thanks."

I glanced at Mary. It was obvious that while she and John didn't understand their son, they loved him. Apple dumplings were a fine, non-prideful way to show it.

Todd helped Mary and me deal with the dirty dishes, something both John and Jake thought amusing. I thought it was wonderful.

"Want to take a walk?" Todd asked after the last dish was dried.

"Sure," I said, aware of a lightness that came over me at the invitation. I could have walked from here to Silver Spring and back.

We turned left at the end of the drive and walked along the edge of the road, the westering sun warming our backs. We didn't speak, just enjoyed the somnolent tranquility. We watched adult purple martens flying in and out of their house, still feeding their fast maturing birdlings. A pair of fat rabbits raced across the road ahead of us, disappearing into a patch of orange day lilies. A crimson streak of cardinal flashed over-head. On a fence post, a mockingbird sang his patchwork melodies, one moment mewing harshly like a herring gull, the next warbling sweetly like a song sparrow or a wood thrush.

We came to the clump of woods I could see from my bedroom window and with unspoken accord turned into it. We walked through the light underbrush until we came to the stream. It burbled breathlessly over mossy rocks, eventually forming a small, serene pool. We sat on a pair of large rocks beside the brook and watched a long-legged water bug walk on water, surface tension holding him successfully aloft.

"I think I'll drive up to Harrisburg tomorrow to visit the Bureau of Vital Statistics," I said apropos of nothing. "I'll ask for a copy of Pop's birth certificate."

"Don't bother," Todd said emphatically. "You won't get it, not even in his Bentley name. They'd *never* give you a certificate in his birth name. Privileged information. I had to deal with the state once about a birth certificate for an adopted person who needed one for a passport. He was an older man who was adopted long before the state automatically issued new certificates in the adoptive name. We wrote letters, went to Harrisburg, practically got down on our hands and knees and begged before they would grant him the proper certificate, *cera impressa*. And that was for a certificate in the person's adoptive name. And he had a sister who could swear he was who he said he was."

"I can swear to who Pop was."

"But you're hardly a contemporary who can swear to his arrival. We had the man's birth name, the date of birth, even the name of the delivering doctor, though the doctor was dead by the time the man sought the papers. It still took us forever."

I frowned. I hated roadblocks in my plans, a Bentley trait if ever there was one.

"Besides," and I could tell this was Todd's culminating argument by the way he leaned into his comment. I imagined him leaning into a jury just this way. "Besides, why would they give you a birth certificate for a dead man?"

I grimaced. He was making a very good point. "I won't tell them he's dead."

Todd shook his head. "And when they ask why you're there instead of him?"

"Maybe they won't ask."

He leaned back, resting his weight on his arms. "I wish I could say you had a good plan here, Cara, but you don't. My advice as your attorney is don't waste your time and gas."

I stared at the pool, brooding, my arms around my drawn-up knees, my braid hanging forward over my shoulder.

"Don't look so discouraged," Todd said. "You've got your meeting Thursday with Alma Stoltzfus."

I nodded. I was looking forward to that appointment, but I still hated being foiled in what had seemed a good plan.

"Now I've got a nonbusiness question for you." He leaned forward until his head was even with mine.

I turned and looked at him expectantly.

"How'd you like to go to a formal garden party Saturday evening?"

I stared. "With you?"

"Of course with me. Do you think I'm into setting you up with other men?"

I grinned sheepishly. "Sorry. I'm just not used to invitations to formal garden parties from my attorney. If you knew Mr. Havens, you'd understand."

"I usually don't enjoy going to these things because I'm not a great chitchat person, but if you'll go with me, it might actually be fun."

Be still my beating heart. "What's the occasion?"

"Each year the president of the Lancaster County Bar Association has a bench/bar reception, and this year it's at The Paddock with outdoor dining and lots of schmoozing."

"And it's formal? Truly formal?"

"Yep. I'll be pulling my tux out of mothballs," Todd said. "And The Paddock is a beautiful home. I think you'll enjoy the evening."

I had no doubt whatsoever. "I promise not to wear beige." I made a little face. "I've recently realized how monochromatic I am."

He laughed. "I don't mind beige, honest. Like I said, it's . . . restful."

Boring, I thought. I took a deep, empowering breath. "Now I've got an invitation for you. My brother, Ward, and his wife, Marnie, are coming up Friday evening. Will you have dinner with us?"

He looked surprised but pleased. "Sure. Sounds nice."

We wandered slowly out of the woods and back down the road. The sun was now hiding behind some clouds low on the horizon, and prisms of refracted light turned the sky fuchsia and orange and fierce purple. I loved the deep, rich silence and the fact that Todd seemed as easy with it as I was.

It was a rude jolt to hear a car speeding down the road behind us. The short burst of a siren as it neared jarred us. We stepped to the side of the road as an ambulance rushed past. As always, I wondered where it was going and who was the needy person at its destination. I breathed a quick prayer.

When the ambulance slowed and turned into the Zook drive, Todd and I looked at each other, fear and uncertainty on our faces.

"Jake!" Todd said, and we ran toward the house.

But it wasn't Jake. It was Mary. She had taken the basement stairs too quickly in the fading light, jars of cooled jelly in her arms, and she'd tumbled to the bottom.

When we reached the house, the emergency medical technicians were already inside checking her. Mary lay half on the basement floor, half on the stairs, her right leg twisted around the upright that supported the railing. There was blood all over the place.

"She cut herself on broken glass," Jake said from his wheelchair when he heard my gasp.

John and Elam stood at the foot of the stairs watching, their faces pale and frightened.

Mary was in severe pain and trying not to show it. She did fairly well—probably much better than I ever would.

"Breathing's okay," said a curly haired young woman with glasses. "Her lungs are clear. Blood pressure's okay too. No bleeding in the ear. The blood appears to be from external wounds."

"Her pupils are equal," said the second EMT, a short, stocky man who was busy applying pressure to a large gash in Mary's right thigh. "Hand me some pads and a couple of cling bandages."

"I missed my step," Mary managed to say. "I was almost to the bottom, but I missed."

The woman nodded. "And your arms were full so you couldn't protect yourself."

"I fell on the jars."

Quickly the EMTs staunched the hemorrhaging.

"We want to protect this leg, Mrs. Zook, but we don't want to straighten it right now. We're also going to put a KED splint on you to protect your back. A fall down the stairs is always dangerous," the young woman said.

"But I only fell three or four steps," Mary said in a weak voice.

"We can't take a risk here in case of spinal or cervical injury."

Working with speed and care, they padded Mary's leg with blanket rolls and wrapped it to hold the rolls secure. In a few more minutes she was wrapped in a splint that went from her head to her hips and closed with Velcro straps down the front. Then the EMTs transferred her to a rigid backboard.

The female EMT positioned herself at Mary's head, the man at her feet.

"On three," she said. "One, two, three." They lifted the backboard.

The woman began to ascend the stairs, and Todd moved quickly to grasp the board and help her with the weight. Elam stepped up to help at Mary's feet. I held the front door, and in no time Mary was in the ambulance. Jake had followed us outside by way of a detour into his apartment to use his ramp. His face was closed and dark, and when he turned to his father and brother and spoke, his voice was harsh.

"Come on. We'll follow her to the hospital."

John and Elam nodded and trailed him to his van, looking back at the ambulance as if they wanted to do something more for Mary. Jake kept his eyes straight ahead and his shoulders rigid. I thought he was struggling to hold himself together—and not just because his mother was badly hurt.

He hadn't been able to help. When it was time to carry her, he'd had to sit helplessly as others lifted her. He'd had to watch his brother and Todd do what he yearned to do. Even I, in holding the door, had assisted his mother while he was forced to endure being useless. He'd had to turn away and roll into his rooms so he could use his ramp. He'd discovered yet another searing limitation of his injury.

My heart ached for him as much as for Mary.

When Jake was in his van, the young woman EMT approached me where I stood with Todd. She kept glancing over her shoulder toward the van.

"Excuse me," she said very softly. "Can you tell me his name? The guy in the wheelchair?"

"Jake Zook," I said.

A smile swept across her face. She doubled her small fist, pumped it discreetly, and said softly, "Yes!"

I watched her, intrigued. "Do you know him?" I asked, realizing that was a foolish question even as I said it. If she knew him, she wouldn't have to ask his name.

"Yes," she said as she turned to the ambulance. "But not really."

Now there was a clear answer if ever I heard one.

The other EMT leaned out of the back door of the ambulance.

"Come on, Rose," he called impatiently. "You're holding us up!"

∙ ∙ ∙

On Wednesday afternoon I went to Todd's office for my appointment. Mrs. Smiley was just as moved by my presence this time as she had been last week.

"Hello, Mrs. Smiley," I said with gusto. "It's good to see you again too. I've missed you. And I love your brown dress. It just matches your brown shoes. But aren't long sleeves a bit warm?"

I got no response beyond a look that would curdle milk, but then I didn't expect any, especially in the face of my phony jocularity.

"Miss Bentley, please have a seat." Her voice was cool and correct, and she gestured to the paisley chairs with a beautifully manicured hand. I noticed her nails were bright red today, with the ring finger of each hand sporting one white and one blue diagonal stripe on the scarlet enamel with a small white star blinking at me as she typed. I didn't know who did her nails, but she clearly knew how to reach that hidden, repressed part of Mrs. Smiley that I could only guess at.

After ignoring me for a few minutes, Mrs. Smiley rose from her chair and nodded briefly at me. "This way, Miss Bentley. Mr. Reasoner will see you now."

How did she know he'd see me now, at this precise moment? I hadn't heard her contact him. I hadn't heard him contact her. Maybe in her other wild fingernail life Mrs. Smiley was a spy and the office was full of sophisticated electronic gadgets that allowed her to snoop on Todd, clearly a man dangerous to the United States. She would call Homeland Security any minute now. I smiled at Mrs. Smiley, imagining her karate kicking a villain from here to Paradise —the small town over on Route 30, not the one Jesus invited the thief on the cross to share with Him.

When I entered his office, Todd rose from behind his massive desk with alacrity, his hand extended in welcome. He showed me to the cozy alcove beneath Kristie's and Mary's paintings. He took a seat beside me on the sofa.

Mrs. Smiley noted our physical proximity and signaled disapproval by a slight sniff as she closed the door.

"I don't think she likes me," I said.

He grinned. "She just likes playing mother hen by protecting me from predatory females."

"Ah." I grinned back. "Of course."

"So how's Mary?" he asked. "Is she still in as much pain?"

"She's still in the hospital, but she's going to be fine. I stopped in for a few minutes earlier today. She has a broken right leg, but the break is clean. They had to wait for the swelling to go down to cast it. She also has several gashes from the broken jelly jars; the ones on her right hip and leg and one on her right forearm are especially deep. They've been stitched, but one's developed an infection. They hope to send her home by the end of the week, and the home-health nurse will come to check on her daily."

"How are they managing at the farm? Are you cooking?"

"On that wood stove? Are you kidding?"

He folded his hands across his stomach. "It is pretty intimidating, I imagine."

"Understatement." I shuddered at the thought of tackling it. "No, they've got a *maud*."

"A *maud*?"

"A maid. A single woman from their church has moved in for the duration. She's living in Ruth's old room. Her name's Esther Yoder. She's this cute little thing about nineteen years old with big dark eyes and rosy cheeks. And I notice that her eyes follow Elam more than casually."

"Watch it, romance writer. You're hatching a plot here." He smiled.

"No," I said. "If I wanted to hatch a plot, I'd go after Rose, who knows but doesn't know Jake. Do you think she's the Rose that Kristie mentioned? The one we're not allowed to talk to Jake about?"

"I'm supposed to know the answer to this?"

"Sure," I said. "I'm paying you to know all the answers or at least to know where to find them."

"Well," he said, settling back against his end of

144

the sofa like he'd finally found a topic of discussion he was comfortable with. "I've done some checking around and have come up with some suggestions for you on trying to find your grandfather's background."

I leaned forward eagerly. "So tell me."

"First, it'd be a good idea to go to the agency he was adopted through and ask them if they'll open his records. They'll probably say no, not without the consent of the Biemsderfers. They should be willing to trace the family and ask on your behalf if they'll agree to open the records."

"I thought of that," I said. "I went to the library yesterday, and the research librarian and I spent some time trying to trace the Children's Home Society of the City of Lancaster: For the Relief of the Poor and the Care of Destitute Children." The long title rolled off my tongue. It'd never make it in today's world of acronyms, but it sounded solid and slightly stuffy and very proper to me, very 1918, like men in neckties and vests and bowlers and ladies with gowns to the floor and gloves and large-brimmed hats. "We found that the agency headquarters burned to the ground in 1926, and all records were lost. There is no hope of any information there."

"Oh." Todd looked slightly nonplussed, though I wasn't sure if it was at my wealth of information or at the fact that I'd beaten him to the idea.

"When I learned there was no help to be had

there," I continued, "I went to Harrisburg to the Bureau of Vital Statistics and talked to them."

"I *told* you that would be a useless trip." He was somewhat abrupt in his comment. "I told you not to waste your time."

"You were absolutely right," I admitted. "But I had to try, you know."

"Why?" he asked. "My word isn't good enough?"

"It's called double-checking," I said.

"You think I don't double-check everything, Cara?"

"I'm sure you do," I said to soothe his ruffled feathers, though why they should be ruffled was beyond me.

He cleared his throat, trying to keep his pique controlled. "There's another very slim possibility, but you could check the newspapers for a birth announcement. I don't imagine there would be one, given that this was probably an illegitimate birth, but . . . " He shrugged.

"I thought of that too," I said. "I went to the Lancaster Newspapers, Inc., offices today and spent some time with the researcher in the morgue. There's not a Biemsderfer mentioned in the paper from 1917 to 1919. In 1920 a Dwayne Biemsderfer married a Rebecca Crum. But I need a birth announcement, not a wedding announcement. And I need a female Biemsderfer, not a male."

Todd sat still, staring at me with surprise, I supposed.

"Next I went to visit Orphan's Court to see if they could help me." I turned to him accusingly. "Did you know that Orphan's Court has nothing to do with orphans and adoptions? It has to do with probate issues and estates. Why in the world don't they just call it Probate Court or Estate Court? It would save innocent people lots of confusion. By the way, Lancaster has a very nice courthouse. I was impressed."

I smiled and sat primly, my bone sandals neatly side-by-side. Mrs. Smiley would have been proud had she seen me. I hoped Todd noticed that my cream pants outfit had a tiny coral flower pattern through it. Not all beige today, though certainly not full of pizzazz.

Todd's fingers, still folded over his stomach, were tapping, tapping. His face was carefully devoid of emotion. Completely gone was the pleasure he'd shown when I first arrived.

"May I ask you a question?" His voice was deadly soft.

"Sure," I said.

"Why did you bother to hire me?"

"For your legal advice."

"Which you've either ignored or not waited to hear."

"You're mad because I went to Harrisburg?"

"I did not say that."

147

"You didn't need to. It shows. You're really used to people doing exactly what you say, aren't you?"

"I did not say that either. Cara, if you're going to run off here, there, and everywhere all on your own, you don't need a lawyer."

"In other words, you don't want to be my lawyer anymore?"

"I did not say that."

"You aren't saying much of anything, are you?"

We stared at each other, jaws set.

"You really like to be in charge, don't you?" I said coolly.

"That's what I'm hired for," he said. "Because I'm the authority."

"So you say." I couldn't help it. Bentley genes.

"If you want to talk about people who like control, you might just want to look at yourself," he suggested, ice in his voice.

"I'm only doing what I do every time I write a book," I said. "I'm researching. We *romance writers* pride ourselves on our research skills."

He ran one hand through his hair, and the curls on the left side of his head leaped to disarrayed life. With his other hand he straightened his already straight tie. I could tell he was struggling for a calmness he didn't feel.

There was a gentle ping from his desk, and Todd spun toward it. "My next client is here," he said.

So that's how she did it. I rose. "Fine."

We walked stiffly to the door. He reached to open it for me.

"What time will you be picking me up Friday night for dinner with Ward and Marnie?" I asked, my voice neutral.

He started. "You still want me to go?"

"Of course. Why not?"

"But we just had a fight."

I almost laughed. "You think that was a fight? That was just a good, old-fashioned clearing of the air."

"It was?"

"If you want to talk fight, you should have seen Mom and Pop when they had one of their rare disagreements. Those were real fights."

I told him the story of the time Pop was going to San Francisco for a convention and Mom wanted to go along and stay for a week or two afterward for vacation.

"We can't do that, Tess," Pop had said, making a unilateral decision just like he made at work all day. "I need to get back to the office as soon as I can. And you can't leave the kids anyway."

I was ten and Ward was twelve at the time.

"I can't *not* go with you," Mom said, her voice crisp and emphatic. That half-strident tone should have been a warning to Pop, but he was too preoccupied with his own thoughts to notice.

Mom plowed on, her voice getting louder and louder. "You have become a workaholic, John. We have to get away together so you can remember who you're married to. And it isn't *business* in spite of what you seem to think!"

He stared at her, unable to believe his gentle wife was screeching, but he wouldn't yield. "No, Tess. The issue isn't open to discussion."

"Then I am also not open to discussion."

And she didn't talk to him for four days. She did all her regular things around the house with a pleasant manner and she joked with us kids and loved us kids as usual, but whenever Pop spoke to her, it was like she had gone deaf.

Finally on the fourth night he came home from work late to find Mom, Ward, and me eating dinner. He stalked up to the table and threw a pair of airplane tickets down in front of her.

"Satisfied?" he roared.

Mom picked them up, read the dates, looked at him and smiled. "Completely. I'll call the baby-sitter tomorrow."

"No more sulking?" he demanded.

"No more dictating?" she shot back.

He grabbed her by the wrist and pulled her out of her chair and into his arms.

"I can't stand it when you're mad at me, Tess," he said, his voice soft and hurt.

"And I can't stand it when you forget me, John." There were tears in her eyes.

He gave her a huge kiss while Ward coughed and gagged expressively. Then with arms about each other's waists, Mom and Pop disappeared upstairs, giving Ward and me a whole evening to watch TV, which we did until our eyes bugged out.

"*That* was a fight," I said, smiling at Todd. "You and I had a mere clashing of wills."

He looked at me thoughtfully. "Cultural divergence due to family background."

"Seems like it."

"A great gulf fixed? Or is there a sturdy bridge we can cross?"

I squeezed his hand, which I found myself holding somehow. "We'll find one."

He squeezed back. "Or build one."

We were staring at each other when Mrs. Smiley opened the door and snorted.

Chapter 7

I liked Alma Stoltzfus immediately. She was just the kind of woman I'd always wanted for an aunt. She laughed easily, talked readily, and seemed genuinely interested in helping me. If she didn't have the information I needed, she would do her best to help me find it.

Her brown eyes snapped and her expressive face showed a keen intelligence. She had legs to die for under a slightly plump, chesty body, and like Pop and Ward, she seemed unable to talk without using her hands. They sliced through the air in whorls and lines and circles, pointing, underlining, explaining. She was hard-pressed to get her spoon full of Tuscany potato soup to her mouth without waving it and losing its contents en route.

While we ate lunch, I told her about Pop and Mom and my family, and she told me about her husband, Art, and their children, Art, Jr., called Bub, Suzanne called Sissy, the twins, Theodore called Ned and Theodora called Dolly.

"I don't know why we named the kids one thing and called them another. I'm sure it says something about Art and me, but I haven't the vaguest idea what, and I frankly don't care. All I care is that Bub and Sissy have given me four of the cutest grandkids you ever saw, three from Bub and one so far from Sissy. When the twins finally get married, I expect several more. Oh, lucky me! Believe me, young lady, there's nothing like grandkids." And she pulled out a passel of pictures.

Nodding and looking, I felt a zip of pain that there was no one I could ever give grandchildren to.

Finally I finished my pasta fagioli and salad and Alma her lunch, and we got down to the purpose of our visit. We pushed everything to one corner of the table, and she unrolled a large chart. Lines and brackets were laced with names and dates, beginning with a single name in 1821, Karl Biemsderfer, and getting progressively more dense and complex as the years passed.

"Lots of fascinating stories here," she said, indicating the upper reaches of the chart. "But your point of interest begins with this generation," she said. "My grandfather's."

I looked where she pointed and read *Dwayne Biemsderfer m. Rebecca Crum.*

"I found their wedding announcement in the newspaper archives," I said. "I was looking for Biemsderfer birth announcements and found this instead."

"Old Dwayne was quite the looker," Alma

said. "I've seen sepia photos of him and Rebecca. Even in those formal pictures, he looks very handsome. I can't say much about Rebecca though. The severe hairstyle of the day didn't do much for her."

"Maybe she had personality," I suggested.

"That's a kind thought." Alma shrugged. "I don't remember Dwayne and Rebecca well enough to comment. They died when I was pretty young." She tapped another set of lines. "Now here's Dwayne's brother, Harold, who married Julia Miller and had five children—my aunts and uncles. There are lots of people for you to trace in this branch of the family, but it will be more difficult and time-consuming because most of them have moved away from Lancaster County. They're literally all over the world because several of them are missionaries."

I stared at Harold's name and the list of descendents that trailed from it. If I had to try and locate all those people, I'd be forever trying to solve Pop's mystery. Of course, I would have the pleasure of traveling all over the world. Look how much fun I'd had since coming here.

"And this," said Alma, finger snapping against the chart, "is the baby of the family and the apple of everyone's eye, at least according to Grandfather Dwayne and my father. Here's Madeleine Biemsderfer who married Enos Lehman."

"What?" I stared at the paper, goosebumps on my arms. I reached out and put my finger on the name, as if that would make it more real. "Enos *Lehman*? Like in *Lehman* Biemsderfer?"

It couldn't be coincidence, could it? *Dear Lord, don't let it be just coincidence!*

Alma looked at me speculatively. "I knew you'd jump at that name, so I checked carefully. They married in 1920, well after Lehman Biemsderfer was born. And their children are listed here. Elizabeth who married Harlan Yost and Joshua who married Kay Proust."

"Of course Pop wouldn't be listed even if he were Madeleine's son." I put my hand to my chest over my rapidly palpitating heart, patting my fingers against my upper rib cage, trying to tamp down my excitement. "Children born on the wrong side of the blanket don't make family trees."

"True," Alma granted, her fingers rubbing over Madeleine's name and freeing the paper of nonexistent wrinkles.

"I need to know more about Madeleine," I said as much to myself as to Alma. "I need to know more about Enos."

"Then you need to speak with Aunt Lizzie. She can tell you as much as anyone about her parents."

"Aunt Lizzie is Madeleine and Enos's Elizabeth? Aunt Lizzie?"

Alma smiled. "Don't get too hopeful, Cara. The repeating of the name Lehman doesn't have to mean a thing. And it certainly doesn't *prove* a thing."

I nodded. "I know." But it did. I knew it did. I felt it in my bones.

"Tell me about Madeleine's line of the family," I said. "What do you know of her parents?"

Alma traced her finger back a generation on her chart to Joshua and Lottie Biemsderfer. She tapped their names for a few minutes while I waited, trying to curb my impatience.

"Lottie was supposed to be a kind woman, and her pictures indicate she was quite lovely, made for the old-fashioned gowns and hairstyles. Joshua, on the other hand, was a stern man, the product of a strict German family, when strict meant rigid and unyielding. That he married the charming Lottie is amazing. I have some letters he wrote to her before they were married. He went West for a time, trying to determine if he'd seek his fortune as a rancher. If he was intimidating in person, and everyone seems to agree that he was, on paper he was a true romantic. The letters are beautiful and full of genuine passion. She drew him back, the flame attracting its smitten moth, and he returned to claim her as his bride and settle here. They were married for fifty years before he died, a truly long marriage for those days when people died younger than today.

"Family legend has it that he was besotted with their daughter Madeleine because she was so like Lottie. He pampered her and loved her, but instead of growing up spoiled, she grew up as charming as her mother. If Madeleine was your great-grandmother, the pregnancy must have broken Joshua's heart. And his background, that old rigidity, and the mores of the day must have made it almost impossible to allow knowledge of the pregnancy to be public."

I sat mesmerized as Alma talked about these people who may have been my ancestors, my family, every bit as much as they were hers. I kept swallowing, trying to control the teeming adrenaline attacking my stomach.

"Oh, Alma," I said, almost breathless with speculation, "what if Madeleine had Pop before she and Enos married? What if Joshua didn't approve of them as a couple, and they decided to take things into their own hands?"

Alma looked at me with kind, intelligent eyes. I knew she'd already thought of several possible scenarios of her own.

"What if," I said, "he was marching off to war? After all, Pop was born in the middle of World War I. It could have been one of those I-might-never-see-you-again things, you know?"

"I've thought of that," Alma said. "And it's definitely a possibility. The other thing that was happening historically was the influenza epidemic, in which thousands of people died. I've wondered if that somehow played into this situation, though I haven't figured out how."

I had a scenario immediately. "Maybe Enos had a brother who was Madeleine's first love and he died of the flu before they could marry." I could see the pathos of the scene as clearly as if I were writing it—which was sometimes with more clarity than if I witnessed it. "Then she had to give away her baby, her only real link to her true love. Enos, devastated by the death of his brother, came alongside Madeleine to comfort her at the loss of both her love and her child, and she fell deeply in love with him. Happy ending."

"I can see why you're a successful novelist." Alma laughed gently at my excitement and handed me a glass of watered-down Coke. "Take a drink, my dear. It'll calm you."

I blushed but I didn't back down on my imagined plots for Madeleine. I wanted desperately for my great-grandmother to have been happy. "I must visit your Aunt Lizzie."

Alma nodded. "She lives at Tel Hai Retirement Community in Honey Brook. I'll call her and tell her you'd like to visit. Then I'll call you and tell you what she says." She turned concerned eyes to me. "I don't think you should just show up, you understand. Aunt Lizzie is old and frail and has a bad heart."

"Of course. I certainly don't want to give her a heart attack."

Then I looked at Alma, my heart on my sleeve. She stared for a moment, trying to understand my expression. Then she nodded and pulled a cell phone from her purse.

I grinned happily as she dialed. Not wanting to seem too impolite in spite of the fact that I listened with an intense excitement that sent little zaps of anticipation zinging thorough my entire body, I busied myself rolling up her marvelous chart.

After their initial chitchat, Alma told her briefly about me. She then put her hand over the phone and said, "She'll see you any night but Friday."

"How about tonight?" I fluttered my hand over my heart. Nothing like being pushy.

A moment later Alma hung up and looked at me.

"Well?" I prompted. My lungs seemed unable to pull in air for the great paralysis that had taken possession of them.

Alma smiled. "Tonight around seven."

Air whooshed out as I recovered my ability to breathe again. "Thank you, thank you, thank you! You have no idea what this means to me."

She patted my hand. "I wish you well. And—" She paused and studied me, "I think I'd enjoy being your aunt or cousin or whatever it is we might be to one another." She held the rolled document out to me.

"For me?" I stared from it to her, stunned by her comment, suffused with affection for her and all the others I hadn't yet met.

"For you. It's a copy." She patted my hand again as I reached to take it. "Just be careful, Cara. I don't want you to build too many castles in the clouds and then get hurt. We don't actually *know* anything yet."

I nodded. I understood her concern although I wasn't certain I could prevent the castle building.

"You don't mind if I pray for you, do you?" Alma asked. "For God's leading and protection over you?"

"Not in the least," I said. "I've been praying about this search ever since I learned there was something to search for. I've even been praying that I find that my family prays."

"Well," she said, "some of us pray anyway."

"The missionaries," I said.

"And a few others of us."

We walked out of the restaurant side-by-side, an easy camaraderie between us.

God, I want her to be my aunt or whatever she'd be. Can she be my aunt? Please?

When Alma halted beside her car, I stopped with her.

She reached to give me a quick hug. "Let me

know what you find out, even if we aren't the right family, okay?"

I nodded and stood watching as she drove away. I climbed into my car, putting the family tree—my family tree?—carefully on the passenger seat. My stomach was still teeming, and my heart was hammering like the tympani at the "Wonderful, Counselor, the Mighty God" section of "For unto Us" in Handel's *Messiah*. I *knew* I was on the right track. I couldn't wait to tell Todd. And Ward and Marnie, I added belatedly.

I drove across the street from the Olive Garden to Park City Mall and went shopping for a dress suitable for a formal garden party. It didn't take long to realize that everything I was attracted to was beige, tan, cream, or champagne. My favorite dress was a soft cream silk that looked great on me, but I wouldn't allow myself to buy it. I was not going to be bland even if it killed me.

I finally settled on a coral column dress that fell from my shoulders to my ankles, skimming my body lightly. I bought new dress sandals in *gold*, not bone or taupe, and earrings of gold and coral that swayed and twisted below my ears. No little gold buttons for the special night. I decided I would carry the beautiful cream cashmere shawl that Pop and Mom had given me for my twenty-fifth birthday, the fabric so fine and delicate you could see through it. Surely cream was okay for a shawl.

As I was leaving the store with my wild purchases, I passed the men's department. I wandered over to the ties and studied them. A wide splash of tans, browns, corals, and crimsons caught my eye. I thought of the monochromatic outfits Todd wore and the ties with the tiniest of patterns. I grabbed a wild one and bought it before I could change my mind. If I had to get rid of beige, he had to get rid of overly buttoned down. It was only fair.

As I drove toward home, I decided I couldn't wait until evening to tell Todd about my time with Alma. I grabbed my cell phone from my bag and dialed his office. Mrs. Smiley answered.

"Mrs. Smiley, this is Cara Bentley. May I speak to Todd, please?" I tried for Bentley imperiousness so she would comply but ruined it by saying meekly, "That is, if he's not with a client."

With a click of her tongue, Mrs. Smiley put me through.

"Cara, what's up?" Todd's voice was rich and vital, and I thought I'd rarely heard a more pleasant sound.

"I met with Alma Stoltzfus," I said. "And—"

"And you're vibrating," he interrupted.

"I am not."

He laughed. "Where are you calling from?"

"I'm on 340. I just got off the 30 Bypass."

"Stop in and tell me what happened. It'd be much better in person."

"I'm not interrupting anything important?"

"I don't see another client for about an hour."

I was still giddy when I pulled into the parking area behind his office and got out. It was strange and wonderful that though I only knew one person in Bird-in-Hand and he was male, I not only felt free to call him, but he actually asked me to stop at his office on a nonappointment basis. I felt like one of my heroines.

It was obvious when I walked in, though, that Mrs. Smiley did *not* share my elation at the unscheduled visit.

"Miss Bentley, Mr. Reasoner does not receive visitors while at work," she informed me. "Only scheduled clients."

"I'm a client," I said, ignoring *scheduled*. "Remember? Just tell him I'm here, please."

She picked up the phone, announced I was there. She stood and moved toward the inner office. She knocked and opened the door.

"Mr. Reasoner," she said as she unhappily ushered me into the office, "you must tell me when you change your schedule. How am I to keep the office running smoothly and efficiently if I don't know your plans?"

"*Mea culpa*, Mrs. Smiley," he said, trying to look properly contrite. The fact that I was standing behind her smiling broadly at his groveling efforts didn't help his attempt to look apologetic. I wiggled my index finger back and forth at him in silent reprimand.

When we were finally seated side-by-side on the alcove sofa, I opened the family tree that Alma had given me. I felt like an ancient Christian unrolling a letter from the apostle Paul, looking for and finding clues to a new life.

"Todd, I've got to tell you! I think I've found my family!"

Todd's mouth quirked in that half smile, and he shook his head. "You're definitely vibrating, woman!"

I looked at him, exasperated. "I am not."

He raised an eyebrow.

My hand pulsed against my collarbone and I relented a bit. "Okay, so maybe I'm excited."

"Vibrating—and no maybe about it."

"Excited," I said with deliberation.

"Can't face the truth, can you?"

"Can't leave well enough alone, can you?"

We grinned at each other and kept staring long after the grins died away. His dark eyes captured mine, and I was trapped in their warmth just like a heroine in one of my novels would be. It was a ridiculous, wonderful moment.

Todd broke first, clearing his throat and saying, "So, tell me all about it."

I blinked. "Right." And I showed him Madeleine who married Enos Lehman.

"Lehman, Todd! Lehman!" My finger trembled just a bit as it pointed out the name. "Just like Pop."

"But don't forget that Lehman is a relatively common name around this area." He bent forward over the chart, studying it seriously, giving the moment its due. "Just because your grandfather was called Lehman doesn't mean he's connected to Enos Lehman. Besides, when was your Pop born?"

"1918."

"And when were Madeleine and Enos married?"

"1920."

"Bit of a time discrepancy there. Isn't two years after the event a long time before a marriage between the principals would take place?"

I frowned at him. "I don't know. Maybe all it means is that we don't have the right explanation yet."

"Maybe." He looked at me carefully. "But, Cara, it could mean a lot more than that." His voice was soft but his point was hard. I knew he meant I needed to remember that there might be no connection.

"Spoilsport," I said unhappily.

"Cara, look at me."

I tore my eyes from the family tree, *my* family tree. It had to be!

"Cara, don't set yourself up for disappointment by believing so strongly with so little information."

"Advice from my lawyer?"

"Advice from someone who cares and who also happens to be your attorney."

We sat quietly for a couple of minutes while I tried to deal with my conflicting emotions. I knew he was right when he said I was jumping ahead without proof. I knew he was right when he said I was setting myself up to be hurt. I knew he was right when he said I didn't have enough information.

But I didn't want him to be right! I wanted God to answer my prayer and make these people mine. I wanted Alma to be my aunt. I wanted to be a Biemsderfer! My passion for wanting these things was unreasonable. I knew it. The need I felt was out of proportion, and I knew that too. But the yearning remained, filling my mind and heart with a craving of extraordinary intensity.

Was it genes calling to genes? Or was it that Ward and I were alone in the world? Or was it a weakness in me that required I get my dream, like a kid who demands a pony for her birthday and won't be satisfied with less, even though she lives in a city in a fourth-floor apartment?

While I sat and lectured myself, Todd continued poring over the chart, studying it with deep concentration. He followed the lines of descent from Madeleine and Enos, until he got to the present. Suddenly he tapped his finger against a name.

"I know an Amos Yost," Todd said.

I looked at the name Amos Yost, son of Elizabeth Lehman Yost, daughter of Madeleine and Enos Lehman.

I turned, my eyes suddenly hopeful. "Will you introduce me to him? He would be Pop's nephew, my father's first cousin."

"If—"

"Right. If."

Todd was silent for a few seconds. "There are probably lots of Amos Yosts," he finally said. "Both Amos and Yost are common Dutch names."

"Yes, but—"

"Yes, but nothing," Todd said. "The truth is that I don't want this Amos to be yours. I really don't like the man all that much."

"Then let me meet him so I can cross him off my list. He does live around here?"

"He lives around here."

"Come on, Todd." I wasn't quite begging since I hadn't fallen to my knees and clasped my hands together, but I was very close to whining.

He cocked his head. "Let me think about it."

"Todd!"

"That's the best you're going to get for now."

And I could tell that it was. But I knew that given time I could talk him into introducing me to Amos. After all, I always got what I wanted out of Pop, didn't I? I decided to take a slightly different tack.

"Do you remember when you were a kid—"

"I try not to," he said wryly.

I refused to be sidetracked. "Now listen to me and don't interrupt." I spoke like a teacher might to her favorite hyperactive student.

Todd raised an eyebrow. "Bossy."

"Absolutely," I said. "Just ask Ward. Now, do you remember when you were a kid and you were going to do something very special and you got this agitated, uncomfortable feeling in your stomach? How it suddenly felt too full and you were almost sick?" I rested my palm on my chest and flapped my fingers up and down against my sternum. "Your heart got all fluttery and your chest got tight, like something was unfurling inside and forcing the oxygen out?"

He looked at me with an intensity that swirled about the room, a blazing energy directed at me. "I've gotten those feelings a lot."

He was not referring to any childhood experience. I knew that with certainty. Suddenly struck by the upset stomach, the fluttery heart, and the tight chest, I swallowed and tore my eyes from his penetrating gaze. I pointed a shaky finger at the family tree.

"That's how—" My voice broke. I cleared my throat and tried again. "That's how I feel every time I learn information that might have something to do with Pop." I was proud that my voice barely shook though my insides were trembling.

"Is that the only time?" he asked quietly.

"The only time?" I stared intently at the family tree.

"The only time you feel that special way?"

I blinked. Did he mean what I thought he meant? "What?"

Todd stared at me a minute longer. I could feel it. Then he abruptly shook his head. "Forget I said that."

As if I could.

He took my hand. "Listen to me, Cara. Please." His voice was now entirely different—friendly, nothing more. Lawyer to client. "I'm worried about you. You're so intense about this search."

I took a breath to calm myself. How could I make him understand?

"All I want to do is find the people who are bone of my bone and flesh of my flesh. I have no family now but Ward." My throat closed and I had to swallow once more, this time against the pain. "I want more."

"I have no family but my father," he said quietly. "Oh, I have some distant cousins on my mother's side that I haven't seen in ten years, so practically speaking, all I have is my father. It doesn't make any difference whether I want more or not."

I stared at him, struck dumb. His loneliness was palpable, though I don't think he realized it. My heart broke for the child he'd been and the man he'd become—alone, hurting, solitary.

"I'm so sorry." I pulled my hand free from his and quickly began rolling the family tree. "I didn't mean for my selfish search to make you feel bad." I looked at him through a sheen of tears. "I never thought that I might be hurting you."

Todd grabbed my shoulders and turned me toward him. "Cara! That's not what I meant."

I shook my head, staring at my lap. Ward and Marnie had warned me about possible problems as I searched, but I'd never imagined one like this, one that hurt someone I was starting to care for, someone who could never find any bone of his bone to love him.

His voice was gentle. "Cara, look at me."

I couldn't. I was embarrassed for my insensitivity.

He took my chin and lifted it, forcing my eyes up.

"You misunderstand," he said softly when my eyes finally met his. "I'm not worried about my lack of family. I'm worried about you! What will happen to you, *in* you, if all you have are Ward and Marnie? If none of this pans out?" And he flicked a hand toward the chart. "I don't want to see you disillusioned and frustrated by what you don't have when you've had so much and you have so much. You've got love and support and people who care. Can't you let that be enough?"

"Oh, Todd." I reached out and rested my hand along the line of his jaw. I felt the hard strength of bone and the soft warmth of skin, an admixture much like what I saw in the man himself. Tough yet tender. "I'll be all right. I will."

He studied me intently for another moment before nodding his head, as if accepting my comments.

With his nod, I suddenly felt awkward with my hand on his face in what I now saw as an unsuitably intimate gesture. I dropped it hastily to my lap and cast about for something to talk about to release the fizz of electricity in the atmosphere. My eyes fell on my purse lying on the floor by the sofa and the flat package lying beside it.

"Oh!" I said brightly. "I brought you a present."

He looked absolutely astounded, and I wondered when the last time was that someone had given him a gift. He took the flat box, its contents obvious by its shape.

"Is this what I think it is?" he asked.

"Probably."

"You don't like this one?" He fingered his tan tie with the thin, thin brown stripe.

"It's not that I don't like it. It's just that you tend to the monochromatic, and I'm offering a change."

"You, Miss Beige, are criticizing *my* wardrobe?" The smile took away any hint of reprimand.

"It's easier to redo you than me."

With a cautious expression, Todd opened the tie box. When he saw the wild splashes of color lying within, his caution turned to incredulity.

"You actually expect me to *wear* this?"

"Of course. You wouldn't want to hurt my feelings, would you?"

"Don't pout at me. I know manipulation when I see it."

"And I know a button-down personality when I see one. Take that tan thing off."

He put a protective hand over his tie. "Now?" He sounded like I'd asked him to strip in front of the Ladies' Missionary Society.

"Now." I lifted an eyebrow and stared, daring him to be brave.

Slowly his hand went to his throat and, with a deep sigh, he loosened the knot and removed the tie. I lifted the new tie and held it out to him.

"How nice you wore your tan suit today." I beamed. "Just like you knew to come prepared."

He rose and walked to the closed door of his small bathroom. He opened it, turned on the light, and stood in front of the mirror.

"Go on," I encouraged. "You can do it. If Mrs. Smiley can have wild nails, you can have a wild tie."

He looked daggers at me via his reflection, but he slid the tie under his collar and began the ritual of making a Windsor knot. As he did that,

I folded his old tie and placed it into the empty box.

He was looking at himself in the mirror, seemingly paralyzed at the rakish sight, when the buzzer on his desk announced his next appointment. He spun around, his tie fluttering with the abruptness of the move.

"Where's my real tie?" he asked, eyes searching the table where he'd dropped it.

I looked at the table and then at him with an innocent expression. "Looks to me like you're wearing the only tie I see. And it looks very handsome."

And it did. The rich colors made the crisp, deep brown of his hair and eyes even more arresting. He seemed to disagree.

"Cara." His voice was low and threatening.

"I'll see you at six for the trip to Tel Hai, right?" I headed for the door with my purse and the tie box with its contraband contents clutched to my chest. "I'm so glad you're going with me to meet Lizzie."

"Cara!" He took several steps toward me, and the glint in his eyes told me he couldn't wait to get me . . . or rather the item I held close . . . in his hands.

I grabbed the doorknob at the same time Mrs. Smiley pulled the door open. I sailed cheerfully past her and a startled client.

"Don't you love his new tie, Mrs. Smiley?" I

173

stage-whispered on my way by. "Matches your nails for style and pizzazz."

I glanced back over my shoulder and saw Todd, his flashy new tie swaying beneath his chin, shaking hands with his client as he glared over the man's shoulder at my retreating figure. I grinned and waved. His eyebrows rose, he shook his head, and I heard, "Look out, woman! I'll get you back," as clearly as if he'd actually said it.

Laughing happily, I went out to the parking lot.

Chapter 8

The day was so lovely that I decided to wait for Todd on the front steps. Rainbow sat beside me, eyeing the grass with alarm. With a sniff she walked to the door and stood, tail straight up, asking to be let back in.

"Get down there on the lawn and be a good kittie, you coward," I told her as I lifted her. She burrowed into me as I walked down the steps. When I leaned over to set her on the grass, she wrapped her paws around my arm, clinging to me, a difficult proposition for a declawed cat.

I put her in the middle of the lawn and stood back to watch. She looked at me in a panic and began walking as quickly as she could back to the porch. She lifted each foot high above the grass, which must have felt strange under her pads. She looked like she was prancing.

"She looks like Elam's Tennessee walker," Jake said as he wheeled around the corner. "He just got a new horse from a dealer that specializes in race horses, especially sulky-trained ones. Blue Grass lifts her legs just like that."

As Jake spoke, Rainbow hit the bottom step and flew up to the porch. She sat in front of the door, casting a begging glance in my direction every couple of seconds. I decided she was safe there and turned my attention to Jake.

"Anything new on your mother?" I asked.

"She's doing much better. She'll be coming home at the end of the week."

Nothing had changed from what I already knew. That was good. "I'm sure she'll like that."

Jake looked unconvinced. "It's not that she won't like coming home," he said. "She just won't like being confined to the bedroom. Mom's a doer, and she's going to go crazy with someone else taking care of her house—even someone as nice as Esther."

"I think Esther's got her eye on Elam," I said, thinking of Jake's dark-haired, gray-eyed, wiry, energetic younger brother.

"Poor Esther." Jake looked genuinely sad.

"Why do you say that? Does Elam have a girl?" I asked.

"He wishes. He's had a crush on Mary Clare Epp for years. I don't think he sees anyone but her."

"And Mary Clare doesn't return the favor?"

"I don't think so. You understand, I only know what I overhear. Not hanging around in Amish circles these days, my sources are very limited. But the last I heard Mom and my sister Ruth talking, it seemed Mary Clare was about to get engaged to young Joe Lapp."

"Poor Elam," I said. "But maybe having Esther here will turn his attention to her." Ever the romantic, I didn't need much of a plotline to perk me up.

"Well, this setup should let them know whether they can stand each other well enough to get married." Jake rubbed absently at a spot on the front of his T-shirt. "I've decided that's the most important thing for a marriage. You need to be able to stand being around each other."

I looked at him and laughed. "Ah, the bachelor who knows all about marriage from observation. Sort of like a childless expert on raising kids."

"I speak the truth as I see it," he defended with a smile.

"What about love?" I asked, unable to resist.

"What about it?"

"Doesn't a good marriage need it?"

He shrugged, his rugged shoulders rising and falling as if the question wasn't even worth asking. "Maybe love is simply being able to stand each other with a little chemistry thrown in for good measure."

"Well, I can tell you one thing, guy," I said. "I don't want to miss the chemistry part. Still, I do think you're right about the getting along part. It's the commonalities that make a marriage flow." Then I thought of Mom and Pop and Ward and Marnie and how dissimilar each of them was from their partners. "I've noticed though that it's the differences that give marriage spice and excitement."

"You want spice and excitement?" He seemed surprised.

"Sure. Don't you?"

He was silent for a minute, his face shuttered. "I don't let myself think too much about things like marriage in a personal sense. I choose to stay philosophical about it. It's safer."

"But dull," I said as I sat there in my boring tan slacks and tan-and-white striped shirt.

He smiled tightly. "Sometimes safe and dull are the way to go."

We were quiet for a couple of minutes while I wondered whether marriage was a possibility for him. I didn't know the extent of his injuries beyond the obvious, and maybe his thought patterns were to protect himself from what he saw as a solitary and lonely life stretching ahead of him. I'd have to ask Todd what he knew.

"Marriage is sort of expected in the Amish culture, isn't it?" I finally asked, reverting to Elam and Mary Clare and Esther.

"Definitely." Jake pulled his stare back from his contemplation of the shimmering haze over the fields across the street. "Faith and family are all."

"How would they look at someone like me?" I asked. "If I were Amish, I mean."

"You mean because you're unmarried or because you're a writer?"

I shrugged. "How about both?"

"As an unmarried woman, you'd be treated

politely, but you'd probably live with relatives. Since you're not a married woman, you'd sit with the unmarried folks at services, which in many districts means with the teens, even if you're much older than them."

I made a face. The idea of sitting with the teens forever didn't appeal to me, and I couldn't believe it appealed to any single Amish woman, no matter how obedient to the church she was.

"More and more unmarried woman have jobs outside the home," Jake said. "But being a writer would still be very rare. And being a published writer would be almost unheard of . . . except for being published in Amish newspapers such as *Amish Life*. But you wouldn't be writing romances. You'd be writing religious stuff."

I decided not to tell him that I wrote about religious stuff in my romances. "How about an unmarried man? Say that Elam decides to suffer for his lost love forever."

Jake shrugged. "Getting married's just the thing to do, and Elam would get married eventually in spite of Mary Clare's rejection. He'd find someone else. That's what Amish men do."

Jake's German shepherd, Hawk, ambled across the lawn and sat beside him. I glanced over my shoulder at Rainbow. She'd seen Hawk, though he hadn't noticed her. Her back was arched, and she looked panicky about the eyes.

"I think I'd better let the cat in before she has

a heart attack," I said, getting up to open the door for Rainbow. At the last minute Hawk saw her bushy tail zipping through the narrow opening to safety. He lunged up the porch steps and plastered his nose against the screen, whimpering. Rainbow was an orange-and-black blur as she dashed upstairs to our rooms and her hiding place under the bed.

I patted Hawk's head. "Sorry, guy. She's not very friendly."

Hawk looked up at me, and I realized I was making an assumption when I thought friendship was what he wanted. Anabaptist nonviolence did not appear to beat in his canine heart.

"Do the Amish ever adopt children?" I asked as I sat on the steps again.

"You thinking of your grandfather?"

I nodded.

Jake snapped his fingers at Hawk, and the dog regretfully left the door to sit by him. Jake's strong hands gently ruffled the animal's hair. "Certainly they would readily take in any child within the community who needed care. I don't know that they'd legalize it the way the English would, but the child would be raised as a member of the family. All the Amish value children, seeing them not only as hands to work the farm but as the future of the community."

Hawk raised up on his hind legs, front legs planted on the arm of the wheelchair, and kissed

Jake wetly on a cheek. Jake made a face as he hugged the animal about the neck. "Ugh! Have you got bad breath! What have you been eating?"

The dog didn't answer but settled happily on the ground at his master's feet.

Jake wiped at his slobbered face and continued the conversation just like Hawk hadn't interrupted. "As far as taking a child from outside goes, if they were approached, I'm sure they'd consider it. It's not a usual circumstance to cross those cultural lines because the gulf is so wide, and they would raise the child never to cross that chasm."

Of course they would. Everyone who adopts raises the child to share their beliefs and values. If you're from a cloistered community like the Amish, you raise the child to the cloister. If you're a Christian, the child's your personal home missions project.

I tried to imagine how our lives would have been altered if Pop had been adopted into an Amish home. How would he have submerged his vibrant, authoritative personality in a peace-loving and submissive culture? What would he have done with that great business acumen of his? What would I be like as a third generation Amish woman? The stretch was too great even for a creator of tales like me.

"You going out with Todd again tonight?" Jake asked, looking wickedly nosey.

I nodded. "We're going down to Tel Hai, wherever that is. Everyone seems to feel it's not too far, so I guess it's not. Do you know where it is?"

"Yep. I'm all too familiar with that area," Jake said. "It's right down the street from where I had my accident. There are these two big hills south of Honey Brook, and in the low part between is the turn to Tel Hai." He sketched the hills with his hand, then looked at me. "That's the infamous intersection."

"How did it happen?" I asked. "A drunk driver?"

He shook his head. "Too much speed, some wet leaves, and someone who ran the stop sign. I braked, skidded, and ended up with my motorcycle on my back."

"Oh, Jake!"

He shrugged. "I survived."

"Jake?" It was Esther, standing in the doorway, pretty as could be with her rosy cheeks and thick hair. I'd noticed that many Amish women had thinning hair, a combination of inbreeding and the constant pulling of the hair into such severe lines, I guessed. But Esther would never have that problem. Why didn't Elam realize how lovely she was? I wondered.

"Jake, Cara already said she wouldn't be here for dinner. How about you?"

"No. I'm going to the hospital now to see Mom so I can get back and still have time to study. I'll pick at something when I get back. Don't worry about me."

Esther nodded. "There'll be extra chicken pot-pie, I'm sure. And I made a lemon chiffon pie."

After she went back into the house, Jake leaned toward me and whispered, "Lemon chiffon is Elam's favorite."

Forty-five minutes later Todd and I came to the intersection where Jake had lost his life as he'd known it. It was just an ordinary country inter-section with open fields on two corners, a house and business on the third, and a thick stand of evergreens with new homes built among them on the fourth. Stop signs were in place to prevent drivers from coming off Beaver Dam Road onto the hills of Route 10 too quickly. But stop signs only achieved their purposes if people obeyed them.

"It's a wonder he didn't die," Todd said. "It was a brutal accident."

We turned onto Beaver Dam Road, and I looked for the house where Jake's angel of mercy lived.

"Martin!" I said as I read the name on a mail-box. "That's where Rose Martin lives!"

"Yep," said Todd. "Personally I think he ought to meet her and thank her, but he's a stubborn guy."

The little valley through which Beaver Dam

Road wound spread out around us, golden in the slanting light of evening. Shortly Todd turned onto the beautifully landscaped campus that was Tel Hai with its cottages, apartments, medical facilities, and rising over all, the white chapel spire pointing all residents heavenward.

My thoughts went heavenward too. *Dear Lord, let this meeting go well. Let Aunt Lizzie give me some concrete information. Let me find the answers!*

As we drove to the parking lot, we were separated from the neighboring Amish farm only by a thin strand of electric fence. I could see the farmer standing on a piece of farm machinery as a six-horse team pulled it through a field. The beauty of the scene barely registered. I was caught in the drama of my quest and hope for impending answers.

"Oh, Todd, this is so great!" I said.

He misunderstood me and thought I meant the facility was great. "My father likes it here. He's got his own little cottage on the other side of the campus, and he can get as involved in the activities offered or be as solitary as he chooses." He paused and then continued in a flat tone. "And with him, it seems solitude wins every time."

I was pulled from my thoughts of Aunt Lizzie by the barely concealed distress in his voice. I looked at him with interest. "Do I detect a bit of disapproval here?"

Todd squirmed and ran a hand through his hair, a move I was learning to know meant agitation. The curls on the left side of his head sproinged free. "I know I'm being ridiculous. He's always been a man who keeps his own counsel, who ignores people and emotion. Why should I expect him to change at this stage of his life? I just keep hoping that he'll get involved in the community activities, maybe even with people since he lives right in the middle of them." He shrugged. "*Casus fortuitus non est supponenous.*"

I waited for a translation, and when none came, I said, "Has anyone ever told you that this Latin habit of yours is a bit frustrating—not to mention bizarre?"

He looked surprised at the acid in my voice. "A fortuitous event is not to be presumed," he immediately translated.

"Thank you." I unsnapped my seat belt. "It sounded better in Latin. Then I didn't know it was in passive voice. We writers hate passive voice."

"Passive," Todd repeated. "That's just the word for Dad. He's a passive man. He's content to let life slide by without even attempting to grab hold of the things it has to offer. Wouldn't that bother you to watch?"

"Probably, because I'm about as compulsive as you. But what's more important, that he be happy with his life or that you be happy with it?"

185

He looked at me with a thoughtful frown. "Can you separate one from the other when it's family you're dealing with?"

Since I didn't know that answer any more than he did, I climbed out of the car. Time to find Aunt Lizzie. After asking a couple of people for directions, we finally ended up in the partial-care wing, third floor, talking with the woman in charge.

"You're the guest who's come to visit Elizabeth Yost, are you?" she asked.

I nodded. "Yes. Great-Aunt Lizzie." I spoke like this relationship was definite, absolute, immutable. I felt rather than saw Todd's unhappiness.

"Well," the woman said, and immediately I knew I had a problem. I glanced at Todd and saw the same response on his face. Surely this wouldn't be one of those so near-and-yet-so-far situations, would it?

"I don't want to alarm you," the woman continued, "but we had to send Elizabeth to the hospital about thirty minutes ago."

"Oh, no!" My first thought was purely selfish. I'd lost my source, maybe forever! Hard on its coattails came more charitable thoughts of the woman herself. "What happened? Will she be all right?"

"She began having heart palpitations to the point that the nurses knew she needed more than we could do for her here. They were afraid of a full-blown heart episode—no small thing for a woman her age."

"No small thing for anyone at any age," I muttered.

The woman spread her hands in regret. "I'm sorry. I hope you didn't travel too far."

"That doesn't matter," I said.

"I know she was very excited about seeing you. She told everyone at dinner that she was having a special guest tonight."

A sudden thought chilled me. "You don't think I'm the reason she had the heart attack, do you?"

The woman looked at me strangely, but then she didn't know why I was here. I looked at Todd, my face bleak. Maybe my coming was a bad kind of exciting, distressing to her, upsetting.

He smiled briefly at me, took my arm, and turned me toward an exit. "Thank you for your help," he said to the woman. "Can you tell us which hospital Mrs. Yost is in?"

"Brandywine Hospital. It's the closest, and they've got good emergency care there."

Todd nodded his thanks and led me outside.

I leaned against the side of his car, feeling the heat of the metal through my slacks. I put a hand to my forehead and rubbed the ache behind my left eye.

"What if is my fault?" I whispered.

"Hey," he said, leaning against the car beside me, crossing one ankle over the other. "It isn't your fault."

"You don't know that."

"True. But you don't know that it is either."

His voice was soft but firm, and I looked at him gratefully. "You're right. I don't." I felt liberated, like a door had been thrown open and the gentle breeze of his logic had blown away my assumed guilt. "I don't know for a fact that Aunt Lizzie's health difficulties today are my fault, and until I do . . . 'Sufficient unto the day is the evil thereof,' " I said, quoting Matthew 6:34.

He nodded. "Good girl. And we'll call the hospital to see how she is after they've had time to assess things. Okay?"

I studied him, my arms folded across my chest. *Lord, I can't believe this guy. He's so nice! I could like him, I mean really like him, so easily it scares me.*

He stared back, his mouth quirked in a half smile. "Are you all right?"

I blinked. "Yes." I stepped away from the car to face him and grabbed the first topic of conversation that occurred to me. "You know what? You need to run your hand through the other side of your hair."

He looked as if he couldn't quite believe what I was saying.

"Half of it's all free and curly," I explained.

"The other half is still sprayed within an inch of its life."

"What?" He grabbed the outside mirror in alarm and twisted it until he could see his reflection. "Oh no!" His hand went immediately to the springy curls, and he tried to plaster them back to the rigidity of the controlled ones.

"No, no," I said, grabbing at his arm. "Free the other side."

He stared at me. "You can't be serious."

"Go on," I encouraged. "You can do it. Let those beautiful curls spring to life. You have to or you'll look lopsided for the rest of the evening."

"Isn't it enough that you make me wear atrocious ties? Do you have to make me look like a leftover hippie too?"

I laughed. "Come on. Free those curls!"

With a groan he ran a hand through the restrained side of his hair. Immediately the curls sprang to exuberant life.

"Look at me," I told him.

He did, his face lemon sour.

"You've got the most wonderful hair," I said. "Why do you keep it a secret? You could have all the women in town lining up to run their fingers through it."

"Yeah, just what I want," he groused, but I could see a sparkle of pleasure peeking through his frown.

"Why do you dislike it? Do you think curls are for girls or something?"

"Well, they're not very professional looking. Do you think a jury or judge is going to listen to a frizzy-haired bozo?"

You, guy, will never be a bozo! For once I was prudent enough to keep my mouth shut.

"You just like it because you don't have to live with it," he continued, enjoying his grump. "You have wonderfully straight hair," he said as he indicated my hair, which tonight hung down my back from a barrette at my nape.

"I might not live with your curls, but I have to look at them. And I like to look at the freed curls. Now, let's go visit your father."

That little sparkle of suppressed pleasure disappeared. Sighing, he opened my car door and walked around to his side.

"You know, Cara, how you talk about what family is? You think it's bone of my bone and flesh of my flesh? Well, you're about to meet bone of my bone. We've shared DNA, genes, and a house, but for as long as I can remember, at least since my mother died, we have not been what I think of as family. We've merely been related."

He looked at me over the roof of the car and repeated in a voice both melancholy and hard, "We've merely been related."

He got in the car and we drove across the campus and parked.

I don't know what I expected in Dr. Milton Reasoner after Todd's bleak comments broke my heart, but it wasn't the handsome, white-haired gentleman who eventually answered the door when Todd rang his cottage's bell.

"Well, Toddy." It was a statement, like Dr. Reasoner was pronouncing the temperature: 78 degrees. Well, Toddy. No surprise, no pleasure, just acceptance.

"Hello, Dad."

The two men stared at each other through the screen while I slowly turned gray from the passage of time. Finally I could stand the silence no longer and spoke.

"Hello, Dr. Reasoner. I'm Cara Bentley." I wore my best smile and most scintillating manner.

Todd looked slightly pained, but he stepped belatedly into the breach. "Dad," he said, "I'd like to introduce Cara Bentley. She's a client."

"I'm pleased to meet you." Dr. Reasoner looked at me with a spark of interest in his eyes. At least I think there was a spark of interest. We were still standing on the porch talking to him through the screen so it was hard to tell.

Suddenly Dr. Reasoner came to himself. "Oh!" He reached for the door. "Please come in, Toddy. And bring your client."

Did I imagine a slight pause before the word "client"?

Todd took the opened door from his father, and

Dr. Reasoner turned into the house. As he walked away, I bumped Todd's arm. He looked at me questioningly.

"Toddy?" I said softly but with as much malice as I could manage. After all, he'd introduced me as a mere client. He deserved to be tormented.

He glared at me. "If you ever tell anyone, so help me I'll triple your billing."

"Nasty, nasty, Toddy," I said with a sly smile.

We walked into a living room furnished with a sofa, a leather recliner, and books. Books were everywhere—on shelves that lined three walls, in piles on the completely uncarpeted floor, on the sofa, on a coffee table, and on the end table by the recliner. They sat upright like in a library, soldiers at attention, or lay flat in high, haphazard stacks, children's block towers awaiting the right vibration level to tumble wildly. Big books, fat books, slim books. Leather covers, hard covers, soft covers. And all looked read, handled, and appreciated.

I wanted to stop and read the titles, but with a firm hand on my back Todd hustled me toward a glass-enclosed back porch. On the way, I glimpsed a bedroom and a den, both rooms holding a minimum of furniture and a maximum of books. The porch was awash with more books piled helter skelter, several open and laid on their faces, spines to the ceiling. The one nearest me was *Alice Through the Looking Glass* by Lewis

Carroll. A glass-topped table that I was certain was meant for summer dining was instead a repository for garishly colored paperbacks, mostly mysteries, espionage, and fantasy. I saw several Dick Francis titles, a smattering of Robert Ludlum and Helen MacInnes, as well as Stephen Lawhead's entire Pendragon Cycle and Donita Paul's dragon series. Face down on the table beside what was obviously his reading chair was the first of Diana Gabaldon's Outlander series, a leather bound copy of *Great Expectations*, and a much-read paperback whose title I couldn't see from this angle.

"Oh, Dr. Reasoner," I said breathily. "You are a man after my own heart."

I heard a gurgling noise from Todd, half astonishment, half alarm. Dr. Reasoner looked at me, startled and uncertain.

"The books," I said, sweeping my arm wide. "The books!"

Dr. Reasoner gave a nod, relaxing now that he knew exactly what I meant. "You love them too?"

"I do. I can't imagine a worse fate than being somewhere without a book."

Dr. Reasoner turned to Todd. "You say she's a . . . " pause "client?"

Todd nodded. "We drove down on business to visit Elizabeth Yost."

I waited for the normal questions and comments, things such as *Do you know her, Dad?* And, *No, Toddy, I don't,* or *Yes, I do.* Or, *Was it a good visit?* But there was nothing. Todd sat in a kitchen chair that he dragged to the porch. His arms were folded, his face set. I sat in Dr. Reasoner's reading chair at his silent insistence as he waved a hand in its direction and bowed me toward it. He took the only other chair on the porch, a webbed folding aluminum one. He proceeded to fold his arms exactly like Todd. The lines of his face weren't as set, though, because he was obviously curious about me.

I immediately became engrossed in reading the title beside me.

"*Beowulf*?" I read in surprise. I picked up the book. "In the original?"

"I don't want to lose my Old English skills." He said it like keeping such skills alive was as common and reasonable as crossing a street at the light.

"How about you?" I said to Todd, waving the book at him. "You ever read this?"

He shook his head. "Milton was about as dedicated as I ever got."

Again the men fell silent while I struggled to make sense of the text in my hands. I looked up, smiling. "How about if I read one of those Harry Kraus medical thrillers instead?" I pointed to a couple of titles on his book-filled table. I indicated a couple of other paperbacks. "I've already read all those Frank Peretti and Ted Dekker ones."

"What did you think of Dekker?" Dr. Reasoner asked.

"Well . . . " And then we had a wonderful discussion of writing styles and plot versus character-driven fiction and which was best and why. Every so often Dr. Reasoner or I looked at Todd to give him a chance to enter the conversation, but he merely sat there, looking somewhat stunned. Finally, when I glanced at him for the hundredth time, he spoke.

"Cara's a writer," he said with all the enthusiasm of a fisherman confessing that the fish had all gotten away. "Published too."

After a minute of astonished silence that Todd had actually spoken, Dr. Reasoner turned back to me. "Tell me how you got started. I love how-I-got-started stories." His brown eyes, so much like his son's, sparkled with anticipation.

I looked at Todd and found him staring at his father, obviously astounded. He felt my eyes on him and turned toward me. I winked and he gave a little snort of surprise and a half smile. This was certainly not turning out to be his usual visit with his dad, I could tell.

"I'd just graduated from college with honors in business administration," I said in answer to Dr. Reasoner's request. "In fact, it was actually graduation day itself. Pop and Mom and my brother, Ward, were all there. Everyone was talking about the future, and several of my friends were telling Mom and Pop their job news. They were going to be teachers and sales reps and engineers. Some were off to graduate school. When there was a brief lull in the activity, Pop looked at me. 'Sounds great, doesn't it, Cara?' He turned back to my friends. 'But Cara's going into the family business, and I'm proud as a peacock.' "

I looked from Dr. Reasoner to Todd. "I still remember the terror I felt at that point. Pop was such an achiever, such a moneymaker, so successful. What would he say when I made my confession? 'Pop,' I said, my mouth so dry I could hardly form the words. 'I don't want to work in the family business. I want to be a novelist. I want to write romances.' "

I looked quickly at Dr. Reasoner when I said the word *romances,* just like I'd looked at Pop, though for different reasons. I'd been afraid of Pop's reaction because he was Pop and I'd always pleased him to this point, always done exactly what he wanted, including majoring in business. I was not exactly afraid of the reaction of a scholar like Dr. Reasoner to my chosen field, but I was slightly intimidated. A man who read *Beowulf* in the original wasn't likely to be at all impressed by *romances*. And I had to admit that I wanted Todd's father to like me. I continued my story.

" 'Is there any money in it?' Pop asked. 'No,' I said. 'Probably not, especially not at first.' 'How about job security?' he said. I shook my head. 'Benefits?' I shook my head again. 'Just the benefit of doing what I love—if that counts. In fact, I already have one novel almost finished. I started it last summer, and I've been working on it ever since.'

"Pop studied me for several minutes while Mom, Ward, and the couple of friends with the courage to stand by me fidgeted in the background. I felt like I was dying a slow death, waiting for his pronouncement. I knew I'd end up writing regardless of what he said, but his response would determine whether writing would be my profession or my hobby, at least for the time being.

" 'I think God's called me to this, Pop,' I said, desperate to make him understand. 'I have all these stories in my head. I see these scenes and I hear these conversations, and these people are so real!' "

Dr. Reasoner nodded his understanding at my last comment, a fact that Todd noticed and frowned slightly over.

" 'Well, Cara,' Pop finally said, 'I think you should do what you want to do, what you feel called to do. You can live at home at no expense for the time being, and I'll bear the expense of keeping you on our insurance for now, but you must earn all your personal money and begin to pay your own insurance as soon as it's feasible. So I suggest you keep your usual summer job as cashier at the Silver Spring Bentley's.'

"So I sent out that first novel and wrote days while I worked late afternoons and evenings at Bentley's. That novel never sold, but my next one did to a flat-fee publisher. By my fourth sale, I was with a bigger publisher on a royalty basis, and soon after that I got an agent. My writing career has been getting better and better."

"I'm so glad he recognized your call," Dr. Reasoner said. "I'm sure he's very proud of you." He glanced at Todd, who was diligently studying his feet. "I've always been so proud of Toddy."

Todd jerked at that, head whipping up to his father, mouth all but hanging open in shock. But Dr. Reasoner had turned back to me and didn't see the struggle between disbelief and joy on his son's face. I did though, and I wanted to cry. How tragic that Dr. Reasoner saw fit to tell me this highly important fact instead of telling the man who desperately wanted to hear it.

"I'd like to read something you wrote," Dr. Reasoner said gallantly.

I pulled my eyes from Todd and smiled at the old gentleman's kindness. "I'll give a book to Todd to give to you."

"Wait!" Todd said, suddenly coming to life.

"I've got one in the car." And he almost dashed from the room. In no time he was back with the copies of *As the Deer* and *So My Soul* that I'd given him.

I sighed a great mental sigh. It was painfully obvious that he had not even cracked the covers. Not that he'd had time to read them yet, but he could have at least taken them into his house instead of forgetting them in the car. He could have at least looked inside the covers, read the first page, even read the last page.

Todd glanced at me as he handed the books to his father, who immediately began reading the cover blurbs. He turned to page one. The porch fell silent. I tried not to squirm. What would a scholar like him think? Did I want to know?

After about fifteen seconds the silence got to Todd. He blurted, "We've got to go. It's a long trip back."

Dr. Reasoner walked to the door with us, reading as he walked. "The cover copy makes these sound wonderful. And I like the hook of the opening. It's obvious you're not working a cash register anywhere these days."

"Nope, not at all." I shook his proffered hand. "It's been a pleasure meeting you," I said sincerely.

I had noticed that he and Todd hadn't touched when we arrived. Not that I expected to see a hug or anything overtly demonstrative, but they hadn't even shaken hands. Nor did they hug or shake hands goodbye. Todd sort of nodded in his father's general direction; Dr. Reasoner sort of smiled vaguely. And then we were gone.

The car had barely begun to move when Todd looked at me with something close to excitement in his face.

"Did you see that?" he exclaimed. "Did you see that?"

"Uh, what?" I asked, even though I knew what he was talking about.

"That visit! That was the best visit I've had with my father in years."

"I was afraid of that," I began, but he wasn't finished.

"And I have you to thank." He reached over and squeezed my hand as it lay in my lap. "Now tell me how you did it."

"How I did it?" I couldn't believe he was serious.

"Yeah. How did you get him to talk to you?"

"All I did was talk about something he likes," I said.

"Books?"

"Books." I had a moment of panic. "You do read, don't you? I mean, if you don't, what do you do in the evenings in your house all alone?"

He turned off Route 10 and onto 340.

"Well," he said, "I work on the lawn. I watch

the Phillies. I do e-mail and Facebook. I explore the Internet." He shrugged. "Stuff."

"But not reading."

He shook his head. "I read the Bible every day and the newspaper. And of course I read lots of legal documents, but fun reading? Not a lot. I think the detail of the reading I have to do professionally has slowed my reading speed so much that reading's not a pleasure."

I stared at my hands, deeply disappointed. Can a writer have a meaningful relationship—now there was a trite phrase if ever I thought one—with a nonreader?

"I saw your face when I gave your books to Dad," he said. "Did you mind that I did that?"

"No, of course not," I said. "It was nice of you."

"Then it was the fact that I hadn't read them that upset you."

He was too perceptive. I took a deep breath. I knew I had to be completely honest.

"I admit that it hurt me that you hadn't even taken them in from the car, let alone begun to read them." I was surprised at the tears that sprang to my eyes as I spoke. This man had too much effect on my heart.

He nodded. "I thought that was probably it."

We were silent for a few minutes, the only sound the soft wheeze of the car's air conditioner.

"Did Pop and Ward read your books?" Todd suddenly asked.

"No. And that hurt me too, but I learned to live with it. At least Mom and Marnie read them."

He turned to me with a challenging expression. "How'd you like to read some of my legal opinions? I've got a great one I just finished on an obscure point of business law in MacKenzie vs. MacKenzie, Inc."

"Mmm," I said thoughtfully. I'd never considered that I was a prejudiced reader too. "Point taken."

He stretched out a hand palm up. "I won't make any promises about reading, Cara. I'm too afraid I'll break them. But I'll always defend your right to write and be proud of you for being published. Can you live with that?"

I looked at him and then at his hand. I nodded. "I can." At least for now. And I slipped my hand in his.

Chapter 9

I lay in bed reading, propped against my pillows, Rainbow asleep beside me. The house was quiet, the darkness outside my screened windows deep and black with no street lights sending funnels of illumination. The night was weighted with heat and humidity, and I yearned for previously taken-for-granted air conditioning.

My new fan oscillated warm air over me, head to toe, toe to head, trying to convince me it was making me cool, but we Bentleys are not that stupid. Rainbow's hair puffed like a filament cheering wave as it moved past her, and every so often she stretched with pleasure.

I was trying to turn my thoughts off enough to fall asleep, but my mind refused to stop skittering, much like leaves helpless before an autumn wind. First Todd, then the adoption search, then the meeting with Alma raced across my mental movie screen. I felt as if I were at a cerebral speed photography screening, image flashing to image.

After reading for a half hour, I finally felt my eyes growing heavy. I closed my book and reached to turn off my lamp. I had maybe five minutes to fall asleep before my mind started up again.

A car roared down the road, its loud sound tearing the stillness. It slowed for an instant, then sped on. Rainbow raised her head, blinking sleepily at the rude interruption of her peace. My eyes snapped open, and hopes of slumber were gone. I groaned in frustration. How long would it be before my busy mind was once again lulled toward dreamland?

The bang was so loud, so unexpected, that I froze in a moment of stunned incredulity. Rainbow gave a bleat of terror and leaped from the bed. She threw herself beneath it to cower in safety, poor baby.

The ice of shock quickly melted, leaving my limbs with a tingling sensation. My heart began to pound, and my breathing became jerky. What had just happened? All I knew was that the sound had been very near . . . scarily near.

I raced to the window. Had the car that just passed crashed? But it wasn't the right kind of noise for a crash. It was one quick loud boom, like fireworks, only there were no lovely bursts of color lighting the sky.

The black night hid whatever had happened.

I grabbed a pair of slacks and a shirt and pulled them on. I could hear John and Elam calling to each other, and I saw Jake's lights flick on and stream out from his apartment, the soft glow illuminating the yard and the road. I looked out the window again, but I still could see nothing amiss, no clue to what had caused the horrendous noise. At least I didn't see a car wrapped around a tree. The only movement was Hawk, let out of Jake's apartment and jumping the rail of the wheelchair ramp, racing for the road.

Feet thundered down the stairs, and the front door slammed open and closed. John and Elam raced toward the barn to make sure the livestock were all right. Jake's door slammed seconds later.

I thrust my feet in flip-flops and raced into the hallway where Esther stood, robe and night-gown falling to her ankles, hair in a long braid down her back, a flashlight in her hand.

"What happened?" She looked dazed.

I shook my head and tore downstairs after the men without waiting to see if she would follow.

I met up with Jake on the drive. He had a strong electric torch that he was using to check out vehicles and buggies. Hawk came to him and poked at his hand, clearly disturbed.

"It's okay, Hawk." Jake ran his hand over the dog's head several times.

Hawk's anxiety lessened though it didn't disappear completely.

I know just how you feel, boy. I wasn't exactly frightened with the three men checking things out, but I wasn't totally at ease either.

"Nothing wrong here," Jake called loudly enough for his father and Elam to hear over the rustlings of agitated animals in the stalls. I could see flashlight beams dancing around in the barn as John and Elam made certain all was well in there.

"My car's okay too?" I asked Jake.

"Looks fine to me."

I walked toward him and kicked something dark and unseen, something that hurt my uncovered toe and clattered as it rolled across the drive. Jake followed the sound with his flashlight.

I picked it up and held it out in my palm. "What in the world?"

He took it. "It's a piece of metal."

Jake sent a beam of light back and forth over the drive and the lawn. Another shard of bent metal showed at the edge of Mary's garden, several feet from where we stood. I crossed the lawn and retrieved it, Hawk coming with me before disappearing into the darkness. I was showing it to Jake when John and Elam came out of the barn.

The two men studied the pieces, one in Jake's palm, one in mine.

John frowned, uncertain what he was looking at, but Elam and Jake moved at the same time, turning their lights toward the road.

A post stood there with a small distorted piece of metal still attached.

"Someone blew up your mailbox?" I was floored. I'd seen rural mailboxes smashed with baseball bats by kids thinking it was cool to be destructive, but blowing one up?

"A cherry bomb or an M-80," Jake said in disgust.

"Aren't those things—cherry bombs and M-80s—illegal?" I asked.

"They are, but you can undoubtedly buy them on the Internet," Jake said. "You can buy anything on the Internet."

"You can?" Elam shook his fading flashlight. "Why would people sell something so dangerous?"

"Because other people will buy them," Jake said.

John sighed. "We can thank *Gott* that it happened in the night when no one was around to get hurt by flying pieces of metal."

"Not that anyone would do it in the daylight," Elam said with an astonishing amount of sarcasm.

John nodded. "Doers of evil love darkness rather than light."

"We should tell the police, Father," Jake said.

John shook his head. "It is just someone wanting to shake up an Amish man. Like we are so easily scared." He made a scoffing sound. "We will turn the other cheek. Vengeance is the Lord's."

"It's not for vengeance's sake." Jake took the piece of metal from my hand, and we all stared at the two mutilated pieces of steel. "What these trouble-makers did is very dangerous. A piece of metal flying fast through the air could hurt someone really bad. It's like shrapnel flying on a battlefield. Whoever did this may do it again to someone else, maybe another Amish family. The police might patrol more often or take other precautions if they knew about this. Maybe they can even trace where the bombs were bought."

John stared at the steel shards for a few minutes. He reached out and touched his finger to a lethal-looking point on one piece. "You're right, Jake. Perhaps it is dangerous not to speak. Tomorrow will you call the police?"

"I will. And I'll get a new mailbox too before Mom comes home. We probably shouldn't tell her about this. It would upset her."

On that we all agreed.

Esther and I brought Mary home from the hospital late Friday morning. I felt so sorry for her because I knew she was in severe pain, her leg in a cast, her cuts barely crusted with scabs. In fact there was a very deep gash on her right hip that they wouldn't let close up. They kept it open to wash it regularly with an antibiotic drip because of an osteo infection that wouldn't go away.

"They say I probably got the infection from something on the cellar steps," Mary said. "But I keep a clean house!"

She was clearly offended at the suggestion of

dirt in her home—more upset about the perceived lapse in her housekeeping skills than about the wound itself. I thought of the manure that came into the house as a natural part of living on a farm. It was impossible to keep all traces of it out. Maybe that had been the source of the infection. Who knew? A visiting nurse would come daily to oversee the antibiotic drip as well as dress the cuts, and Mary was to be confined to bed for some time.

Elam and John had come in from the field and were waiting for us when we arrived. They carried Mary inside and up to the bedroom she and John shared. She was barely settled when the home-nurse showed up.

"Rose!" I said in surprise as I let in the woman EMT, now dressed in the blue uniform of the Lancaster Home Health Group. "Do you moonlight as an emergency tech or as a visiting nurse?"

She smiled. "You remembered me."

"That's because I already knew who you were. Or guessed it anyway. You are Rose Martin, right? The woman from Jake's accident?"

She nodded. "Just don't let Jake know, okay? He doesn't want to meet me for some reason, so let's not tell him who I am. I'm just Rose, his mother's nurse."

I liked her with her curly brown hair and those sparkling hazel eyes beaming through her glasses.

"He's still at school right now," I said.

"School?"

"Millersville University. I'm not certain when he finishes classes today, but I'm sure he'll try to get home as soon as possible. Like the rest of the family, he's concerned about Mary."

"It was wonderful to finally see him the other night," Rose said, eyes dancing. "Did you know that for some time I thought he had died in the accident? I even put up a little white cross at the scene as a memorial. I felt so badly that I, a nurse, hadn't been able to save him. I think that's why I became an emergency tech. I wanted to be sure that it would never happen again. Then I found out he was alive after all. Taking down that little cross was one of the happiest things I've ever done."

"And now he won't meet you."

She shrugged. "It's a pride thing, I think. But I tell you, it's made me intensely curious about him. That's why I asked for this case. I knew from the ambulance run that she would need home care, so I spoke to my supervisor. To my surprise she said okay."

"What are you doing working all the way up here if you live way down there?"

"I don't live at home anymore," Rose said. "When I got my job with the Lancaster Home Health Group, I moved to Bird-in-Hand. I've been here about six months now. I joined the emergency squad as a way to meet people."

"Is it working?" I was fascinated. I'd never thought of such a means to making friends.

"Oh, yes," she said, laughing. "I've met some very interesting people."

I led Rose upstairs and introduced her to Mary, John, Esther, and Elam, not mentioning that she was the Rose from Jake's accident. After speaking briefly to everyone, Rose firmly sent all of us but John from the room.

"I need to run the drip over the wound," she explained. "Mary doesn't need an audience."

As we left, I looked over my shoulder at Mary, so frail in the great bed. John sat beside her on the edge of the bed, his large, calloused hand holding her smaller, work-reddened one. He reached out and pushed her long, unbound hair back from her face in a loving gesture that he would never normally let another person see. It was a sign of his concern for his wife that he didn't realize he still had an audience.

Jake arrived home while Elam, Esther, and I were at the table eating the ham loaf and whipped potatoes Esther had prepared for the noon meal.

"Is she okay?" he asked immediately. "Was the trip home hard on her?"

"She's fine," said a voice behind him, and we all turned to find Rose at the foot of the stairs. "Esther? John asked that you bring some broth up to Mary and sit with her until she falls asleep.

If you ask me, the trick will be to get some of the broth in her before she falls asleep. He'll come down as soon as you go up."

Esther jumped to do as she was asked, and I turned to Jake.

"Jake, this is Rose, your mother's visiting nurse."

Jake stuck out a hand, and I watched as his fist swallowed Rose's small hand. I wondered how she felt actually touching the hand of a man she thought for some time was dead.

I helped Esther prepare a tray for Mary, putting a dishcloth under the soup bowl to make the tray surface slip-proof. I added a glass of ginger ale and some saltines while Esther ladled the warm broth.

"Here, I'll carry that." Elam took the tray from Esther as she walked toward the steps.

Esther beamed, but I thought he offered more because he wanted to check again that his mother was all right.

I turned from watching Elam and Esther go up the stairs to watching Jake and Rose talk by the front door.

"I'll be here about the same time every day," I heard her say.

He mumbled something in response that I couldn't make out, and then he reached out and pushed open the screen door for her. He rolled onto the front porch after her and watched as she climbed into her car with its Lancaster Home Health Group logo of a blue cross inside the black outline of a house.

Feeling a little unnecessary at the present moment, I went up to my rooms and began working on the series proposal my agent wanted from me. I always enjoyed working up the bare bones of a plot and establishing the characters that lived within it. I worked happily for what seemed only a few minutes when I happened to look at my watch and saw it was 5:30 already.

I flew around, getting ready for Ward and Marnie's visit. I was pulling my hair back into a wide gold barrette when my cell phone rang.

"Cara, it's Marnie. We're behind schedule, but we're coming! The babysitter was late. I'm going to blame it on her rather than my husband. We're on Route 100, not too far from Exton. We'll pick up Route 30 from there. We took the Commadore Barry Bridge over the river. What do you think? An hour from here?"

"Give or take a few minutes. Why don't you meet us at the restaurant instead of coming to the farm first? I'll call and change the time of the reservation. We can come back here after dinner."

"Sounds good," she said. "But tell me. What's this *us* we'll be meeting? Is he really coming with you?"

"Who?" I asked innocently. I could hear Ward

in the background yelling, "What? The lawyer's actually coming? Cara's got a real date?"

"Don't give me that 'who' stuff. You know who I mean," Marnie said.

"Oh, you mean my lawyer," I said, trying to sound offhand about the whole matter. "A real date?"

"Ignore your brother. He means well even when he talks too much. So we're going to meet him?" Her voice was eager.

I watched a gray car turn into the drive. "He's pulling up out front as we speak."

"I can't wait," she said. "I told Ward the guy would come. In fact, we had a bet, and I just won."

"You bet about me and Todd?"

"About whether you'd actually have the courage to invite him."

"Ah, I'd forgotten," I said. "Ward thinks I don't have any guts."

"Poor mistaken baby," Marnie said affectionately. She was probably looking at him as she spoke.

"Poor mistaken idiot, you mean," I said with a smile. "I love it when I prove him wrong."

"I know I should say something about you two being too old for sibling rivalry, but I love it when you get him too."

"Marnie!" Ward said in the background. It was interesting how my brother couldn't resist taking part in any phone conversation he was around, whether he was an intended participant or not. "What about your wifely duty to be true to me?"

"My dearest heart," Marnie said to Ward, her voice so clear that I knew the comment was for me too. I could almost hear her eyelashes fluttering as she spoke. "Never for one moment doubt my resolve to always fulfill my wifely duties. You are the king of my heart. But sometimes," and her voice lost all its honey in favor of vinegar, "it does the king good to get his ego knocked by one of those he perceives as his ladies in waiting!"

I laughed at my sister-in-law and thought again how much I loved her. "We girls must stick together," I agreed.

I gave her directions to the restaurant. "See you soon." And I hung up.

I went down to meet Todd, glad for time alone with him. Tonight he was wearing an olive green sport shirt and olive green slacks two shades deeper. Mr. Monochromatic. I, for my part, was wearing a soft yellow dress that I had gotten the day I met Alma and had bought my lovely coral gown. I hoped he would notice.

"Hello," Todd said when I opened the door to him. "Will you tell Cara I'm here?"

I blinked.

"Not that I wouldn't mind having dinner with

someone as lovely as you and wearing yellow, no less. But I'm committed for the evening to a woman who wears beige. *Ipso facto*, she must still be inside somewhere."

I let the screen door swing shut behind me. "Cute," I said. "Now let's go buy you an aloha shirt so we can pep up *your* wardrobe too."

He looked pained. "Over my dead body."

"I really do want to go shopping," I told him as we walked to the car. We got in and he began to back out of the drive. "Marnie and Ward are going to be late, so we have some time to kill. Let's go to Bentley Mart."

"Okay," he said. "I could pick up a few things there myself."

The Lancaster Bentley Mart wasn't all that far from the farm, but it was a world apart. The road on which the farm was located was quiet and rural, lined with snarls of raspberry canes and honeysuckle or cleared to the edge so there was room for the six-horse or six-mule teams to turn without going on the road. Fields of golden winter wheat stood awaiting harvest and the rows of corn now reached to my thighs. Alfalfa grew almost tall enough for the cutting of the first of three crops grown over the season.

Amish women in bare feet mowed their lawns with push mowers while their children weeded the vegetable patch. Boys pushing scooters ran errands, and a girl who looked remarkably like

Esther flew down the road toward us on roller blades. It wasn't until we were driving passed her that I realized it actually was Esther, a pharmacy bag hanging from one hand. We waved as we passed.

By contrast, Bentley Mart sat on Route 30, just east of Lancaster City, in a sprawling shopping area. Discount stores, entertainment complexes, and motels lined the highway. Traffic was heavy, requiring full concentration to navigate. Tour buses, travel trailers, out-of-state drivers, and locals who actually knew where they were going vied for position. It was a relief to park in the Mart's vast parking lot, but I was very unhappy to look up at the sign and see that the second E in Bentley was burned out.

"Look at that," I said to Todd. "Disgusting."

He glanced at me, amused. "I wouldn't let it ruin my night," he said. "If it was a traffic light that was burned out, then we might have a problem."

"Mmm."

We went into the store and I was struck by a feeling of clutter. I hate clutter. We always designed the interior layout of Bentley Marts to avoid even the look of congestion. I shuddered. Something wasn't right here.

When I went to the film department, there was no one to help me.

"I used to work this counter," I said, irritated. "There's always supposed to be someone here because of the value of the cameras. It helps prevent shoplifting."

"You worked here?" Todd asked.

"No, not this store. One in Silver Spring, near home."

But there was one thing that made me very happy. I found a Choice Books rack, and there were my books *As the Deer* and *So My Soul*.

"At least they're doing something right," I said, patting my titles proprietarily.

I moved on, only to realize a few steps down the aisle that Todd wasn't with me. I turned and saw him reading the cover copy of *As the Deer*. Perhaps his father's perusal and comments had made him curious. At one point he looked up and frowned at me. I smiled back, especially cheered when he picked up *So My Soul*. He read some more, and then opened to the first page.

I came to stand next to him.

"It says here that you're a bestseller," he said, pointing to the words on the cover.

I nodded.

"It says here that you teach writing all over the country."

I nodded again. "At writers conferences."

"It says here that this book's in its tenth printing in less than two years."

"Twelfth by now," I said. "Over 100,000 copies sold."

"You have review comments on the cover that

make you sound like the best thing since sliced bread."

"People have been very nice about these books."

"They aren't fluff, are they?"

"No. Did you think they were?"

"You said you wrote romances." He looked like I had been purposely deceiving him.

"I do. But a romance doesn't have to be shallow, you know. After all, isn't love the strongest and most noble of human emotions? An emotion that God feels toward us and the attribute of God that led Him to send Christ for us?"

"Hmmm." Todd read again for a moment. He looked up. "As the deer pants for streams of water, so my soul pants for you, O God," he said, quoting Psalm 42, the source of the titles.

"You got it," I said. "Come on. I want to hit the computer aisle for a minute. I always check out the computer aisle at Bentley's."

When we got there, my smile faded. I stood around waiting for someone to help me. Not one person materialized. I knew that when Pop and Ward decided to carry a choice selection of computers, they decided that the only way they could compete with the computer megastores was to offer unparalleled sales help. That's why I always checked the aisle. I wanted to be certain help was truly available.

Todd stood beside me but paid no attention to me. He was reading chapter one of *As the Deer*.

"Excuse me," I called to a salesperson walking by two aisles over. "Can you help me?"

"That isn't my department," he called back, not slowing his pace.

In an attack of pique, I began typing on a computer. Immediately a Warning: you have performed an illegal act sign lit the screen.

"An illegal act, my foot," I muttered. "I haven't had time to do anything illegal yet. Not that I would, of course," I added piously.

Suddenly Todd began to read aloud.

Marci watched the moon's light fall across the heaving black waves. The lunar radiance burned a path to her feet, shimmering in the wet sand as each wave receded, the soft luminescence like a highway to God. She put out a foot to step on the light. But as she moved, so did the lambent stream.

He looked up and studied me like he hadn't seen me before. I stared back, a slight smile on my lips. He shook his head slowly.

"You're a surprise every time I see you, Cara Bentley. And this is no exception." He waved the book in my face.

"Does that mean you're impressed?" I said.

"Most definitely," he said. "Most definitely."

I feared I was vibrating again. I who never vibrate.

"Are you interested in a computer?" The monotone male voice came from just behind me. I jumped and spun to find an older man in a red Bentley Mart shirt staring absently at me.

I nodded yes, and the man did everything in his power to ruin the pleasure I had wrapped about myself like a fleecy blanket at Todd's comment. He was rude, abrupt, ill-informed, and acted like he was doing a great favor by deigning to speak with me. After he told me for the fifth time that the large number of gigabytes meant a modem of great strength, I walked away.

"Lady, did you ever think about doing a little homework before you come in to make a purchase this size?" he called after me. "Then you'd know what you were doing."

"That man's an idiot," I hissed as I stalked toward the exit. "I can't stand incompetency!"

"Well, slow down and wait for me," Todd said. "I have to pay for the book."

"I'll give you another, for Pete's sake," I groused.

"Nope. I want the next printing to say 100,001."

I waited for him at the big exit doors. "Thanks," I said when he walked up with a little bag with *As the Deer* stuffed in it.

He nodded. "My pleasure. Did you know that

the moonbeam over the water at your feet is caused when the angle of incidence is equal to the angle of reflection?"

I looked at him. "No, I didn't know that, Mr. Physics Professor. Did you know that scientific explanations kill the romance of a scene?"

He draped his arm companionably over my shoulder. "No, I didn't know that. But then I always thought it was the company that made a situation romantic."

"You have a point there," I said, my heart turning somersaults.

We met Ward and Marnie in the restaurant lobby and were barely seated before I started telling Ward all about my disastrous visit to the store. I had worked myself up to full Bentley choleric steam when Todd leaned toward Ward.

"She's a little bent out of shape over an unqualified salesclerk," he explained with just a touch of condescension. "And some clutter."

Fat lot you know, I thought unkindly, giving him a look that would scorch asbestos. He smiled placidly back, which ratcheted my anger up several notches.

"The man called me *lady* like it was the crudest epithet he could come up with," I snarled.

Todd and Ward exchanged a man-to-man glance that made me want to gnash my teeth. I could almost forgive Todd because he didn't know what was going on here, but Ward! He was being his usual smarmy self, bless his little heart.

"And what did you say to rile him so?" Ward asked with a smirk that was a very close relative to Todd's condescending expression.

"I told him gigabytes had nothing to do with modems. And they don't. Every idiot knows that."

"And your tone of voice?" Ward asked in an absolutely infuriating one of his own.

I decided I didn't want to answer that question. I was afraid I didn't meet the biblical standards of speech seasoned with grace. Then or now.

"Listen, Ward," I said instead, drumming my fingers. "If you're running all our stores the way that store is run, we're going to be out of business in no time. Pop must be rolling over in his grave."

"All *our* stores?" Todd asked, his condescension turning to shock.

"I'll check on things tomorrow," Ward said. "You know that's not the way we do business, Cara."

"Cara *Bentley*. Bentley Marts." Todd looked stunned. "Bentley Marts is *you?*"

"I think you should fire that store's manager and all the personnel. Send the human resources people and the industrial engineering people up from headquarters to give that store a thorough overhaul. And they need a new *E* in their outside sign."

"Consider it done," Ward said, eating his salad.

I nodded. "Good. Thanks."

"You guys are Bentley Marts?" Todd repeated, still reeling.

"Yes," I mumbled around a mouthful of greens dashed with raspberry vinaigrette.

"And you never thought to tell me?" His surprise was quickly becoming pique.

"Ward made me promise not to."

"But I'm your lawyer, for heaven's sake." He was definitely out of sorts.

Marnie entered the fray. "My husband is afraid of fortune hunters," she explained. "He's certain that Cara will fall in with unscrupulous villains who will take advantage of her and steal her money."

"Take advantage of Cara?" Todd looked at Marnie in disbelief. "Our Cara?"

I liked the sound of *our Cara*.

"I know," Marnie said. "But in spite of overwhelming evidence to the contrary, he always thinks of her as his little sister."

"And he always thinks he knows best," I explained with a do-you-believe-it sniff. "He always has."

"I do," Ward defended. "Going incognito was a good plan. I still say it's my job to protect you. Who knows what kind of people might suddenly claim to be related to us?"

Todd ate his Caesar salad in silence, the romaine

224

crunching beneath the strength of his wonderful jaws. He frowned in a combination of irritation and deep thought. "How many stores are there?" he finally said. "If I might ask."

Marnie saw his expression and offered sympathy. "I know how you feel, Todd. When I first realized that Bentley meant *that* Bentley, I was shocked too," she said. "And if it makes you feel better, Ward didn't tell me until we'd dated for almost a year."

"See," I said, patting Todd's hand. "Only a week. You're way ahead of the curve."

Somehow that comment didn't calm him as much as I thought it should.

"But don't let the money bother you," Marnie said, patting his other hand. "They're remarkably normal and nice for being filthy rich."

"There are 45 stores," I said, answering Todd's question.

"Soon to be 47," Ward corrected. "Two more open next month, one in Virginia and one in Rhode Island."

"Don't expand too rapidly, Ward," I cautioned around a sesame seed roll. "You know what that can do to a business. There are always megachains going bottoms up. I'd rather you moved a little cautiously until you're used to things without Pop. You don't want it to look like you're trying to prove something to the world now that you have the CEO's office."

For the first time Ward looked unhappy with me. "Cara, I say this with love and affection. Butt out."

"A bit outspoken," Marnie said to Todd, "and very Type A. But nice."

"Millionaires?" Todd asked.

Marnie sipped her tea. "Several times over."

"She tells people she earns her living by writing," Todd said.

"I do," I snapped. Butt out, my eye. I was a Bentley too.

Marnie grinned compassionately at Todd. "Paradigm shift time?"

"Big time," Todd muttered.

"They hardly ever yell at me," Marnie said. "I don't think they'll yell much at you either."

Todd looked at me. "Why didn't you tell me who you were? Couldn't you trust me?"

I looked into his unhappy eyes, blinking so I wouldn't stare too hard and drown in their depths.

"It had nothing to do with trust," I said.

He looked unconvinced.

"It didn't! I honestly don't even think about Bentley Marts most of the time. The only reason we're talking about it now is because that store was so bad. If it had been up to snuff, I'd never have thought about it at all."

He glanced at me briefly without saying anything. I thought how much easier this explaining would be if I could just write it down and then rewrite and rewrite until I was saying what I wanted instead of what popped out.

"Todd, you know as well as I do that I have been consumed with this adoption search." I leaned toward him. "And then there's Mary's accident. And my book proposal." I leaned closer. "And you." It was almost a whisper.

I wasn't even certain Todd heard me. He was staring, frowning, into his water glass like he was looking for a clear thought in its crystalline depths.

I looked at him unhappily. I didn't know what to say to make him understand that I wasn't trying to deceive him about who I was. In my mind I was Cara Bentley, writer, not Cara Bentley of Bentley Marts. The one was me. The other was just something that had happened to me because of other people to whom I happened to be related.

"Come on, Todd," Ward finally said. "Don't be mad at her. I mean, look at her." He waved a hand in my direction.

Todd's eyes swung to me. I stared back, my heart in my eyes.

"She's beautiful and rich," Ward said. "I can't hide the one, but I can try and protect her from the other."

Todd sighed. "Well, she's beautiful all right," he said, his eyes still on me. "I knew that from the first. It'll just take a while to get used to the second."

"But you'll try to get used to it? Please?" There are times when begging is most appropriate.

He nodded his head at me, the corner of his mouth quirking up. "I'll try."

I beamed.

Chapter 10

T he Paddock looked like something from a fairy tale. The house, a large, early nineteenth-century brick farmhouse restored to its original splendor, had candles lit in every window. The deep front porch was filled with hanging flower baskets and planters of geraniums and ivy. Mature beeches, maples, and oaks shadowed the lawn, and evergreens stood sentinel as they had four centuries ago when the first German settlers came to this abundant valley. A white, split-rail fence edged the property.

The large front lawn was covered with round tables, each laid out with white linens, silver, and crystal for eight. Flowers in a medley of summer colors blazed as centerpieces. White covers draping to the ground sheathed the chairs completely. To the left, in front of an immaculate barn, was a wooden dance floor, beside which a quintet of musicians was playing.

"Oh, Todd!" I breathed as we walked up the drive. A teen in a tux jacket, dress shirt, bow tie, jeans, and white tennis shoes had taken our car, and we were able to appreciate the full effect of the setting as we walked.

I tucked my hand in the crook of Todd's elbow

and thought again how handsome he looked in his tux. He'd even let his curls arrange themselves in a less rigid manner. A good sign, I thought, because it meant he was listening to my suggestions and preferences. And he was willing to forgive me for being rich.

"Everything looks lovely," he agreed, surveying the grounds. "But not half as lovely as you."

I turned and found him looking at me in a way that made my breath catch. I was suddenly very glad I had spent the time and money to buy this coral dress. I wasn't boring tonight, though I wasn't sure I'd made it all the way to sophisticated—or ever would. It had taken me forever just to successfully pull my hair back into a figure eight chignon that actually stayed in place.

As I had told Rainbow while I brushed out yet another failed attempt with my hair, "Now I remember why I let it hang down my back or wear it braided. Elegance is too much work!" But tonight it appeared worth all the effort, right down to the sprig of baby's breath tucked in it.

Todd spent most of the evening introducing me to people whose names I would never remember. The women sparkled in sequins and shimmered in silk. The men looked substantial and well cared for in tuxes. I didn't realize there were so many lawyers to be had, let alone so many in one county.

"That's our host," Todd told me shortly after we arrived.

I looked where he indicated and saw a big man who was speaking with a powerful voice. I could hear its boom even where we were, although I couldn't make out the words. He had a full head of dark hair with silver at the temples and a marvelous smile that he used freely. He was obviously a man who liked his position as president of the county bar association, talking to everyone, glad handing, laughing easily, whispering compliments to the ladies and delighting in their blushes and simpers.

"I bet he could charm the birds from the trees," I muttered to Todd as I watched him lean over to whisper into the ear of a stout, well-corseted older woman. She listened for a moment and then leaned back and laughed like a young girl.

"Amos, you are a liar," she said, her upper-register voice carrying. "But I love it. I love it."

"Judge Wallace Brubaker's wife," Todd whispered. He pointed out the judge, who was more than equal to his wife's girth and was busy talking to a slim, carefully coiffed woman in a swirling sea-green silk number. "And talking to the judge is Jessica, Amos's wife."

"Shall we go pay our respects?" I asked, turning in their direction.

"No rush," Todd said. And he led me to the bar

where he got us each a Perrier with a twist of lime.

We made a leisurely loop around the yard, enjoying the setting and watching the people. Amos's voice rolled over us wherever we were.

"He is a bit noisy, isn't he?" I asked.

Todd made a noncommittal noise in his throat just as Amos laughed raucously. The man he was with turned a brilliant shade of red, visible even from our distance.

"Does he often make people uncomfortable?" I asked.

"Only when he has a reason to. Otherwise he is, as you noted, a charmer."

When we finally reached Amos, he turned his charm on me.

"My, my, Todd," he said, taking my hand in his a little bit too enthusiastically. "Where have you been keeping this lovely young woman? You look absolutely beautiful, my dear, in that dress the color of sunrise."

The color of sunrise? Give me a break. But I simpered with the rest as he patted my hand and gave the impression I was the only woman in the world.

"May I present Cara Bentley," Todd said, standing at my shoulder and looking as frosty as January rime at the edge of a lake. "And Cara, this is our host, Amos Yost."

"Amos," I said and dipped my head politely while I tried to reclaim my hand. Then his name registered. My breath caught in my throat and I spun to Todd.

"*My* Amos Yost?" I wanted to yell. "My maybe uncle or cousin or something? And you didn't tell me?"

Todd grasped my arm and smiled at me very sweetly. Too sweetly. He reached out, put a finger under my drooping jaw and pushed my mouth gently closed. Then he turned back to Amos. "You've done yourself proud here tonight, you and Jessica. The place looks absolutely wonderful. I know Cara is impressed." And he squeezed my arm. Make that pinched.

It might have hurt, but it was a wise move on Todd's part. It brought me out of my stupor in short order. I shot him a look of pure venom before I turned back to Amos.

"I am most definitely impressed, sir. It looks like a fairyland, and I'm delighted to be here."

I let my anger at Todd simmer in the back of my mind while I looked at Amos with great interest. If he were my Amos Yost, Pop would be his uncle. Could I see any physical resemblance to Pop in him? Maybe they were somewhat alike in the barrel chest, but the biggest similarity wasn't so much in appearance as in manner. He shared with Pop—and with Ward, come to think of it—that indefinable but palpable charisma that made everyone listen when they spoke and act upon their suggestions with due haste.

But that didn't mean he was related to me. Lots of people had charisma. Pop's hallmark had been affection for just about everyone, and his genuine caring tempered the force of his great personality. And much as I groused about Ward, I could see that same respect for people developing more and more in him. I think it came because both men appreciated people as created in the image of God. I would have to get to know Amos to see if he had that family trait.

"Jessica," Amos said to his wife. He reached out and touched her arm to get her attention. She was again talking to Judge and Mrs. Brubaker. "You remember Todd Reasoner? And this is his guest, Cara Bentley."

Jessica Yost turned to me with a smile. Suddenly her expression congealed and she stared. If such a thing as an aura existed, and if I could actually see hers, she would have been pumping out red. Her demeanor was wrathful and full of a combination of disbelief and violation. I blinked at the animosity that rolled toward Todd and me at flood speed.

Almost immediately she caught herself and became once again the gracious-though-distant hostess I'd seen all evening from afar.

"We are delighted that both of you have joined us this evening." Her recovered smile looked genuine.

My mind swirled. Had I imagined that hostility? And why? Whether or not we proved to be related, I was certainly no threat to her.

"I was telling your husband how lovely everything is," I said.

"Wait until dark and the little lights in the trees come on." She gestured and I noticed for the first time the strings of lights wrapped around the tree limbs. "Fairyland," she said.

"I look forward to it," I said.

She nodded and then turned with what seemed to be relief to speak to some other people who were wandering up to greet their host and hostess. With a nod of his head, Amos turned away too.

Todd tucked my arm into his and started to walk. I took a couple of steps and then dug in my heels. I stared at my feet, trying to decide how one murdered one's date and got away with it.

"You louse!" I hissed when he turned to see why I wasn't following him. I didn't scream or raise my voice. We were surrounded, after all, by lots of well-dressed people. The way I felt at the moment, I'd be happy to humiliate him in front of his peers, but I didn't want to embarrass myself. "How could you do that to me?"

"Smile, woman," he returned, a phony grin pasted across his mouth. "We're having fun on a lovely summer evening. And let's walk. We won't look quite so much like we're fighting if we move around a bit. We are fighting, aren't we?"

"We sure are." But I let him take my arm and lead me in another circle of the yard.

He sighed. "I was afraid of that. But at least I'm learning to recognize the real thing. That's a hopeful sign for someone as repressed as me, right?"

"Not repressed. Buttoned down," I corrected in a snarly voice.

"Ah. Buttoned down. Right."

I made the mistake of looking at Todd. My eyes might be sparking with anger, but his were puppy dog worried, and all because I was angry at him. I turned my head abruptly. He affected me too much.

"I didn't tell you because I didn't want you to get your hopes up," he said. His voice was soft, caring, like the whisper of the breeze that floated through the trees above us.

"So instead you let me get hit across the head with a two by four! You should have warned me."

He nodded. "I probably should have, but I chose not to."

"You chose? *You* chose?" My voice shook. "You had no right, Todd! It's my potential family."

"I know. And I knew you'd probably be furious with me. But I'd do the same thing again." He glanced at me. "At least I think I would," he said wryly.

"But why, Todd? Why would you do that to me? People don't hurt people they care for."

He cleared his throat self-consciously. "I know how much you liked Alma, and I was afraid you'd claim Amos as your own as you've done with her. And quite frankly, I don't want *him* to be yours."

"You don't want him to be mine?" I stopped to put my hands on my hips as I glared at him. He took my elbow and pulled me along, completely ruining my attempt to wilt him with my pique. "Why? Are you jealous?"

He was suddenly genuinely smiling. In fact, he was laughing his fool head off, something that did *not* make me feel any better, especially since I deserved the laughter after making such an inane comment.

"Jealous?" he repeated. "Oh, no. After all, he's probably a cousin or something. Besides, you've got better taste than to ever be hoodwinked by someone like him."

"Just by someone like you," I muttered.

He grinned and took my hand. "Cara, I know how important finding your family is to you and how much you want them to be nice people, but I've got to tell you that I just don't like Amos. I don't trust him. He's always got an angle. I've faced him often enough in court to know he's expedient instead of ethical, more interested in accruing billing hours than giving solid legal

237

services. He spends more time furthering his career than serving his clients."

"And yet he's president of the local bar association."

Todd nodded. "Politics."

I took a deep breath and studied Todd thoughtfully as the shimmer from the just lit fairy lights fell over his face. I was still angry that he hadn't told me about Amos, but there was an even more basic question at issue here. Did I trust him? Even when I disagreed with what he'd done, did I have confidence in him as a man? Did I trust his motives? His opinions? Did I believe that he thought his actions were for my benefit, not his? Could I rely on his advice? His obvious affection for me? Did I trust him with my future?

And how would I know I was right, whatever answer I came up with?

My staring must have made him uncomfortable because he began fiddling with his bow tie. Then he ran his finger under his collar. "This shirt is slowly choking me to death. I must have gained weight since the last time I wore it."

"How long ago was that?"

"Five years. I told you I didn't like chitchat so I usually avoid evenings like this."

"You've probably filled out a bit since then. Matured."

He nodded. "I used to be quite skinny."

I eyed his shoulders. "You're not skinny now." I smiled. Not broadly, but enough that he knew I wasn't about to bolt on him or burn him at the stake.

His sigh of relief reached all the way to his toes. He grabbed my hands. "Cara, I have nothing but my instincts when it comes to Amos. I have no evidence that I can present to you to encourage you to go slow with him, no evidence that proves he's really not a very nice man. I thought maybe if you saw him in action for a bit before you met him, before you knew who he might be, you'd be able to make a better judgment about how involved to get with him. Assuming he's the right Amos Yost."

I nodded. This whole discussion could well be moot. We had stopped walking and stood in a circle of two under a ring of giant hemlocks. From tiny cones and tinier seeds these giants had grown. From tiny trusts and small reliances grew solid relationships.

"I can see that my actions look selfish to you," he continued. "And looking at them in hindsight, they look foolish to me too. I shouldn't have let you get a shock like that. If the truth be known, I was probably just trying to protect myself."

"Protect yourself?"

"I don't want him in your life because if he is, I have to deal with him too. And I don't want to deal with him any more than I'm forced to in court." He ran his thumbs, slightly rough but so tender, across the backs of my hands. "It seems that more and more anything that touches you touches me."

"Right," I said, mildly sarcastic. "As you never fail to tell everyone, I'm your *client*."

His thumbs stilled. "That is not the alliance to which I refer, and you know it."

I glanced up at the towering evergreens and then looked at the intent face of the man before me. I chose to trust.

"I accept what you say about how you see Amos, Todd. And because I'm coming to know you well, I accept that you're probably right in your judgment about his character. He's not the greatest guy in the world, and I'm not going to be all that delighted to have him for a relative."

His shoulders relaxed and he opened his mouth to speak. I beat him to it.

"But—and it's a big but, at least to me—I have to make my own judgments. You have to give me that freedom. You want me to trust your instincts. Well, you have to trust mine too. You can't decide unilaterally what's good for me. Ever. If there is to be anything significant between us, you must be able to live with that truth."

Todd stared at our clasped hands and was silent for a few minutes. Then he nodded slowly. "Fair enough."

I smiled brilliantly at him. He was such a good guy.

He didn't smile back. "This trusting the other guy to make sound decisions isn't easy for a pair of controllers like us, is it?"

I looked up at the soaring hemlocks again. Little seeds. Little trusts. "No, but it's necessary. That is," and I swallowed hard, "if we want our friendship to go any further."

He looked me straight in the eye. "I want. I want very much."

My bones turned to liquid. "Me too," I whispered. "Me too. But I'm not a controller. I'm the one Bentley who isn't."

"Right," he said on a laugh.

I was about to protest, but his hug was warm and enveloping and I forgot. It was also over too soon. Slowly we walked hand-in-hand back toward the dinner tables and the other guests. As we moved toward the bar for another Perrier, Judge Wallace Marley Brubaker grabbed Todd's arm.

"Son," the little man said, "I've been looking for you. I've got to tell you how impressed I was with your work on MacKenzie vs. MacKenzie Inc. Your brief was a masterful presentation of your arguments, very cogent and well-written."

"Thank you, sir," Todd said. Pleasure oozed from his every pore. "Coming from you, that's a great compliment."

The men began talking shop, and I stood patiently, hoping dinner would be served soon. Late dinners might be elegant, but the sound of my growling stomach indicated how long ago lunch had been. It also shattered any illusion I might hold that I was as genteel as the setting.

"I'm afraid those two will be at it for some time, my dear. We might as well make the best of it."

I turned and found Mrs. Brubaker, pouter pigeon body corsetted and stuffed into a gown of the most lovely blue I'd seen in quite a while. Her blonde hair was fluffy and her gown too ruffled and frou-frou, but her eyes were intelligent and aware.

"I'm Hannelore and he's Wally," she said, indicating the judge.

I smiled, delighted that Hannelore was rescuing me. Now I wouldn't have to look like Todd's not-too-bright appendage for the duration of his conversation. "I'm Cara Bentley."

"And what do you do, Cara? I assume you have a profession? All the young women do these days."

"I'm a writer."

"Of what?"

"Romances."

"Romances? I *love* romances." She got a faraway look in her eyes, not uncommon with romance readers. Suddenly her eyes widened. "Cara Bentley?"

I nodded.

"Oh, my dear!" She giggled. "This is so exciting. Stay right here," she ordered. "Don't move. I'll be right back."

When she returned, she had two women with her.

"Judy, Pat, this is Cara Bentley." She said it like I was a recently discovered, strange life form.

Judy and Pat immediately grabbed my hand in succession and shook it vigorously.

"It's a pleasure," Pat said.

"A real pleasure," Judy concurred.

"We belong to a book club," Hannelore explained.

Pat nodded. "There are five others of us, but they're not here."

"They're not in the legal professions." Judy obviously pitied them this lapse.

"We meet every month," Hannelore said. "And last month guess what book we discussed?"

"*As the Deer*," all three women said in unison.

"And we loved it," Judy said.

"All except Mindy." Pat made a face. "But Mindy never likes anything unless it's so dark and obscure that you can't understand it."

"I just finished *So My Soul* last week," Hannelore said.

"Me too," Pat said. She was a handsome woman in her forties wearing a black number like Audrey Hepburn wore in *Breakfast at*

Tiffany's. "I want to know where you found the hero."

"You liked Scott?" I said. "Me too."

"But does he exist?" Pat asked. "Is there a Scott out there? I sure haven't found him if there is."

"Pat's single," Hannelore said as if I couldn't figure that out. "She's a lawyer—a marvelous lawyer—and she scares most of the men away. Too strong."

"But I wouldn't scare Scott," Pat said, accepting Hannelore's assessment of her without batting an eye. "That's why I want to know if he even exists."

It was Hannelore who answered the question. "He exists," she said emphatically. "But he's already taken."

"Aren't they always," Judy said. Her hair was so black it was almost blue and she had the most vivid and unusual blue eyes I'd ever seen. She looked somewhat like a husky minus the tan markings. Her dress matched her eyes.

"Judy's a judge," Pat said. "She's been on the bench for five years now. She was married, but the jerk couldn't stand her success and left her for a beautician."

"A beautician twenty years younger than me," Judy added.

"So you see why we want to know if Scott exists in real life," Pat said.

I never knew how to answer that question,

especially when asked by mature, successful, professional women who should know better. Heroes were larger than life, magnifications of all the qualities we wanted or dreamed of in our men. They were stronger, more resilient, more understanding, and more sensitive. They were braver, wiser, more loving. They never got killed because, obviously, if they did, they couldn't be the hero. And when the chips were down, they always came through for their women. In romances especially, heroes were way beyond mortal. They had to be for the happily ever after to be satisfying. Who would read a romance where the heroine, strong woman that she was, married a weak man?

"I don't know if Scott exists or not," I said. At that moment Todd's arm brushed my back as he gestured about something to Judge Brubaker. I smiled. "Real men tend to be human with flaws that require trust and understanding on the part of their women. But I guess we never live up to the heroines in romance novels either."

"I disagree," Hannelore said.

We all looked at her with her fifty-something body and her fluffy blonde curls.

"You think we live up to the heroines?" Pat asked.

"She says that because she's never seen me when I wake up in the morning." Judy made a face. "Bed head, bleary eyes, *non compis mentis*."

We all laughed.

"I'm not talking about the heroines," Hannelore said. "I'm talking about Scott. He exists. I know he does." She swept her hand wide in her enthusiasm. "And there he is!"

We turned en masse to follow her pointing finger, and there stood portly Judge Brubaker.

"My Wally," Hannelore said. "Scott in the flesh."

Judge Brubaker flushed though he had no idea why we were all staring at him. Hannelore went to him and kissed his cheek. Again he flushed, but he looked quite pleased with his wife as he slid his arm about her ample middle. They made me think of Mom and Pop, and I had to swallow the lump in my throat.

"Beauty is certainly in the eye of the beholder," Pat whispered in my ear. "But I'm still jealous that she even thinks he's Scott."

"Of course there's Todd." Judy eyed him speculatively.

"That there is." I smiled at him. "And he comes pretty close."

"But he's too young for us," Pat said with a exaggerated sigh, grabbing Judy and pulling her away. Judy gave a small wave and the two women disappeared into the crowd.

When it was finally time to sit down for dinner, Todd and I found our table. We had a pleasant, but uneventful meal making small talk with our table mates. The only time things got really interesting was when one of the wives confessed to liking romances, and she and I had a pleasant conversation that clearly bored or appalled everyone else.

The candles on the tables, the fairy lights gleaming about the property, the women in formal dresses, and the men in tuxes gave the illusion of a more gracious, genteel era when one dressed for dinner each evening, ate multiple course meals served by retainers, and lingered over clever conversation instead of rushing away to the mall. I loved the glamour of it all and planned a scene in my next book where my heroine attended just such a gala.

The waiter removed my dinner plate with the remains of chicken topped with crab imperial, green beans seasoned with bacon and a sweet/sour sauce, julienne potatoes, and grilled tomatoes. Unfortunately he stepped back at precisely the same time as the waiter at the table behind us. Their collision sent what was left of my dinner onto my lap.

"Ack!" I stared at the stain spreading over my beautiful sunrise dress and thought I should have worn the old cream number I'd bought for last year's Romance Writers of America convention. Its loss would have been no big deal.

"I'm fine," I hastened to assure everyone, especially the young man who had deposited the food on me. He looked stricken. "It's okay. Really."

I mopped at the mess while Todd picked up my dish from the ground where it had bounced and swept the dinner debris off my lap back onto the plate. My romance-reading friend dunked her napkin in her water glass and handed it across the table to me. I dabbed a bit at the ugly blotch, but in the dimness I couldn't see clearly.

I stood. "I'll just go up to the house and see if I can get something to put on this to keep the stain from setting."

"Soda water," a lady suggested.

Everyone nodded agreement at this positive recommendation, and I started across the lawn, making a detour to the bar for the soda water.

We were seated at one of the tables furthest from the house. As I made my way through the company, I realized Todd was walking with me. He took my elbow and smiled at the people we passed, just like it was normal for his date to have big stains running down the front of her dress. I noticed Amos and Jessica spot us and felt warmed by their look of consternation at my ill fortune.

"Will it come out?" Todd asked.

I looked down and made a sad face. "I doubt it."

"But it's such a beautiful dress." He was genuinely distressed for me.

"You just like it because it's not beige," I said.

"No," he said. "I like it because you're in it." And he tucked my arm tightly against his side.

We went inside where I asked the first person we saw the way to the bathroom.

"I think it's down there," the girl said vaguely. "But I've never been here before. I'm part of the caterer's staff."

"I'll find it," I said with more confidence than I felt.

"I'll wait right here," Todd said, sitting on a deacon's bench in the front hall.

After a couple of turns I found the powder room and went to work on my dress, not an easy task when the skirt was too slim to hold over the sink. By the time I was finished, I had a wet streak from waist to hem, sort of like a skunk's stripe, only down my front instead of my back, deep orange instead of white, and made of water instead of fur. I wasn't sure that the greasy blob from dinner wasn't preferable, especially since it was probably still there, buried under all the wet.

Shaking my head, I left the powder room and trekked down the dimly lit hall back to the front of the house.

"Hey, Morgan! What are you doing? We're waiting!"

The voice was that of a young man, and the tone indicated that he was not very happy with Morgan.

"Yo, Morgan! I'm talking to you, girl!"

I couldn't resist the impulse to glance over my shoulder and see who was yelling and whom he was yelling at.

A very large but considerably younger version of Amos Yost was stalking down the hall toward me. Obviously he was the yeller. The problem was that I saw no yellee. Unless he was yelling at me? It certainly seemed so, the way he was glaring at me.

"What are you planning to do, crash the party?" His voice got nastier.

I looked up and down the hall again, but there was no one in sight but him and me.

"Are you talking to me?" I asked hesitantly.

He sneered at me. "Oh, that's cute. Just who else would I be talking to? Do you see anyone else?" He grabbed for my arm.

I jerked away and frowned at him. "Hands off, buddy!" I said in my best Bentley hauteur.

When he stepped toward me, I stepped back and felt the wall behind me. I tried to slide along it, ready to call for Todd—scream for Todd if need be.

The kid reached for me again, and as his hand closed over my arm, he froze. His eyes narrowed and he stared at me, looking me over from head to toe. I slid a step along the wall, uncomfortable under his scrutiny.

"I don't believe it," he muttered. He looked flabbergasted.

"What?" I asked in spite of myself.

"Hey, Pip," he yelled suddenly. "Come here! You gotta see this!"

If he could call for reinforcements, so could I.

"Hey, Todd," I yelled. "Come here! Quick!"

Another young man, presumably Pip, appeared behind my captor. He didn't have the bulk or look of the one staring at me with unfriendly eyes. He had, in fact, a strong resemblance to Jessica Yost.

"What do you want, Mick?" asked the new-comer. "Oh, you found her. It's about time."

"Who's he?" I asked the bigger kid. "Your brother?"

I got no answer.

"Come on, Morgan, you're holding us up! And what are you wearing that ridiculous dress for?"

"It's not ridiculous," I said, stung. "And I'm not Morgan."

I looked pointedly at my arm where Mick had it in a death grip. My skin around the edges of his hand was white from the pressure, and I thought that tomorrow I might well have a hand-shaped bruise. "Don't you think it would be a good idea to let go of me?"

"Oh. Right." Mick released me just as Todd came into the hallway. He looked wonderful, my hero, though by now I didn't think I needed rescuing. I'd figured out who I was talking to, thanks to the memorized family tree. Mick was undoubtedly Michael Yost and Pip was Phillip. Morgan was their sister.

"Who's he?" Mick demanded, looking at Todd. "What's he doing here? And who in the world are you?"

"Mick," Pip said, "just leave Morgan there. If she doesn't want to come with us, there's no rule that says she has to. I'd rather go without her anyway." He looked at me like he expected me to complain about being abandoned. And I guess if I were Morgan, I might have. As it was, I looked from him to Mick and answered Mick's questions.

"He's Todd Reasoner. We're here for your father's dinner party. And I'm Cara."

"Anything wrong?" Todd rested a hand protectively on my shoulder.

"I don't think so," I said. "I think it's a case of mistaken identity."

By now Pip was staring at me over Mick's shoulder like he couldn't believe his eyes. "It's not Morgan . . . but it is." His voice was full of awe.

"Who's Morgan?" Todd asked.

Mick glanced at him and then looked back at me. "Our sister."

"And I must look like her. Right?" My heart was tripping at a fantastic rate, and I brought a hand up to keep it from pounding out of my chest. I looked at Todd to see if he understood the possible ramifications of a resemblance here. He looked at me with a crooked eyebrow that said I understand but don't jump to conclusions. He gave my shoulder a squeeze.

Suddenly a girl with long brown hair and long slim legs came barreling around the corner and down the hall behind Mick and Pip.

"What's keeping you two?" she demanded. "I've been waiting out in the car. It's getting later by the moment, and I don't want to miss the beginning of the movie because you two are too dense to tell time."

Then she saw me. It was as if someone had punched her in the stomach. Her mouth made a small "O" and a little *oof* sound emerged. I suspected that I looked exactly the same.

In fact, I did look exactly the same. Certainly there were slight differences. The shape of our eyes wasn't quite the same, and my hair appeared to be a little lighter than hers, though she had just washed hers and it hung long and dark with moisture down her back and almost to her waist. And she was younger.

But looking at Morgan Yost was like looking in a mirror. And it gave me goosebumps.

The five of us were clustered in the hall, staring, when suddenly Amos and Jessica were there, Amos swearing under his breath as they came up behind Todd and me.

"Who are you?" Morgan asked when she could finally talk.

I swallowed, trying to get enough moisture in my mouth to speak. "I think I might be your long-lost cousin."

"Really?" Morgan looked surprised.

"Neat!" Pip looked impressed.

"Rubbish!" Mick looked furious.

"Oh, dear." Jessica looked worried.

Amos snorted. "We will talk in my study." And he stalked off down the hall and around the corner, obviously expecting everyone to follow.

We all did. It was that family charisma.

The three kids sat on the navy-and-white checkered sofa in descending order by size—Mick, Pip, Morgan. Jessica sat in a navy wing chair while I sat in an overstuffed white chair piped in navy. Todd sat on the arm of my chair, a very comforting support. Amos sat behind his desk in an executive's chair covered in blue leather. The navy rug was deep and plush and had sweeper marks across its surface. A watercolor of a sleek Nittany lion hung over the sofa, and various service and award plaques hung in clusters on the walls. However, the pride of the place was a photo of Amos shaking hands with football coaching great Joe Paterno. It was a Penn State alumnus's dream office.

"I know all about you," Amos began, his eyes on me cold and accusing. "Tel Hai called. So did Alma."

"I was very sorry that your mother had to go to

the hospital," I said. "Alma told me she's doing well and was expected back at Tel Hai today now that her heart is regulated. It was a matter of medication."

"Medication, my foot." He put his hands on his desk, palms down, and leaned forward. "It was *you*."

I jerked as though hit. Todd put a comforting hand on my shoulder.

"Amos, that's not true and you know it," he said.

"No, I don't know it," Amos said. "Mom had been doing quite well until she came along." And he pointed at me.

"She wanted to see me." I sounded desperate that he believe me.

"Ha! She's a senile old lady. She doesn't even understand why you were coming. But *I* know."

Suddenly something felt very strange here. What did he think he knew? "Why do you think I wanted to see your mother?"

He all but sneered. "Her money, of course."

"She's wealthy? I didn't know that."

This time he did sneer. "Do you honestly expect me to believe that?"

We Bentleys weren't used to being called liars, and my spine stiffened. "You might try. It's the truth."

"Cara came to me as a client because she was looking for her family and needed advice on

Pennsylvania law regarding adoptions," Todd said. "She has been following leads carefully since she's been here. She has not indicated in any way that she seeks anything from her family but acquaintance."

"Well, we're not her family, and even if we were, we wouldn't want any acquaintance." Amos's voice was heavy and final.

I thought about the call from Alma he'd mentioned. Surely she didn't call random people about something like this, but I didn't challenge him. It wouldn't do any good; that was obvious.

"I don't know about us not being her family, Daddy." Morgan got up from the sofa and walked toward me, studying me intently.

I glanced at Amos, and while he didn't look happy with his daughter, neither was he going to stop her speaking.

"Look at her, Daddy. She's me. Or me in what? Twenty years?"

Thanks a lot, I thought, and could feel Todd's enjoyment of my scowl at the unintended barb.

"How old are you?" Morgan asked.

"Thirty," I said. "How about you?"

"Eighteen. I graduated this year."

"Are you going to college next year?"

She nodded. "Penn State, main campus."

"What will you be studying?"

"English and journalism. I want to write."

My skin prickled. "I'm a writer."

"Really? What do you write? Are you published? How did you get published?"

"That's enough!" Amos roared.

I flinched but Morgan didn't. "We'll talk later," she said to me quietly. "When he's not around."

I nodded and opened my evening purse. I pulled out a little gold case and extracted a business card. "Here. It's my cell phone number and the address where I'm staying." I smiled at her. "I just made them today in case I saw anyone important tonight."

"Thanks," she said, and with a challenging look at her father put the card in her shorts' pocket.

"Morgan," Amos said in a taut voice, "you will not contact this woman. Do you understand me?"

Morgan nodded but made no promises.

Strong-willed parents breed strong-willed children, I thought as she took her seat beside Pip.

"Dad, Morgan's right," Pip said, also apparently not intimidated by his father. "There's a family something here. There has to be with a resemblance like theirs. Aren't you at all curious about it?"

"I already know about it," Amos said. "She claims she's the descendant of an illegitimate child of my grandmother."

"Yeah?" Pip looked intrigued. "So it's not you that was adopted?" he asked me. "You're not Mom or Dad's kid?"

My horror at such a thought was second only to that of Amos and Jessica's. I tried not to shudder as I shook my head.

"Not me," I said. "It's my grandfather who was adopted. He's the one whose family I'm trying to trace."

"And you think we're yours?" asked Pip. "And you've met Aunt Alma?"

"I'm tracing everyone I can find who is or was a Biemsderfer."

Pip nodded. "Well, that's us a couple of generations back."

"Pip," Amos said, heavily authoritative. "We do not have illegitimacy in our family."

Pip didn't seem impressed by the claim of familial purity. "Dad, who cares if your grand-mother had a baby before she was married? She's been dead for years. Besides, it happens all the time."

"That does not make it right!" Amos all but shouted.

Somehow I didn't think the issue of having sex outside of marriage was what Amos saw as wrong. It was that his grandmother had gotten caught, that his family had had to deal with it then and was having to deal with it now. And most important, his reputation might get besmirched by this bit of family history, though I had to agree with Pip. Who cared at this point?

I realized how overwhelmingly important appearances were to my cousin or uncle or whoever he was. Expedient rather than ethical, Todd had said.

Jessica had sat quietly through the conversation so far. Now she spoke to me, her eyes hot with contained resentment. "When I was introduced to you, I was absolutely shocked. I knew you were out there." She waved her hand vaguely. "We've known you were looking ever since Alma called. She said there was an uncanny similarity between you and Morgan. But when I turned around and saw you right here in my own yard . . . " She let the sentence trail away, the horror of my presence speaking for itself.

I nodded. "I can only imagine," I said. "I had no idea I was coming to your home . . . that The Paddock was your house."

Amos suddenly stood, and with that movement he took control of the conversation once more. He walked out from behind his desk, and Jessica sank back into her chair, looking sorry she had spoken.

Amos came to a stop a few feet in front of me, standing too close, trying to intimidate me by making me look up at him. I refused to cooperate, looking instead at his belt buckle. I wasn't a Bentley for nothing.

Todd stood and moved to the front of the chair we occupied. When he turned sideways to offer me his hand to help me rise, his movement forced Amos to step back. I looked at Todd gratefully.

"Listen here, whoever you are," Amos said when we finally stood face-to-face, eyes close to level. "I forbid you to see my mother. I absolutely forbid it."

I looked from Amos to Jessica and then to the children, especially Morgan. I felt a burning behind my eyes. I'd had such hopes. To have them dashed like this, especially after Alma had been so kind, was very painful.

"And one other thing," Amos said, his voice low and threatening. "If you ever try to insinuate yourself into my home or family again, you will regret it."

Insinuate. Ugly word, I thought.

Todd bristled immediately, but I laid a hand on his arm. "Let's go," I whispered. "It doesn't matter."

But it did . . . it did . . . and I was desperate to get out of there before I began to cry.

Chapter 11

Todd was so gentle and kind to me when he brought me home that Saturday night and then again when he picked me up for church Sunday morning. There's something quite terrific about a man who supports you even when he doesn't necessarily go along with your objectives.

For church Mr. Monochromatic was all in tans, from the tan-and-white stripes of his shirt to his tan slacks. I had on tan too, so we sort of looked like a matched pair if you discounted height, hair, and gender. I had added some color to my cotton knit dress with a necklace of multi-hued wooden beads Marnie had given me. It was only the second time I'd worn it in spite of having it two years.

"So you don't blend in with the woodwork completely," she'd told me with a loving wink.

"We Bentleys don't blend," I'd told her as I hung the beads about my neck.

She'd laughed. "That's one of the truest things you've ever said!"

Smiling, I fingered the beads as I climbed out of Todd's car. Heart relatives like Marnie were so much nicer than blood relatives like Amos —assuming he was indeed a relative. So why did

Amos and the rest of the Biemsderfer clan mean so much to me? And what was wrong with me that they did?

"I had a thought last night," Todd said as we walked across the parking lot toward the church.

I refrained from making a smart-mouth remark because he looked so serious.

"It occurred to me," he continued, "that God is a proponent of adoption."

"I've thought about that too. Jesus and Joseph? Raising the Son of God must have been a tall order. And there's Pharaoh's daughter and Moses and Eli and Samuel."

"Well, if it was good enough for Jesus, why isn't it good enough for you?" His question was asked conversationally, not confrontationally.

"But Jesus knew His Father. He knew His eternal background."

Todd frowned. "Okay, I'll give you that. But how about this? When we believe in Jesus, the Bible refers to us as adopted children of our heavenly Father. I always liked the old King James phrase 'adopted in the Beloved.'"

"What are you trying to tell me, Todd? That Pop's adoption has a spiritual parallel, and because it does, I shouldn't be looking for our birth family?"

"No. But maybe I'm suggesting that your adopted family should be enough."

I thought about his comment all through the

worship service. It was one of those Sundays when I heard little the pastor said, but I knew God was very close. I thought about Amos and Jessica and their rejection of me. I thought of Alma and her friendliness, but I also thought of her not mentioning to me my resemblance to Morgan, though she'd told Amos about it. I thought of Morgan, who wanted to be a writer, and Pip, who wondered aloud if I were the child of one of his parents. I thought of Mick, who didn't bother to talk to me after his initial response in the hallway. I thought of the branch of the Biemsderfers who no longer lived in Lancaster County but were scattered around the world. And I thought of Mom and Pop and Ward and Marnie and little Johnny.

And I realized that generation to generation doesn't have to be blood generations. In theory, family should be bone of my bone as well as heart of my heart. But if you had to choose, maybe love and acceptance were more important than DNA.

When we left the service, I said, "You know I think adoption is good, don't you?"

He quirked an eyebrow. "Do you? Sometimes it seems you're almost trying to undo Pop's adoption with this great drive to find your blood family."

I gave his comment careful consideration before I answered. "No, I don't think so. That would say something negative and unfair and unjust about my great-grandparents, and I'd never want to do that. From everything I've heard, they were wonderful people. Great-Grandfather Bentley was a doctor and Great-Grandmother was an artist. I have some of the most beautiful hand-painted china that she did. Painting china was popular with the ladies in those days, you know."

"Um, no, I didn't know." Todd's mouth twitched.

"Now why am I not surprised?" I grinned at him. "Most of the ladies who painted were no-talent dilettantes, but Great-Grandmother Bentley's work is absolutely wonderful. If she lived today, she'd be an artist in great demand."

We stopped to avoid getting bowled over by three little stair-step brothers running out the doorway of the Sunday school wing. One ran so close that my skirt swayed in the breeze he created.

"I'm sorry," their mother panted as she ran after them with a fourth little boy in her arms. "But at least they like to come to church."

"See how much they look alike?" I said as I watched the boys disappear into the parking lot. "That's genetics. Great-Grandmother Bentley might have been talented, but it didn't rub off on me. What abilities did Pop's birth parents have that we know nothing about? That's one of the strange things about adoption: who do your abilities, your talents, your likes and dislikes come from? Was there a Biemsderfer somewhere who liked to write?"

"Does it matter?" He shrugged.

"Doesn't it?"

I was still mulling these ideas over as Todd and I stopped for something to eat on the way home following the service.

"It's like Pop's a coin with two sides," I said over a burger and fries. "I know the Bentley side. I'd like to know the Biemsderfer side too. I think for some who search, there is a driving need to find where they've come from, an intensity that is painful and overwhelming and utterly compelling. The need for roots is an unhealthy compulsion for some because they think it will fix all the problems in their lives, and of course it won't. Locating the Biemsderfers isn't that all-consuming for me, probably for two reasons: I'm not the adopted person, and I love my family. I'm not looking to replace them. But I can't deny a compulsion to find out about the Biemsderfers, even the ones who are all over the globe."

"In spite of the fact that an omnipotent God allowed the Bentley side of Pop's coin?"

"I'm not denying our side of the coin. Truly I'm not. I appreciate and love my family too much to do that. It's just that I can't deny the other side either."

I was swallowing my last fry when my cell phone rang.

"This is Elizabeth Yost," a voice told me when I answered.

"Oh, Mrs. Yost," I breathed, looking at Todd with excitement.

"Jessica?" Todd said in surprise.

I shook my head and mouthed, "Aunt Lizzie."

"I want you to come and visit me," she said. "I was so disappointed we missed each other on Thursday. Sometimes this old heart gives me such trouble, and at the most inconvenient times. But I'm feeling fine now, and I want to meet you. Alma has told me all about you."

"I'd love to come, Mrs. Yost," I said. "But Amos asked me not to." Now that was a kind way of explaining his uncompromising order.

"I'm Aunt Lizzie to you, child. And I don't care what Amos says."

I liked this woman already.

"He's always trying to tell me what to do," she continued. "I'm not senile yet, and I make my own choices. After all, I'm the mother here; he's the child."

Referring to Amos as a child made me want to laugh out loud. He was very much a petulant little boy who demanded his own way.

"Please come. I want to meet you. And I want to tell you a story."

"When do you want me?" I asked.

"How about later this afternoon?"

"Later this afternoon?" I repeated with a look at Todd. It didn't strike either him or me as odd that I expected him to come with me. He nodded. "We'll see you then," I told her.

"I think," I said to Todd as we drove to the farm, "that it's okay if I look for family if I don't *need* them, if I can function without them. If I find them and they accept me, I'll know a fuller life. If I find them and they reject me, like Amos did, I'll know sadness. But it's not the end of the world. My life is still rich and full—full of people I'll love and who love me. I keep thinking of what St. Paul wrote: 'We are hard pressed on every side, but not crushed; perplexed, but not in despair; persecuted, but not abandoned; struck down, but not destroyed.' That's me and how I feel about Amos."

I felt tears rising again, as I had frequently since we'd left Amos's last night. "I feel struck down by last night's events, but I'm not destroyed. I realize more strongly than ever that if I were looking for my birth family to make me whole, I'm looking in the wrong place. Only God can fill my deepest longings because only He understands them. People come and go, but God is forever."

"He's there when you don't know who your family is," Todd agreed. "And He's there when you do, but they don't necessarily give you much emotionally."

I looked at him sharply, ready to give sympathy since he was obviously speaking of his situation. But he was already distracted.

"Would you look at that!"

I looked and saw the entire Zook drive was full of buggies.

Todd pulled to the side of the road. "I'll have to let you out here," he said. "I don't want to get in the middle of all that. But I'll be back in a couple of hours. Why not try to get a nap?" He looked at the circles under my eyes. "I'd say you didn't sleep very well last night."

"I'd say you're right. And I'd also say my eraser stick isn't working as well as it should."

"Oh, one thing I want to mention before I forget." He looked at me with concerned eyes. "There are wisps of rumors in the legal community that Amos and Jessica are having trouble with one of their sons. It's all vague, no specifics."

"And given your affection for Amos, you haven't tried to find out any details, right?" I refrained from noting that guys tended to let the most interesting pieces of information go unexplored.

"I don't like gossip. But think about it. Do you want to get involved with a family that has a kid who's trouble?"

"Like legal trouble?"

"I don't know."

"It must be Mick. He was very sullen and angry

last night." I pictured him slouching on the sofa, arms folded across his chest. And he was the one who grabbed me.

Todd leaned over and kissed my cheek. "Just another piece of information to tuck away in that overactive mind of yours."

"Overactive is good," I said as I climbed out of the car. "The alternative is boring."

He laughed and I watched him drive away. Then I threaded my way up the drive and inside. The large open room that filled the downstairs was full of people, some of whom, I'm sorry to say, weren't using deodorant on this very hot June day. The men in their black Sunday suits and white shirts occupied the living room end of the house and were talking in Pennsylvania Dutch. The women occupied the kitchen end of the house, fussing over food, and also talking in Pennsylvania Dutch.

When I came in, everyone fell silent, the hush sounding terribly loud to my embarrassed ears. Everyone smiled and nodded politely to me, and Elam gave a little wave before returning to his conversation with two other young men. Esther walked over.

"They're here to visit Mary," she explained. "They're taking turns going upstairs."

"I see all the buggies," I semi-whispered, "but where are all the horses?"

She giggled and answered in the same sotto

voce manner. "They're tied behind the barn at a special hitching rail Elam and John set up."

"Ah." I nodded sagely. "You guys are so practical!"

Just then an older woman in a royal-purple dress, black apron, black shoes and hose, and white kapp appeared at the bottom of the steps.

"She needs a nap," the woman announced and everyone nodded. "We should eat."

I slipped upstairs to my rooms as the men began filing into the kitchen to fill their plates with the cold food prepared yesterday since cooking on the Sabbath was prohibited. I wondered if Elam's Mary Clare or his rival young Joe Lapp were here, but the only one I could ask was Jake, and he seemed to be hiding out in his apartment.

As I entered my room, I wondered if any of these people knew Mary's secret. What would they think if they knew she painted? And worse yet, sold her work to the English through Kristie's efforts?

I changed into khaki cropped pants and a white shirt and was sitting in front of my fan reading; Rainbow was draped on the back of the chair. I heard a knock at my door. It was Esther, looking worried and unsure of herself.

I hurried to her. "Come in, Esther. What's wrong? Is Mary all right?"

Esther shook her head. "She's in a lot of pain

today, and she's run out of medicine. Could you call her doctor and ask for more? It'd save me running down to the phone shanty at the end of the road."

"Sure." I pulled out my cell phone and dialed the number Esther gave me. In a remarkably short time, the doctor returned my call and agreed to call in a refill. When I hung up, I asked, "Who's going to pick this up?"

"I can skate down for it," she said.

"But it's Sunday! You shouldn't skate on Sunday, should you? And you shouldn't go to the store on Sunday either." Surely both were anti-*Ordnung.* "Besides you're caring for the guests. Let me go get it, okay?"

She bent and picked up Rainbow, who had left her queenly perch and was wrapping herself around Esther's ankles. She buried her face in the cat's soft fur. "I'd do it for Mary."

"I'll go." I reached for my purse and keys. Esther smiled her thanks. We put Rainbow on the bed and with a final, "Remember the litter box, baby," I followed Esther downstairs.

I was afraid I wouldn't be able to get my car out of the drive with all the buggies that were there, but the men had graciously left room for either Jake or me to back out. I walked to my car and reached for the door handle. I missed on my first grab. I had just extended my hand again when I realized something was very strange

271

about my car. The handle was lower than it should be.

I stepped back, looked, and with a gasp realized all my tires were flat. All four of them!

I bent and looked more closely. My skin crawled. In each tire were long slashes where someone had taken a knife and cut and cut and cut. I stared in shock. My tires! Someone had purposely sliced my tires. Why? Who? I looked at all the buggies but quickly dismissed that idea. Not one of the Amish guests. Aside from the fact that they were peaceable folks, there was no privacy to do the deed. Surely slashers liked—needed—privacy.

I looked back at my car and was overwhelmed. *Why me? Why my car?*

I turned to look at Jake's van. His tires were fine. No one had done anything to his vehicle. Just to me. To my tires. And whoever it was hadn't been satisfied with a single cut. Far from it. I shivered in the shimmering June heat.

I pulled out my cell phone and made two calls. First, I called the police. Not that I expected they could find who had done the vandalism, but they needed to know it had been done. Then I called the automobile club.

"Tell whoever comes to bring four new tires," I told the dispatcher.

"Four?" Disbelief edged her voice.

"Four."

The police came quickly, pulling into the drive. I stood with a sturdy-looking officer beside my wounded car answering questions for his report. We were surrounded by men in black suits and broad-brimmed hats who had come streaming out when the police car pulled in. Jake sat supportively by my side, his hand holding Hawk in place.

"Don't worry about Mom's medicine," he told me. "Hawk and I'll go get it as soon as we're finished here."

I nodded gratefully. I'd discovered that if I spoke, I was having trouble controlling the quaver that insisted on wobbling uninvited through my words.

"A blown-up mailbox and slashed tires within three days," the officer said.

The Amish men murmured their notice of that fact too. John and Elam looked especially concerned.

"You're sure you don't know anyone who has a grudge against you?"

"Me?" I shook my head. I felt very tired. "I just moved to Bird-in-Hand a little over a week ago. The only people I know are the Zooks, Todd Reasoner, my lawyer, and Amos Yost, a lawyer in Lancaster. Not much in the way of suspects, I'm afraid."

Mick Yost's sullen face flashed but I couldn't give his name to the police just because he was an angry kid. I wished I knew what his rumored problem was. If he had a record for petty violence, I could suggest him as a suspect, but if he was just mad at the world . . .

The police were preparing to leave when the AAA service truck pulled into the drive. Jake, the Amish, and I watched as the serviceman began work on the first tire.

"Wow," he whistled. "Somebody did a number on this!"

Somehow his awe at the cowardly attack made me feel ill. I turned and walked down the drive. I could feel eyes following me as I continued down the street and into the woods.

There were no problems here before you came. That was undoubtedly what they were thinking. The police never visited Mary and John before you came.

I pushed through the underbrush until I came to the stream. I collapsed on one of the rocks and felt vulnerable.

I didn't like the idea of violence on the Zooks' farm any more than their congregation did. John and Mary, Elam and Esther were part of a people who believed in nonviolence, and even worse, they had a house full of guests of the same persuasion. Nothing evil should happen near them—any of them—especially if it were because of my presence. Granted this was nothing compared to the Nickel Mines school shootings, but this was here and this involved me.

Is this my fault somehow, Lord? Does someone want to hurt me? Scare me? But why?

I knew Amos didn't like me, but slashing tires was not the work of a man like him. He would never stoop to something so petty. If he decided I was in the way, he'd go all out. One of Lancaster County's counterparts to Tony Soprano's goons would show up to take care of me.

Not that I actually thought Amos would do something like that. He was used to political power and intimidation, to legal pressure and manipulation. If he decided to go after me, and it was a very big if, he'd go that route.

So maybe it was just random violence. My car, like the mailbox, was just a handy target for some kids who had no sense and a streak of malice.

I don't know how long I sat staring at the burbling stream, the chattering rush of water soothing my tattered spirit with its gentle whispers. The tightness in my shoulders loosened somewhat. I closed my eyes and took deep, cleansing breaths. Still I was more than glad when I heard a concerned voice behind me.

"Cara, are you all right?"

I turned and watched Todd, solid and safe, come to me. He sank onto the rock beside me and reached for my hand.

As soon as his fingers closed around mine, tears burned my eyes, breached my lower lids, and fell. He put his arm around me and pulled me to him until my head rested on his shoulder.

"Shush. It's okay," he whispered as he patted me gently on the back. "It's okay. You're okay."

I sniffed and smiled through my tears. For a guy who wasn't used to emotion, he was doing all right. "Someone slashes my tires and you say it's okay. Some lawyer you are."

I felt as much as heard his little burst of laughter. "A smart-mouth remark. Why am I not surprised? I knew you were a gutsy lady."

I didn't feel very gutsy. "Why would someone do that to my tires, Todd?"

His arm tightened around me. "It wasn't you, Cara. Never think it was you."

"But it was my car!"

"Just because it was there."

"Do you really think so?"

"What else could it be? You're not the kind of person to have enemies."

"You met me less than two weeks ago and you already know this?"

He ran his hand over my hair and said with quiet assurance, "I know this. So don't cry, sweetheart. Don't cry."

I nodded and said, "I won't." But I did. Buckets. All over his blue shirt, turning one side into a mass of wrinkles. I looked at him apologetically.

"I think I'm crying as much over Amos's nastiness last night as I am over the tires." I sniffed. "Up until now I was trying to be brave about it. But it hurts! I'm not used to people not liking me."

I sat up, sniffed again, and wiped at my face in a mostly futile effort to erase the tears. My cheeks felt hot and puffy. I knelt and leaned over the stream. I took a handful of water and splashed my eyes, my cheeks. The coolness felt good. I took a quick drink.

I sat back on my rock, pulled my sandals off, and lowered my feet into the stream.

"Yo! Cold!" I pulled my feet out of the water and then tried again.

Todd reached forward and lowered his hand into the water. "It's not cold."

"Oh, sure," I said. "You're only sticking your hand under. Hands are tough. They can take it. It's feet that complain."

"Not mine." And so saying, he took off his shoes and socks and stuck his feet in the water. "Yo! Cold!"

We grinned at each other as we sat on the rocks with our feet dangling in the creek, slowly turning blue.

Todd cleared his throat. "I had an idea after I left you today," he said. He fell silent and watched his feet slowly paddling.

I turned to him. "Do you think you'll share it?"

He looked at me and then back to the stream.

"It's about the adoption, isn't it?" I said. "And you're not sure you want to tell me?"

He took a deep, fortifying breath. "What if opening more doors somehow brings you another unpleasant episode like last night?"

I studied the shifting light playing across the flowing water. "I've thought about that possibility. It's a matter of deciding whether the return is worth the risk."

He arched his eyebrows at the unspoken question.

I grinned at him. "What do you think?"

He sighed. "That's what I was afraid of."

I bent over and caught a handful of water. I flicked it in his direction.

He looked with great interest at the deep-blue splash mark on his jeans leg. His eyebrow quirked and his jaw hardened. "I don't know after treatment like that." And he sent a cascade of water my way with his foot.

I gasped as the deluge caught me in the chest. My shirt was drenched and clung to me.

"Sorry," he said with a huge grin, obviously as sorry as a bully who'd taken the lunch money of some poor little kid. "I didn't mean to kick quite that much."

"Why, you!" I made my hand a scoop and gave him a face full. I was pleased to see him choke and sputter, but my pleasure turned to consternation as he sent another great spray my way. Now it was my turn to choke and splutter.

I jumped into the creek so I could aim head on. I cupped my hands and threw, water flying. I got him squarely in the chest and crowed with pleasure. How do pacifists feel, I wondered as I tried unsuccessfully to duck his retaliatory measures, about water battles? And on Sunday?

Next thing I knew we were both in the stream dashing water at each other at a furious pace. We were wet, cold, and laughing, and my tears were forgotten. I never even saw the mossy rock that my foot slipped on, but I felt myself start to fall.

"Ack!" To keep from tumbling I grabbed the nearest object, which happened to be Todd. Suddenly both of us were sitting in water to our waists.

"My wallet!" Todd moaned as he felt his back pocket.

"Look at it this way. You're just laundering your money."

"Ha ha." He pulled his wallet out of his pocket and tossed it onto the rock where it leaked a steady stream. "Like that would ever happen."

"I don't know. Seems to me I've read about just such activity."

"Attacking a whole profession because of a few. Unfair and unjust." He dipped into the stream with joined hands and poured the captured water over my head like he was ladling soup. Water dripped from my nose and ran off my chin. "Why, I might as well say all writers are plagiarists."

"A scurrilous attack!" I was laughing so hard I could barely get the words out. I cupped my hand and sliced it along the surface of the stream, sending a great arc of water into Todd's face. It happened to get him with his mouth open in laughter and on an indrawn breath. He coughed and wheezed as the water flooded down his throat.

"Serves you right!" I said, though I began clapping him on the back in sympathy. The pats were pretty weak because of my laughter, but they helped curb his coughing.

I sat back, leaning on my hands, out of breath, and exhilarated. My braid trailed behind me in the stream. I couldn't remember the last time I'd done something so absolutely foolish and fun.

Todd slowly rotated until he was facing me, and I knew he had great plans for revenge. He reached around me and grabbed my braid.

I grabbed his hand. "Dunk me and you're a dead man!"

I expected him to try to pull me under, but instead he pulled me slowly toward him. I looked up, surprised. Our eyes met and held.

In a flash the frivolity dissapated and the atmosphere between us was as laden with electricity as the air is with ozone after a lightning strike. I couldn't have moved if my life depended on it. As it was, I could barely breathe. It was as if all the oxygen had been burned off by the atmospheric charge, and there was nothing left to draw into my lungs.

A fly buzzed between us and Todd blinked, reluctantly releasing my hair. "Come on, Cara," he said softly. "We'd better get out of here before we catch pneumonia."

He stood and pulled me to my feet. We climbed onto our rock, brightly lit and warmed by a shaft of sun streaming through an opening in the canopy of leaves. Water streamed from our clothes, forming pools that flowed into rivulets that became little waterfalls that fell back into the creek.

I was conscious of Todd's every movement even without looking directly at him. I knew he bent one knee, curling the leg around himself. He raised his other knee and rested an elbow on it. He stared thoughtfully at the water for a minute and then turned to study me.

I pulled my braid over my shoulder with assumed nonchalance and squeezed. Water poured in a little torrent. I began working the rubber band that bound the plait, but it was wound about by hair and snarls. I felt myself go cross-eyed as I tried to unravel the tangled mess.

"Here, let me." Todd pulled my braid back

over my shoulder. "Turn sideways," he ordered. I did and he struggled with my hair.

"Now tell me what you were going to tell me before we got sidetracked," I said. We definitely needed something ordinary to talk about to discharge the surge of current arcing between us.

He cleared his throat. "Well, I was thinking about adoption papers and . . . Ow!" I heard the smack as the rubber band snapped him. "And you'd better not be smiling," he said grouchily.

I wiped the grin from my face. "I'm not."

"Right." He went back to wrestling with the rubber band. "In the earlier part of the twentieth century, adoptions weren't sealed like they were later, after 1924."

Hope stole my breath. "What are you saying?"

"There's a possibility that your pop's papers might be filed along with all the other civil records from 1918 in the Prothonotary's office."

"You mean I could just walk in and ask to see the papers and they'd show me? I could find Pop's birth and adoption records?" I was floored.

"Maybe," Todd said. "I don't know. It's just something that occurred to me. You'd have to go find out."

"Where?" I tried to turn to look at him, but my braid in his hands prevented it.

"The Prothonotary's office is in the courthouse in Lancaster."

I nodded. I knew where the courthouse was. "What in the world is a prothonotary?"

"You and Harry Truman. He's reported to have asked the same thing, expletive added, when he met one in Pittsburgh at a campaign stop."

Nice to know a president and I thought alike, expletive aside.

"We elect them here in Pennsylvania."

"Good for you staunch citizens, but what in the world is one?"

"It's the person who watches over all the civil records." With a satisfied grunt he finally pulled the rubber band free. He began carefully unbraiding my hair.

"Then why don't they call him the Keeper of Civil Records in the Civil Records Office?" I grumbled. "It's as bad as Orphan's Court."

"Thank you, Todd," Todd said. "That was very nice of you to come up with such a wonderful idea for me."

I could feel him spreading my hair out to the sun. I smiled. "Thank you, Todd. It was very nice of you to come up with such a wonderful idea for me. You are absolutely the best lawyer a woman could want. I will go to the courthouse tomorrow and check it out."

"Mmm," he said. His strong fingers combed my hair, catching every so often on knots, but it felt wonderful regardless. Mom had often combed my hair for me when I was a child, and few things meant love and security more. I closed my eyes and gave myself up to the pleasant sensation.

The sun fell warmly on my face. The leaves hung hot and still above, and the stream frolicked beside us. I opened my eyes, looked into the branches overhead, and saw a catbird land on a branch. His melodious trill filled the air as he sang with all the joy within him. I smiled and my eyes slid shut again.

I woke when the sun had moved off me. I wasn't chilled; it was impossible to be chilled in the heat. I was just aware that time had passed, though I had no idea how much. I was also aware of Todd's touch still on my hair and of my head resting against his knee as he sat with his legs bracketing me.

"Enjoy your nap?" he asked softly as he brushed my hair back from my forehead.

I nodded. "Was I asleep long?"

"Only a few minutes. Maybe it'll get rid of those bruises under your eyes."

"I think I need more than a few minutes for that."

A honeybee hummed beside me and flew on; a mosquito buzzed next to my ear. A squirrel chattered at us from overhead.

I sighed with contentment. "Do you treat all your clients with such excellent care?"

Immediately his hands stilled. "No," he said.

"Only the special ones." But just like that, in spite of his nice words, the magic mood was gone.

I sighed, this time at my stupidity. I should have kept my mouth shut. I sat up straight, feeling the weight of my hair fall over my shoulders and back. "I guess we'd better get going if we want to see Great-Aunt Lizzie."

Todd glanced at his wrist and nodded. "My fortunately waterproof watch tells me you're right."

He gathered up his billfold and the contents he'd laid out to dry, and we walked down the quiet road back toward the house. We weren't dripping too badly by now, but we were a sight, clothes wrinkled, my hair wild and all over the place, Todd's curls in a riot of unruly brown all over his head.

I stopped walking abruptly. "The company! I can't walk through the living room looking like this. They'll stare and think terrible things about me."

Todd eyed me. "I don't know. I think you look kind of cute."

I grinned. "Thanks, but I probably look like a reprobate to them. What am I going to do? I have to change. I can't go visit Lizzie like this."

When we reached the edge of the yard, I had an inspiration. "Come on." I grabbed his hand and dragged him toward Jake's door.

Jake's expression was priceless when he saw us.

"We fell into the stream," I explained.

"Obviously."

"And I don't want to walk through the living room in front of everyone."

"I don't blame you. It is, after all, Sunday and you both look very un-Sabbath-like."

"So I thought you could get Esther for me."

"And she?"

"Could get some clothes for me."

In a minute Jake had Esther, who took one look at Todd and me and was torn between laughter at how bedraggled we looked and horror that we had participated in such activities on a Sunday. And I could only imagine the "activities" that crossed her mind. But she was sweet and helpful, and in a short time I had dry clothes in hand. I shut myself in Jake's bathroom and changed. I pulled my hair back in a loose ponytail and wrapped it with a scrunchie I found in the bottom of the purse she'd also brought for me.

By the time I emerged from Jake's bathroom, I looked quite presentable, but I couldn't say the same for my date.

"Jake, have you got a shirt Todd can borrow?" I asked. The blue one he had on was a woven cotton, and the water had done a number on it.

The men eyed each other and decided that a

large knit polo shirt would do as well on one as the other. As far as jeans, Todd would just have to dry out as he went. He went to Jake's room to change, and I heard a cry of anguish.

"His hair, I bet," I told Jake. "The curls. Wild." I whirled my hand around my head.

"Makes him look less buttoned down," Jake said.

"My feeling exactly. But," and I grinned sympathetically as Todd strode into the room looking grumpy, "he doesn't agree."

Jake had given Todd a red shirt, and between the bright color and the unchecked curls, he looked better than ever. He turned as red as his shirt when I told him so, but he didn't stop grinning from the farm to Tel Hai.

Chapter 12

I was very nervous about meeting Aunt Lizzie. I kept replaying Amos's words, feeling their heat and fury.

"I forbid you to see my mother. I absolutely forbid it."

"Am I making a mistake?" I asked Todd as we drove past the peaceful Amish farms on Beaver Dam Road. "Should I have listened to Amos?"

"I think you're doing the right thing." He slowed for the turn into Tel Hai. "Mrs. Yost wants to see you. She invited you to come, and she has every right to select her own company." He reached over and squeezed my hand. "Don't worry."

Father God, it's not that I want to worry; it's just that I do. Please calm my fears and help us to have a good visit!

Once again we made our way to the third-floor, partial-care area, but this time the attendant led us directly to Lizzie's room.

"She's been looking forward to your visit all day," the attendant said with a smile. "I'm just glad someone is visiting her! It makes me angry that her family ignores her like they do. There's a niece who visits her every so often, but she lives up in Camp Hill. That's a pretty good trip, so she doesn't come as often as Lizzie would like. But she comes more frequently than the son."

That's Alma, I thought. She comes but Amos and Jessica don't.

"Lizzie is one of my favorite people," the attendant said. "In fact, everyone here loves her. But then I'm sure you know how wonderful she is."

I merely smiled, thinking an explanation would be much too complicated.

"Come in," a tremulous voice called when we knocked.

We walked into a large room filled with furniture, personal treasures, books, and Aunt Lizzie. The overall effect was of too much for the confined space, but even so it seemed a pleasant place to live. As I glanced around, I realized that she'd had to weed her possessions to a bare minimum to fit them into this space. How did you do that when memories were attached to so many things? I could just imagine her saying, "I'll keep this pretty piece of porcelain my husband gave me, but I'll get rid of the one my parents gave me. I'll keep this book I love, but I'll give away that one that I also love."

How hard it must be, that putting away of life.

A love seat and an easy chair sat at right angles near the door, ready for company. A bookcase hugged one wall, and she could have won a competition with Dr. Reasoner for getting the most books into a limited area. Her bed was against the back wall of the room, and a dresser faced it. Photos sat on the bookcase and the dresser, and what looked to me to be original watercolors hung on the walls. Several beautiful petit point pillows sat on the chairs and the bed, and I wondered if Lizzie had done them herself. A rug in fragile creams, roses, and greens was echoed in the window treatments, bedspread, and slipcovers.

Lizzie sat in a rocking chair beside the window. She'd been reading a Readers Digest condensed book. She put it down and rose slowly to her feet. "I read lots of these now," she said, pointing to the book. "I don't have enough time left to read the unabridged versions, you see. I'm eighty-seven, and there's so much more to squeeze in!"

She walked across her room slightly unsteady, but her eyes were keenly alert as they looked Todd and me over.

"Now I know you must be Cara Bentley," she said to me. "And Alma was right. You do have the look of Morgan about you. But who's this?"

I introduced Todd.

"Your lawyer?" Aunt Lizzie said. "My, my. I don't know many people who come to call with their lawyer in tow."

Todd took the old woman's proffered hand and shook it. "I'm here tonight as Cara's special friend. And yours." The smile he gave her would have stolen my breath, and it tickled me that Aunt Lizzie wasn't entirely immune either as she preened at his attention.

"Ah," she said as she indicated we should sit on the love seat. "I know all about special friends. That's how Harlan used to describe himself until the day we married. After that he said he was a privileged friend, a very privileged friend." And she sank into the easy chair and sighed. "I miss that man. I truly do."

I studied Aunt Lizzie. If we were related, as I believed we were, she was Pop's sister. I was seized by a feeling of disbelief. All my life or at least as far back as I could remember, our family had been the four of us, five when Marnie joined us. To think that there was a woman out there who would have expanded that circle was almost beyond comprehension.

But if I looked like Morgan, Aunt Lizzie did not look like Pop. She was petite to his huge, even considering the fact that she had undoubtedly shrunk with age. She had delicate features to his strong ones. And she was a reader to his doer. I was somewhat disappointed at the lack of family resemblance.

Then she put out her hand in a gesture that was so Pop that my heart stopped.

"Do that again," I whispered.

"What?"

"That hand movement. Please."

And she did it again, just the same. The hand was considerably smaller, the nails delicate and cared for as his never were, but the movement was all Pop.

"My mother used to make that gesture all the time," Lizzie said.

"So did Pop," I said. "And so does Ward."

"Who is Ward, my dear?"

"My brother." And I began talking about my family, telling her stories, making her laugh and, when I told of Pop's death just a few months ago, making her cry.

When I finally ran out of steam, she said, "I have wondered for years if my brother was happy." She looked at me through misty eyes. "It is a great joy to hear just how happy he was."

"You believe Pop was your brother?"

"I have no doubts, my dear. No doubts. I know it. And now I will tell you my story." She leaned back in her chair and stared at the middle distance, seeing her own mental pictures, her own scenes as she recounted her tale.

"My brother Josh and I had a happy home. Mom and Dad loved each other and us very much. We laughed a lot, but I always thought there was a touch of sorrow about Mom that I couldn't understand. One time when I was about nineteen, old enough to be brave and young enough to be foolish, I asked her what made her sad, especially around the same date every November. She wouldn't tell me. All I knew was what we all observed: the beginning of that month was always very difficult for her, but by Thanksgiving she was usually back to her normal self."

I leaned forward. "Pop was born in the beginning of November."

Lizzie nodded. "I eventually learned that, but not for many years. In fact I was 55 when I learned Mom's story. My father was already several years gone, and she was dying. It was the beginning of November—"

"Sit down, Lizzie," Madeleine said. "Stop fussing over me."

Liz sat. "I'm only trying to help, Mom."

Madeleine smiled the best she could for November, which is to say not very convincingly. "I know. But it drives me crazy."

Liz nodded and watched her mother. The older woman lay on pillows, looking weak, fragile, brittle enough to break into pieces if touched. Her weight had dropped precipitously in recent days, and she was having trouble keeping anything down. She was dying rapidly with no possibility of reversal.

The thought of losing her mother made Liz want to weep. No, to wail. Her mother was her friend, her confidant, her sounding board. No matter what Liz's problem or need, her mom had always been there. She had taught Liz to pray, to trust God, to believe in Jesus, to accept loss as part of life when Liz's three-week-old daughter, Abigail, had died of crib death.

"Did we sin that God had to punish us so?" Liz had cried.

"No," her mom replied, and she put her arms around her weeping daughter. As she hugged Liz fiercely, she paraphrased the words of Jesus: "This happened that God might be glorified."

And because her mother said it, Liz believed it and survived with her faith intact.

"This is my last November," Madeleine said in a voice that was stronger than it had been in recent weeks.

Liz made a disclaiming sound and a quick hand movement of denial.

"Yes, it is, Lizzie. But it's all right. I don't mind. Novembers have always been a time of deep pain for me. Enos tried his best to help me, and I loved him for trying. He'd hold me and love me and whisper soothingly in my ear. But he never understood how or why I felt such pain year after year even though he knew its cause. Always my heart breaking. Always a bit of me dying."

Liz looked at her mother and dared to ask for the first time in many, many years the question she'd asked at nineteen: "What causes you such hurt, Mom? What tears you away from us at this time every year? What is it that breaks your heart?"

"It's your brother, dear."

"Josh?" Liz couldn't have been more surprised. Josh was a wonderful person. In fact, he was the person she admired most in the world next to her mom. He set a standard of Christian living that was without peer, and his wonderful sense of humor prevented her or anyone from thinking him too holy, too pure for real folks to like.

"No, no, Liz. Not Josh. Lehman."

"Lehman?" Liz stared at her mother. "I have another brother? And his name is Lehman? But that's our last name." She began working dates in her mind, but try as she would, she couldn't see when another child had been born to her parents. "Was he stillborn? Or impaired somehow? Is he in an institution somewhere? Why do you never talk about him?" she finally asked.

"One doesn't talk about illegitimacy, Lizzie, especially not to one's daughter."

Liz felt the world tilt. Her mother, a paragon of Christian virtue, a gracious example of a woman worth far more than rubies, was saying she was involved in an illegitimate pregnancy? Madeleine Biemsderfer Lehman? The pope might as well announce he had become a Baptist. Her husband might as well say he'd welcome liver for dinner.

Madeleine smiled sadly. "You should see your face, Lizzie. Then you'd understand why you don't know about Lehman. But it's my last November, and someone has to know. Someone has to keep his memory alive!" The last was a whisper.

As her mom lay back on her pillows, her eyes closed, her breathing labored, Liz studied her. She tried to comprehend a brother besides Josh . . . and all the ramifications.

The thought of her mom with another man besides her father was too awkward, too terrible for Liz to consider. Her parents had loved each other with such commitment and passion. Yet there was an out-of-wedlock child.

"It was World War I," Madeleine said, her eyes still shut. "Enos was to go to Europe. A doughboy who would save the world from the Kaiser. We were already very much in love, and the thought of the separation was a knife in our hearts."

"How old were you?" Liz asked.

"I was sixteen and Enos was nineteen. And we ignored God and took what we wanted, which was each other."

It was hard for Liz, even at fifty-five, to imagine her parents in bed together within the bonds of holy matrimony. Trying to imagine them as hormonally driven teenage kids desperate over an impending separation and the possibility of

Enos's death on a foreign battlefield was beyond her. But at least there was no other man. For that Liz was intensely grateful.

Madeleine's lips curved in a sad smile. "I finally understood that I was pregnant three months after Enos had shipped out. My parents were understandably upset—a massive under-statement if ever there was one."

Madeleine's face filled with regret. "I've always felt so terrible for what I put them through. Mother cried and Father grew more taciturn than ever. They took me out of school and kept me home for the remaining months of my pregnancy. They refused to let me write Enos, and they wouldn't give me any of the letters he wrote."

Madeleine's voice shook as she remembered the anguish of those days.

"I was so distraught with worry for Enos, for his safety, and for what he must think of me for not writing. And I was eaten up by guilt that we had done things out of God's order. We knew and had willfully disobeyed. How could God forgive us? It's a wonder I didn't miscarry from the emotional stresses. I delivered a healthy baby boy on November first. But I never held him. They wouldn't let me. For my own good, they said." Madeleine's face contorted with pain.

Liz took her mother's cold hand. "It's all right, Mom. It was long, long ago." Of course it wasn't all right. And in spite of the years—what? Sixty-two years? The wrenching separation was still a heart wound that hemorrhaged, especially in November.

"My parents were adamant. Adoption was the only possible way to deal with the situation. I was too weary and frightened to offer much protest. My one independent action was selecting the name for the birth certificate: Lehman Biemsderfer for Enos and me."

Liz stared out the hospital room window. "So I have a brother out there somewhere? A full blood brother." *What was he like? Was he happy? Did nice people raise him? Did he survive the Depression? World War II? Was he married? Did he have children, grandchildren? Would I ever know?*

Madeleine saw the questions in her daughter and nodded her understanding. She was all too familiar with them because she'd asked them daily for more than 60 years. "Open my Bible to Proverbs 3, will you?"

Liz did so and found a picture of a chubby baby boy propped up on a blanket embroidered with baskets of flowers.

"Lehman," Madeleine said. "It's the only proof I have that he exists beyond my imagination."

Liz looked at the sepia print and her heart turned over. *This adorable child was her brother!* No wonder November was awful for her mother.

"When he was almost six months old," Madeleine continued, "I went to the agency that had placed him. I was desperate. Enos was still somewhere in Europe, and I hadn't heard from him for so long that I doubted he could still love me. I knew he was probably still alive only because I hadn't read of his death in the paper, but that was all I knew. Mother and Father were still reeling from what I had done to them, and my baby was gone. I had nothing! Please, I pleaded with the people at the agency. Please get me a picture of my baby or I will surely go insane. They took one look at me and believed. A month later this photo arrived for me."

Madeleine reached out and ran a gentle hand over the cracked and faded print. "As long as I had the picture, I knew I would survive. I knew I wouldn't forget. I knew God would care for him. That's why it's in Proverbs 3. 'Trust in the Lord with all your heart.' I did that every day for Lehman. I did it for you and Josh too, but I saw what was happening in your lives. I talked with you and prayed with you. Lehman I could only trust to God."

Liz, herself the mother of a son who was ignoring God, knew all about trusting to God those who, for whatever reason, couldn't be influenced.

The women sat quietly for a while, thinking, praying, wondering.

When she felt strong enough, Madeleine took up her story once again.

"When Enos finally came home from the war, my parents forbade me to see him. I was barely eighteen, sheltered, living with the consequences of the one great rebellion of my life. But I knew I loved Enos. I sent him messages through my brother, Harold. Enos sent love letters back, so I knew he loved me and felt anguish over Lehman too, especially over the fact that he hadn't known and hadn't been here for me. When I turned twenty-one, we ran off and married. My parents were furious, especially Father."

Liz thought of her grandfather, a German in the old tradition, fierce, strict, unemotional. How had her mom ever had the courage to defy him?

"The first Christmas we were married, my parents refused even to accept a gift from us. By the second Christmas you were born, and you were the one who broke the barrier. They loved you, Liz. And then Josh came. And one day when you were five, Mother broke down and told me she prayed every single day for Lehman. We cried together that day, she and I, a mother and a grandmother weeping over a boy we would never know but would always love."

"How many years older than me is Lehman?" Liz asked.

"Six years. He was born November 1, 1918. And I still pray every single day for him, just like I do for you and Josh. And I pray for his family, just like I do for yours and Josh's."

Madeleine grasped Liz's hand, her expression desperate. "Lizzie, you must keep praying for them." It was an order and a plea. "Someone has to keep praying for them because we don't know who raised Lehman. We don't know if anyone taught him to love God and to follow Jesus. Promise me, Lizzie. Promise me that you will pray for your brother and his family every single day of your life. Promise me that he won't be forgotten. Promise me, Lizzie. Promise me!"

"Oh, Mom!" Tears poured down Liz's face. "It will be an honor to take on that responsibility." Liz leaned over and kissed her mother. No wonder there was such depth to her mom's walk with God. Great pain and great grace had forged great intimacy. "Now you must calm down. You're making yourself sick."

"I am sick. And it's November. And Enos isn't here to help me. My one hope is that I am forgiven in Christ. I have at least learned that over the years. When I sorrow now, it's only loss, not guilt and regret. Christ has borne my guilt, and He helps me with my pain." A slight smile touched her pale face momentarily.

Liz's tears fell onto her mother's pillow, her face, her nightgown. "Every day for the rest of my life I will pray for Lehman and his family. For my brother."

Exhausted, Madeleine fell back on her pillow and went to sleep.

"She never woke up." Aunt Lizzie smiled sadly at Todd and me.

The three of us sat silently in the gathering dusk. My heart broke for Madeleine and her years of sorrow, and I found myself swallowing, trying to control my tears. What she had missed by not knowing Pop!

Finally Lizzie spoke. "I kept my promise. I have prayed for Lehman and his family every day for more than twenty-five years."

"That means you've been praying for me." I leaned forward and laid my hand on hers. "Thank you, Aunt Lizzie. Thank you. And from now on, I shall pray daily for you and your family."

Aunt Lizzie smiled sweetly. "It will be nice to have someone praying for me." She leaned forward and tried to rise from her chair, but her legs seemed to have trouble bearing her weight.

"Is there something I can get for you?" I asked, rising.

"Over there on the end table by the window. My Bible."

I handed her the requested book and sat down. Aunt Lizzie riffled through the pages.

"Proverbs 3," she said and took out an old photograph. She passed it to me.

I stared at the chubby baby on the embroidered

blanket, holding it so Todd could see too. Once again I had to blink back tears. Todd's arm slid around my shoulders and pressed comfortingly.

"Aunt Lizzie," I said through a throat tight with emotion. "I know this picture. Mom had a copy of it on her bureau for as long as I can remember. 'For when John gets too big for his britches,' she always said. 'Then I can remind him that he's nothing but a grownup baby, just like the rest of us.'"

I traced the baskets of flowers with my index finger. "And we still have the blanket. It's a family treasure. Great-Grandmother Bentley did the needlework on it, and she and Great-Grandfather Bentley brought Pop home from the adoption agency wrapped in it. Since then, each generation of Bentleys has brought their children home in that blanket. Mom and Pop brought Trey home in it, and Trey and Caroline brought Ward and me. Ward and Marnie wrapped Johnny in it to bring him home even though it was July and eighty-seven degrees. I've always known that someday I'll use it for that same purpose."

"You've actually seen the same picture and have the blanket?" Aunt Lizzie's face was alight with amazement. "As if we needed more proof."

I nodded. "I'll bring the blanket next time I visit so that you can see it. The background is cream, the baskets are a soft aqua, and the flowers are worked in pinks and roses with light green leaves. I'm sure the colors have faded over ninety-plus years, but it's still very beautiful. And the moths have never gotten it."

"You're coming to see me again?" My Aunt Lizzie looked at me with eyes bright with hope. It broke my heart that there was such surprise in her voice.

"Of course. And I'll bring Ward and Marnie and Johnny too."

"My cup runneth over," she said, and I thought that Amos deserved a good kick in his posterior. And I immediately remembered I'd promised to pray for him and Jessica.

Ouch.

My first prayer for them would be that they'd realize how wonderful his mother was and come visit her as she deserved.

Todd and I were silent as we walked from Aunt Lizzie's room to the car a few minutes later. In fact, we didn't talk until we pulled into the drive at Todd's dad's cottage.

"I have a question for you, Cara," Todd finally said as he put the car in park.

I held my breath. I knew he had been almost as moved as I was by Aunt Lizzie's story, and I couldn't imagine what was bothering him.

"Why do you think Pop never tried to find his family? From what you've told me, you have a drive to know and understand your genetic her-

304

itage. Didn't he have the same compulsion? And if not, why not?"

"I've wondered about that myself," I said. "And I can only come up with one answer. He didn't care where he came from."

Todd frowned. "But he was a creative and imaginative person. Why wouldn't he be curious about his birth family?"

"I don't know exactly." I searched for the right words to explain what was only a feeling. "Pop was very secure in himself. He was one of those people who are born confident. Most people have gaps in their self-confidence, some little chinks, some gigantic holes as big as the Grand Canyon. A few, though, seem born without that internal uncertainty. Because of this, they take life and mold it to their dreams without questioning their right to do so and without questioning their abilities. Pop was one of those. He never debated with himself about who he was. He always knew."

"Does that make those people terribly difficult to live with?"

I had to admire his delicacy in how he worded his question. He asked about people who were extremely confident—a vague, amorphous collection of faceless beings rather than his real concern, my pop.

I nodded. "They can become very controlling and assume they know what's best for the whole world. If these people don't develop a heart for others and a heart for God, they can be very intimidating and calculating, very manipulative. If they don't have people who are strong enough to challenge them on their attitudes and behavior, they can overwhelm others and not even recognize the pain they've caused. But they don't need the holes in their lives filled because they don't have holes."

"And adoption searches are often ventures in hole filling."

"Uh-huh. At least this search is for me. But Pop was confident that being a Bentley was great. He was confident that opening the first Bentley's store was great. And he was confident that expanding the chain was great. And Ward is the same way. He doesn't understand why I want to know about the Biemsderfers. He doesn't feel the holes."

"I thought that was because he saw family in terms of heart, not body and bone."

I pushed some straggling hair back into my ponytail. "I see family in terms of heart too, but I also think it's body and bone. And I feel the body and bone holes. Ward doesn't. And apparently Pop didn't either."

Todd opened his car door and climbed reluctantly out. "Well, let's go visit some body and bone."

"Todd." I laid a hand on his arm as we walked

up the sidewalk. "There's heart here too. You just need to learn how to see it."

He looked at me skeptically but said nothing.

We knocked on Dr. Reasoner's door just as we had a few nights ago. A slow steady shuffle sounded, and Dr. Reasoner appeared on the other side of the screen.

"Toddy."

"Dad."

I poked Todd in the ribs.

"Oh. Dad, you remember Cara Bentley, my client?"

"Ah," he said. "Of course I remember the client. Come in. Come in." He turned to walk back into the house, assuming we would follow.

I poked Todd in the ribs again. "You've got to stop introducing me as your client," I hissed. "I'm beginning to think I'm going to get billed for all the extra hours we spend together."

He turned a broad grin on me. "Of course you're getting billed for all those hours. How else can I afford the cabin I want on a lake in Canada?"

I quirked an eyebrow. "If you think I'm paying so you can flee the country to get away from me, you're much mistaken, guy."

Suddenly Todd's grin faded and his eyes darkened. He slipped his arm around my waist and bumped his hip against mine, lifting me clean off my feet. I made a little squeak of surprise. He

307

spun me effortlessly until I was standing with my back against the side of the cottage. I could feel the bricks through my cream knit shirt. He placed a hand against the wall on either side of my head, trapping me. Not that I was trying to escape.

"Todd," I said breathlessly. "Your father's waiting."

He ignored me. Well, he actually ignored what I said. Me he paid lots of attention to. He leaned over and kissed me.

As kisses go, I don't know how it would rate on a scale of one to ten. I haven't had lots of experience, so I can't make a sound judgment. But I do know that as far as I was concerned, and I was, after all, the one who counted, I felt it all the way to my toes. I also realized very quickly that I had been under-writing my heroines' responses to my heroes.

Todd drew back and gave a devastating smile. "I've been wanting to do that for some time now, probably since the day you gave me that ridiculous tie."

"Really?" It was all I could do to get one word out.

His wonderful eyes glommed onto mine, and I saw all sorts of wonderful possibilities written there. "Really," he said.

I looked at him a minute longer and then threw myself into his arms. "Again."

A discreet cough pulled us apart. Arms still wrapped about each other, we turned to see Dr. Reasoner standing at the door watching us.

"Toddy," he said conversationally, "I must insist you stop ravishing your client on my front porch. What will my neighbors think? I have, after all, a reputation to consider." And he turned and walked inside.

I felt Todd stiffen. Glancing at him, I realized he thought his father was criticizing us.

"Todd, he was teasing," I said softly.

Todd frowned. "Teasing?"

"Didn't you see the twinkle in his eye?"

"Twinkle? In Dad's eye?" He looked through the screen at his father's retreating figure, trying to wrap his mind about this alien thought.

"Trust me on this," I said, going up on tiptoe and kissing his cheek. "You'll see."

We sat in the same seats in the glassed-in porch that we had occupied on our last visit. I glanced with great interest at the end table beside my chair and saw that *Beowulf* was gone. So were *Great Expectations* and *Through the Looking Glass*. In their places and obviously read were *As the Deer*, *So My Soul*, and George Eliot's *Silas Marner*.

"Wow," I said, pointing. "You've got me in excellent company."

"I must tell you, Cara, that I enjoyed your books very much. You have a distinctive and delightful style."

If I weren't already glowing like an incandescent bulb from Todd's kiss, I would have from that compliment.

"Marci and Scott are memorable characters," said Dr. Reasoner, professor of English and authority on literature who liked my books! "And you show their development as both humans and believers very realistically. You also develop their love in a delightful, thoughtful progression."

"You have no idea what your words mean to me, Dr. Reasoner." I hugged them to myself, metaphorically spinning like a top or, better yet, Maria as she serenaded the sky in *The Sound of Music*. I really wanted to ask him to write the wonderful words down so I'd have them forever, but it seemed a bit premature in our acquaintance to ask for endorsement copy. "Thank you very much."

He nodded his head in acknowledgment. "I made one very interesting observation." He glanced from me to Todd, who was following the conversation with great interest, and back to me. "You write about love as if you are acquainted with it."

I felt myself blush, sitting here in front of Todd and under his father's obviously assessing eye. "I've lived all my life observing it," I managed.

Dr. Reasoner lifted an eyebrow in question, an expression I'd seen on his son's face many times.

"My grandparents who raised me," I explained. "Theirs was a great love affair."

"So by observation you've been able to capture both the emotional and volitional aspects of love. I find that amazing."

I blinked. "You do?"

"I do. Love is so difficult to define, to portray. You have captured the essence of what I think of as love." He glanced hesitantly at Todd, as if he weren't certain about speaking his mind in front of his son. "I know that while I was reading, I realized I hadn't missed Catherine so much in years. You made me yearn again for what I thought I had forgotten."

I must have looked distressed because he hurried to say, "It was a *good* missing, my dear. A bringing to mind of all the joy we shared."

His eyes grew misty with reminiscence. "Catherine taught me that sharing love makes you more than you are alone. That's how I know you got Marci and Scott right. They made each other more than they were alone." He smiled. "Catherine taught me laughter, something I hadn't known before her—or after her for that matter. When she died, my life lost its joy. I became the morose and melancholy man she had thus far prevented me from becoming."

He glanced again at Todd, but he turned to speak to me. "I think it was hard on Toddy, the lack of laughter. I tried for his sake, but I didn't know how to be other than I was . . . than I am. I'm afraid his growing up was shadows instead of sunshine, and I regret that more than I can possibly say." He smiled sadly at me, as if he were asking my forgiveness.

Together he and I turned to Todd, who was sitting with his mouth hanging open, staring at his father. In a reversal of last night, I reached over and pushed his jaw shut. He blinked and looked at me. I rested my hand along his face for a moment, smiling at him, reminding him from my heart that there was much more than body and bone between him and his father. It was just that neither of them knew how to see it yet.

Again Dr. Reasoner turned from Todd to speak to me. "From the day Catherine died, I have prayed that Toddy would find his sunshine. I see his mother's laughter in him, but I've never known how to release it. I can't even talk with him much less make him laugh. Perhaps, Cara," he said hopefully, "in you I'm seeing the answer to my prayer."

I was overwhelmed by his words. Speechless, I stole a glance at Todd and saw he was as confounded as I.

"And now," said Dr. Reasoner, slapping his legs briskly. "Let me get you two a bowl of ice cream." And he rose and left the porch.

Todd watched his father leave, his face a study in conflicting emotions. Hope, disbelief, wonder, anger, bemusement, affection all flashed through his eyes. He looked at me and shook his head, unable to articulate what he was feeling. He reached for my hand and gripped it fiercely.

Ah, Lord, teach this man about heart and family. In fact, and I glanced toward the kitchen, *teach both of them.*

"He prays for me!" Todd's voice and face were full of wonder. "Like Madeleine and Lizzie prayed for your pop. I never knew he did that, never would have imagined it in a million years."

I nodded. "One of the things I've grieved over most since Mom and Pop's deaths is knowing that no one is praying for me with the same concern and commitment I'd taken for granted all my life."

"You want someone to pray for you?" He ran a hand gently down my cheek. "I'll pray for you."

"Don't say that lightly," I said. "It's too precious a promise."

"And not one to be broken," he agreed. "But praying for you will be easy. You're the one with the hard job. You promised to pray for Amos and Jessica."

"I know. I think it's going to force me to stretch myself spiritually in ways I never foresaw."

We sat silently for a few minutes. I could hear Dr. Reasoner opening and shutting the refrigerator and the cupboards. I heard the chink of dishes and the schuss of pretzels being poured into a basket.

"Cara, why did he tell you all those things instead of me?" Todd asked suddenly. There was hurt and a slight edge of anger in his tone.

I shrugged. "Because he knows me better?"

"What? He's only seen you twice!"

"But he read my books. He's seen into my heart."

Todd looked at me skeptically.

"You'll see what I mean if you ever get around to reading my stuff."

"I am reading your stuff," he said in a huff. "I'm halfway through *As the Deer*."

"And don't you feel you know me better by reading it?"

He took a moment, obviously trying to find an answer. "Well, I guess I know that you like Coke better than Pepsi because your characters always drink Coke."

A burst of air escaped, half amusement, half frustration.

"Isn't that what you meant?" he asked, his eyebrows drawn together.

"Not quite," I said. "But knowing me isn't the real issue here, is it? It's how can you and your dad get to know each other."

His shoulders dipped. "I haven't figured that one out in thirty years."

"Well, we'll just have to work on that, won't we?"

He raised his eyebrow and smiled. "We will?"

I raised my own eyebrow and smiled back. "We will. I'll ask your father a question. He'll answer. Then all you have to do is ask why. Now go help him carry the ice cream out."

He blinked.

I jerked my head toward the door to the house. "Two hands, three bowls. And pretzels. Go."

To my surprise, he went. To Dr. Reasoner's surprise too, if the look on his face when they returned to the porch was any indication.

When we were eating our ice cream, I asked innocently, "Dr. Reasoner, aside from *As the Deer* and *So My Soul*, what has been your favorite book you've recently read?"

When he answered, I looked at Todd. For a minute he stared blankly back. Then he sat up straight and looked at his father.

"Why?"

Dr. Reasoner looked at him in surprise. "Why is it my favorite?"

Todd looked at me in a slight panic. I inclined my head ever so slightly.

"Yes," Todd said. "Why is it your favorite?"

"Well," Dr. Reasoner began.

The conversation lasted thirty minutes, and I was very proud of Todd. His eyes didn't glaze over once.

Chapter 13

I woke up Monday morning tense and irritable. As I lurched into the bathroom and turned on the shower, I tried to analyze my bad mood. It didn't take long until I had the answer. In a word: change. And worse, change beyond my control.

Three months ago I was safe and secure in Pop's house, writing away as I'd done for the past eight years. Then poof! Pop was gone.

Three weeks ago I was safe and secure in what was now my house, then poof! I finished my novel and had to face the reality of being alone.

Three weeks ago I might have been alone, but I felt secure in who I was—a Bentley with a proud and wonderful heritage. Then poof! I wasn't a Bentley. None of us were, from Pop on down.

Three weeks ago I slept in my own bed in the bedroom that had been mine for essentially my whole life. Then poof! I was living on an Amish farm in a little village that was schizophrenic, half of its citizens living in a parallel universe, the other half enjoying the prosperity the fantasy half generated in tourist dollars.

Three weeks ago I had a small family I'd known and loved all my life. Then poof! I had relatives coming out my ears, and a significant number of them seemed to not like me.

Three weeks ago I was Cara Bentley, spinster, not exactly happy over my single state but not losing any sleep over it either. Then poof! I got a new lawyer, and suddenly I was enamored with brown curls and strong jaw lines.

I adjusted the shower temperature and told God a few of the things that were simmering in the back of my mind.

How come I have to deal with so many changes of such magnitude all at once? You know I hate change! Couldn't we have dealt with one, maybe two at a time?

But I recognized quickly that I couldn't have any one of them without the others. They were a package, and they were giving me a headache.

Except for Todd. He made me smile.

I let the water beat on my head and slide down my face and shoulders and race down the drain. I felt a significant amount of my stress slip away with the water. I turned my back to the spray and lowered my head, pulling my hair aside. The sharp needles of spray massaged my neck, easing the tension in my taut muscles.

As I shampooed my hair, I had a most electrifying thought, an epiphany of sorts. The notion appeared out of the blue between squeezing a blob of Pert in my palm and massaging it into my hair. I raised my hands to my head in a daze.

As I worked the shampoo to the tips of my hair, I pondered and wondered.

What if my obsession with Pop's adoption papers wasn't just for the purpose of discovering where we came from? What if it was for the purpose of teaching me lessons I'd never learn any other way? Lessons like letting go of the past, moving on, adapting to change? Lessons like reaching out even when it was uncomfortable and stretched me way beyond my usual boundaries?

I'd glibly told Todd that Pop had never searched because he wasn't interested in his heritage. He was secure in himself with things as they were. While I still thought that was right, maybe there was more to it than that. Maybe God knew that three generations later I would need something drastic to get my life out of the comfortable rut it had fallen into, something so dramatic that I'd make changes in spite of my predilections.

Maybe God knew these things? No maybe about it. This was God I was thinking about. If I were right, God had planned that I find those papers in the bottom of that box of pictures—papers that would turn my life upside down, papers that should have been in Mr. Havens' office with the rest of Pop's things.

Another snippet of a psalm floated through my mind: *"I will instruct you and teach you in the way you should go."*

I pondered this radical idea as I dressed in a tan denim skirt and white, scoop-neck knit shirt with a brown leather belt and sandals. I wondered about it as I sat at my desk and stared at the crisp, clear view out my window. A cool front had blown in overnight, and the humidity was temporarily gone. The sky was a brilliant blue, and the far fields were as crisp and green as the leaves on the great maple in the front yard.

Maybe my narrow view of what I will accept in my life is clearing some, Lord, just like the atmosphere outside. Please help me with these changes, the wonderful ones like Todd and Aunt Lizzie, and the difficult ones like Pop and Mom being gone and Amos not liking me.

By the time I went down for breakfast, I was feeling excited about life's possibilities once again. So much for my prescience.

The first things I saw were a pair of hens lying on the kitchen counter. Their throats had been slit, and they were lying there waiting to be plucked and cleaned. I knew full well that the family killed the poultry they ate, but I hadn't been on the farm long enough to witness this particular farm reality. I turned my back on the gruesome sight as Esther came down the stairs from Mary's room.

"Dinner?" I said, gesturing to the hens.

"I guess so," Esther said. "There's not much choice."

Something in her voice made me look at her closely. "What do you mean? Is something wrong?"

"Elam found them lying on the front porch with their throats slit when he went out to milk the cows this morning."

It felt like ice slid down my back. "Another act of vandalism?"

Esther shrugged, her great eyes wide, her normally rosy cheeks pale. "I guess. I don't know about vandalism. I've never seen anything like this before."

"Except for my slashed tires," I said grimly. "And the blown-up mailbox."

If possible, Esther's eyes got bigger.

The front screen door slammed and Elam walked in. He took one look at Esther and frowned. "Has something else happened?"

She sighed and shook her head. "Your mother keeps asking me what's wrong. I try to act natural, but she can tell I'm upset. And I can't lie and say everything's fine."

"Is she okay?" He looked toward the stairs.

Esther nodded. "She's sleeping. Yesterday all the company wore her out. She'll sleep until Rose comes. And then Kristie is coming."

Elam nodded.

"Elam, what do she and Kristie do? I've seen pictures, drawings, and paintings, and I don't think Kristie did them," Esther asked.

The implication hung in the air, and I looked at Elam to see what he'd say. How much did he know?

"Don't worry about Mom's sketches," he said. "She's been doing them as long as I can remember."

"But Elam—"

"It's Mom's little secret, Esther. And we want it to remain a secret." He looked at her with steel in his gray eyes.

"Does the bishop know?" she whispered.

Elam shook his head.

Esther was clearly torn.

"It's like a hobby for her," he said. "She draws something and sticks it in her book. They're not hanging anywhere." He gestured to the barren walls as if the fact that his mother wasn't doing anything beyond the drawing itself meant everything was fine. "It's like Father's wood carving or your quilting."

"But the wood carvings are toys for children," Esther said. "And quilts have a useful purpose." Unspoken was the assumption that artwork was worthless because of lack of practical purpose or spiritual use.

"It's just Mom," Elam said. "Don't let it bother you. As for Kristie, she's become Mom's friend. That's all."

I looked at him to see if he was being disingenuous, but I didn't think so. He really didn't know Mary was selling her work and that Kristie was acting as her agent.

But how could he not know?

Easily, I realized. Where would he be to see Mary's pictures for sale? Or see them hung on a wall? The separate universe in which he and his people moved automatically kept Mary's secret without her having to do anything more heinous than keep silent.

Shoulders hunched as if she still wrestled with her conscience, Esther turned back to the hens. I stared at the lifeless bodies. A far more pressing issue than Mary's paintings gnawed at me.

"Do you think the hens have any connection to my slashed tires?" I asked Elam.

He shrugged, but it was obvious the idea had crossed his mind.

"Should we report it to the police?" I asked.

"No." He was emphatic. "Father and I don't want to do that. We'd rather just accept the loss." He placed some mail on the table.

"Turn the other cheek?" I asked. "Give him your cloak?"

"Exactly." He eyed me carefully as if he were looking for sarcasm or ridicule. He seemed satisfied that I was merely stating nonviolence principles. He nodded. "If you're okay, Esther, I have to get back to work."

Suddenly her pale cheeks flooded with color. He had come to see how she was doing. "I'm fine," she said, eyes aglow. But he was looking at the mail.

You're an idiot, Elam, I thought. I don't care how nice Mary Clare is. Esther's just the girl for you.

"Couple of letters for you, Cara," he said, holding them out to me. "And one for you, Esther. From Ammon?"

Esther grabbed her letter, blushing furiously. "It's from my mother!"

"How do you know? You haven't opened it yet. Maybe it's from Ammon."

"I recognize the handwriting." Her voice was breathless.

"Then Ammon is even dumber than I thought." Elam let the screen door slam behind him.

Since Esther was a brilliant red, I decided the kindest thing I could do would be to read my mail and make believe I didn't notice the effect Elam had on her.

I slid my finger under the flap and opened a card from Marnie. *Sometimes life throws curve balls,* it read on the cover. An absolute harridan stood at the plate as the ball whizzed by. *But you managed a home run anyway,* read the inside. The harridan wore a giant grin as she ran the bases.

"We like him," Marnie wrote. "Definitely a home run."

I was still grinning when I opened my second letter.

You were told not to visit her. You were warned. Now you will suffer. Like the chickens.

I stared at the block printing on lined paper torn from a spiral notebook and felt like spiders were crawling all over me. I threw the letter down and started rubbing my arms like I was brushing insects away.

Don't look! I ordered myself, but my eyes went of their own volition to the hens. They had been thoroughly bled, but in my imagination I saw red welling up and spilling from the wounds at their throats.

God, am I that undesirable a relative?

I picked up my threatening letter and went to my rooms. I got my cell phone and called Todd's office. If I ever needed advice from my lawyer, it was now. Some comfort too.

"Mrs. Smiley, this is Cara Bentley. May I speak to Todd, please."

A slight clearing of her throat was her only sign of disapproval. I wondered in passing what color her fingernails were this week. "I'm sorry, Miss Bentley. Mr. Reasoner is not available."

"It's really important, Mrs. Smiley. How can I reach him? Does he have a beeper? Or is he in conference?"

"He's in court and cannot be interrupted."

I glanced at the clock: 11:15. "They do break for lunch, don't they?"

"Well, yes."

"I'll find him then." I clicked off and gathered my things. I wanted to go to the courthouse anyway to visit the Prothonotary's office. Time for the old two birds with one stone bit.

Not that I needed more proof of Pop's origins than Morgan's and my amazing resemblance and Aunt Lizzie's picture, but Amos needed hard evidence.

Well, I'd show him. I'd give him legal confirmation he couldn't refute. I'd present proof in a manner that meant something to him—if Todd's idea worked.

I'd been to Lancaster County Court House before when I went to Orphan's Court with such high hopes. I took my ticket from the machine in the nearby parking garage and found a slot for my car on the third level. The courthouse was in the middle of downtown Lancaster City at the intersection of Duke and Orange Streets. Approaching the main entrance, I glanced across the street at the graceful colonnade at St. James Episcopal Church. It was a lovely sight in the midst of the concrete and brick of the business district, a delight to the eye.

I reached for the door of the courthouse only to

have someone grab it out of my hand and move to barge through. I turned to glare at the rude person and found myself face-to-face with Amos Yost.

I inclined my head slightly, the barest politeness I could imagine.

"What are you doing here?" he hissed with no attempt at civility.

I felt like saying, "None of your beeswax," but I remembered about speech being seasoned with grace and kept my mouth shut. I even kept silent about the letter currently burning a hole in my purse instead of shouting, "Your son is psychotic!"

"I told you not to visit her." Amos's voice was like tiny pellets of hail beating on me, cold and stinging, but ultimately ineffective and not damaging.

I squared my shoulders. "She invited me." I regretted my compulsion to answer as soon as I spoke. I should have ignored him completely. I should have been smart enough not to defend myself to him and so begin a he-said, she-said exchange.

"She's a senile old lady," he said in a brutally dismissive tone. "She undoubtedly told you the strange story of my grandmother's baby. I bet she even showed you a picture, didn't she? Ah, I can see by your face that she did. And you thought you'd found the perfect way into her affections by claiming the baby in the picture was your grandfather."

I didn't tell him I had seen that picture almost every day of my life and that Ward and Marnie currently had the blanket and had brought Johnny home from the hospital in it.

I stared at Amos for a minute, wondering what it was like to be so nasty and to speak of your own mother with such cruelty. The affection in our family had been so genuine that people like Amos were hard for me to comprehend.

"Excuse me. I have business in the courthouse." I tried to reach around him for the door, but he shifted just enough to block me.

"You think I'm kidding when I tell you to leave my mother alone, do you? Ever heard of a restraining order?"

I looked at him in stunned disbelief. A restraining order? He saw me as that dangerous? That greedy? That threatening?

I heard a group of people walking up behind me. I waited until they were almost to me. Then I said very loudly, "Excuse me, sir. You're blocking our way."

Since five new people pressed up behind us, Amos had no choice but to move. I walked into the courthouse with a calm I didn't feel and turned left. I was walking blind, going anywhere to get away from Amos. When I felt a hand on my arm, I spun around, furious.

"Don't touch me!" I hissed.

"Okay," Todd said, slightly taken aback. "If you feel that strongly about it."

"Todd!" I grabbed his arm to hold myself up. Now that he was beside me, I was shaking like the proverbial leaf. "I thought you were Amos."

He studied my face for a brief moment, and then slipped his hand under my elbow. "Come on." He led me to a cafeteria where he found a table in a corner. He seated me facing the wall.

"All right. Give. What happened?"

Willing my chin not to tremble, I reached into my purse and pulled out the letter. Silently Todd read it. When he looked up, his eyes were hard and angry.

"What's this about chickens?"

"Two had their throats slit this morning. Elam found them on the front porch."

He looked at the letter again. "You don't think Amos had anything to do with this, do you?" He ran his hand through his curls, but they were so naturally combed now that they barely showed the strain. "A man in his position surely wouldn't stoop so low. It'd be professional suicide if it ever got out."

"I'm more inclined to think it's Mick."

"Makes more sense than Amos, who would be more subtle."

I shivered. "He wasn't very subtle a few min-

328

utes ago. He threatened me with a restraining order to prevent me from visiting Aunt Lizzie again."

Todd nodded, not surprised. "That's more what I would expect from him. Use the law, not petty crime." He patted my hand. "Don't let the threat bother you. I'll take care of it."

I smiled my thanks. "But he still gives me the willies," I added.

Todd glanced at his watch. "I have to be back in court in five minutes. I'll stop at the farm as soon as I'm finished, okay?" He pushed back his chair and grabbed his briefcase. "Will you be all right?"

"I'm fine," I said. "Now." I smiled my best smile.

The smile must have worked because he suddenly leaned down and kissed my cheek, looked surprised at himself, and left.

I bought myself a bottle of iced tea and a bagel and cream cheese. I munched as I thought. When I was finished, I had no more answers than I'd had when I began eating, but I was ready to visit the Prothonotary's office.

Back in the lobby I found a directory that sent me to the second floor right, almost to the end of the hall. I passed Orphan's Court and the Register of Deeds and came to the Prothonotary. I entered and waited my turn for assistance before a long counter.

"How can I help you?" a pleasant woman in wire-framed glasses asked.

"I'd like to look at papers from 1918," I said.

The woman blinked. "Did you say 1918?"

I nodded.

"You'll have to go to Archives for them," she said. Though why I should want papers that old was clearly beyond her.

"Okay. Where is Archives?"

She sent me down the hall and down some stairs, down another hall, and down some more stairs.

"At the bottom of the stairs you can go right or left," the woman said. "I don't know which way will give you the material you want, but there will be people there to help you."

I thanked her and followed her directions, going from the new part of the courthouse to the old in the process. I eventually found Archives and came to a T, just as the woman had said. I looked right and left and saw no one. I turned right.

I entered a large room full of bookshelves rising rank upon rank from floor to ceiling, from one end to the other. The shelves were full of books of bound legal documents. 1887 Orphans Court. 1916 Orphans Court. 1901–1905 Marriages. 1926 Marriages.

Marriages, I thought. I searched the shelves for 1923. I found the heavy book I wanted and slid it from its resting place over rollers that allowed easy access to the ungainly records. I carried the book to a counter and started leafing through it.

The legal record of long ago love was fascinating to me. Widowed farmers, young clerks, thirty-year-old spinsters, divorced seamstresses —their personal stories were reduced to the equivalent of name, rank, and serial number. Every so often in the margins were the signatures of parents giving permission for underage children to marry. Apparently underage meant through twenty.

Some of the questions asked on the various documents raised more questions in my mind.

Is the applicant an imbecile, epileptic, of unsound mind, or under guardianship as a person of unsound mind or under the influence of intoxicating liquor or narcotic drugs?

If you were any of these things, would you admit it?

What is the relationship of parties making this application, if any, either by blood or marriage?

If the wrong answer meant you couldn't get a marriage license, would you answer truthfully?

I flipped page after page until suddenly, there it was:

Statement of Male:
Full name: Enos Adam Lehman

Statement of Female:
Full name: Madeleine Elizabeth Biemsderfer

I traced Madeleine's name with my forefinger. Five years after Pop's birth, she and her Enos had finally married. It was overwhelming to try to imagine the heartache of those five years, pain beyond measure for Madeleine and Enos as well as for her parents, Joshua and Lottie. I thought for the first time of Enos's parents. Did they ever know about Pop?

I closed the marriage license book and rolled it back into place. On a high shelf I found the 1918 Orphan's Court book. I felt compelled to look at it even though everyone told me Orphan's Court meant estates. I found a stool and stepped up to slide the book from its place. The cover was torn and dusty. I lugged the heavy volume to the counter and started leafing through.

With no great surprise, I saw that the book did indeed contain records of estates where the legatee was a minor and the estate was placed under the financial guardianship of an adult. At least the Orphan's was a complete misnomer.

I sighed, but I was glad I'd doublechecked. It wasn't that I didn't trust Todd and all the other people I'd talked to at the courthouse. It was just that I liked to see things for myself.

After I climbed back on the stepstool and slid the bound journal back into place, I decided there was nothing more for me in this room. I went back to the foot of the stairs and turned left. A lady saw me coming and met me in the doorway.

"May I help you?" she asked. Her nametag read Annabelle.

"I'm looking for the adoption record of my grandfather," I said.

Immediately Annabelle looked distressed. "I'm sorry," she said, and I could tell she really was sorry. "All adoption records are sealed. It's impossible to gain access to them without a judge's order, and such an order is difficult to obtain without mutual consent. I'm afraid I can't help you."

"I know all about the sealed records," I said. "But I'm looking for records from 1918. I was told that adoption records going back that far may not be sealed."

Annabelle looked at me with interest. Her eyes narrowed as she considered my comment.

"You may be right," she said. "I think records were purged under judge's orders of all adoption documentation going back to 1924. But adoption papers before that may still be in the public records."

I tried to still the flutter of anticipation in my stomach. I couldn't let myself get excited yet. Still, in spite of my stern self lecture, I found myself holding my breath expectantly.

"If there is anything still available, it would be in the Trust Books," Annabelle said.

"What are they?" I asked.

"They're the bound prothonotary records. And they would be locked in a storeroom down the hall."

She turned back to her desk and got a handful of keys. She searched through them with quick fingers, selecting a silver colored one. She walked up the last flight of stairs I'd come down, and I followed. Halfway down a hall, she stopped before a door and inserted the key. She turned it and the door swung inward. She reached around the corner and touched a light switch. A weak light shone over multiple file cabinets and more shelves full of books of bound documents.

"Have you worked in Archives long?" I asked.

"Ten years," Annabelle said. "I find it fascinating."

I was very grateful for her longevity on the job. A new person mightn't have known about these records, or if she did, she wouldn't have been able to walk unerringly to the right shelf. In no time I had a volume in my hands that included papers from 1914 to 1920.

"Bring it out to my room where you'll have better light," Annabelle said.

"Really? I can just sit and read it as long as I want?"

"Sure." She led the way back to the hall. She shut off the light and relocked the door. I trailed her down the steps, the heavy book under my arm.

Soon I was settled on a stool under a strong light, flipping pages. Everything in the book was written in old fashioned longhand by a pen with a thin nub and a person with a neat hand. Once in a while I saw an inkblot, but whoever had recorded these papers was very particular and precise, a good civil servant.

As I read, Annabelle and the world receded, and decisions and petitions made almost a century ago took center stage. I was fascinated by the declarations of dementia and insanity that gave the care of property and money into the hands of another. I read Bills of Divorcement. And I found adoption records.

There was no careful wording of things, no protecting of the participants. All the pertinent facts were spelled out clearly for anyone and everyone to read.

In re Adoption of Jonathan David Brewer.

In re Adoption of Eliza Tansy Duncan

In re Adoption of Lehman Biemsderfer.

I sat stone-still for a minute, one hand on my heart and the other on the page before me. Even though I knew already where Pop had come from, was totally convinced I had met his family for both good and ill, seeing the actual legal document moved me. I blinked the tears away lest any splash onto the page and blur the spiky hand-writing.

June 15, 1918. Petition of John Seward Bentley and Mabel Brooks Bentley his wife of Lancaster City, PA setting forth that they are desirous of adopting as one of their heirs Lehman Biemsderfer, the minor child of Madeleine Biemsderfer of Lancaster City. He was born on November 1, 1918. That the child is now in their home and has been there since February 4, 1919 and was placed there by The Children's Home Society of the City of Lancaster. That they will perform all the duties of parents toward said minor, and that the mother of the said Lehman Biemsderfer has consented to said adoption. Affadavits of said consent attached to the petition.

And now August 20, 1919, upon consideration of the foregoing petition and statement and it appearing to the said court that the welfare of the said minor will be promoted by the said adoption and the Society in whose hands the child was originally placed consents thereto, the prayer of the petitioners is granted and it is ordered and decreed that the said Lehman Biemsderfer shall assume the name of John Seward Bentley, Jr. and herefore shall have all the rights of a child and heir of the said John Seward Bentley and Mabel Brooks Bentley respectively, and he shall be subject to the duties of such a child.

Attest Herman F. Walton, Prothy.

Such cold legalese. Such far reaching ramifications. Such changed lives. *Pop,* I thought, *it's all here. Here's your birth mother's name and your adoptive parents' names and both of your given names. All the ties, all the people who made you what you were, all except Enos. Do you know that I've met several of the family living today? Do you care? You wouldn't like your nephew Amos—you never had much time for unkind people or people full of their own importance. But you'd love your sister, Lizzie. She and Mom would have enjoyed each other so much. And your niece Alma. Very nice too.*

But just as Ward and I never knew Trey and Caroline, you didn't know Madeleine and Lizzie and the others. Life's like that, isn't it? Full of absolutes that we can't change.

I became conscious of Annabelle standing beside me.

"Did you find what you were looking for?" she asked.

I nodded. "My grandfather. He raised me."

She leaned over and scanned the page. "Amazing. Right there for all to see. I'm glad you found it."

"Me too." Massive understatement. "Can you make me some copies?"

"Sure." She picked up the book and carried it to a copy machine at the foot of the stairs. Soon I had five copies in my hand, and Annabelle was carrying the Trust Book back to the locked room where she'd gotten it.

By the time I got back to the farm, I was desperate for someone to talk to about my discovery. I was so delighted to see Jake and Rose that I almost ran from the car to them. Rose sat on the second step of the front porch and Jake was in his chair beside her.

"Look!" I said, thrusting my papers under their noses. "I found it."

Then it dawned on me that they had been having a serious discussion, and I had interrupted.

"I'm sorry," I said, pulling the papers back just as each put a hand out for them. "You were probably discussing Mary."

"We weren't," Jake said. "But I think it's a good time to be interrupted." He gave Rose a look that was half challenge, half tease.

She nodded agreement and looked calmly at me. "So, Cara, what were you trying to show us?"

Grinning, I held out the papers again. "Pop's adoption papers!"

"I thought you already had them," Jake said as he bent for a look.

"I have a set given to my great-grandparents, but these are different. These are the court documents that have everyone's name in them —even Pop's mother. This is the absolute proof that Pop was born to Madeleine Biemsderfer."

"And?" Jake said.

"And now we know where he came from. Now we have family."

"And you didn't before?"

I looked at him, exasperated. "A genetic family. DNA and all that."

"Ignore him, Cara," Rose said with a smile. "He likes to play devil's advocate."

Jake looked at her in surprise. "I do?"

Rose rolled her eyes. "Have you ever listened to yourself? You're the one who challenges everything, including my care of your mother."

"Well, it's just that I've been around hospitals a lot."

"Um. And you're an expert now."

Jake scowled. "I've learned how important it is to ask questions."

Rose scowled back. "Tell me about it." But her mouth quirked up and ruined the scowl. She turned to me. "So what will you do now that you have this information?"

"I can prove to a major skeptic that the relationship is real. That will be a satisfying experience."

"Have the family members you've met been nice?" Rose asked.

"Most have. The skeptic hasn't."

"Is he responsible for the slashed tires and the dead hens?" Jake asked.

I frowned. "I don't know. But I find it hard to believe an adult would do things that are so juvenile."

"So who are the juveniles?" Rose asked.

I stared at her. This was one logical lady. "There's Morgan who looks just like me. And there are two boys, Mick and Pip."

Jake leaned back in his chair, elbows on the arms, hands clasped chest level. "So which one?"

"Mick wasn't very pleasant to me the one time I met him. In fact he was cold and threatening." I thought of his hand on my arm and could almost feel the pressure.

"See?" Jake said. "A suspect already."

Rose stood. "I've got to get going. I have a couple of more stops before my day's finished. But Jake, I still say that you can't claim Jesus was a nice man." And she left.

"You can't say Jesus was a nice man?" I stared after Rose. "Of course He was nice."

Jake gave a huff that was as close to a laugh as he got. "You've come in on the middle of our conversation. Somehow we got talking about what we believe. She believes Jesus is the Savior of the world."

"Me too," I said.

He nodded. "Them too." And he waved toward the house. "But I'm not certain. I said maybe He was just a nice man. Rose says He can't be. Did you know that she's a very opinionated woman?"

"Rose?" I thought of her sweet demeanor and gentle care of Mary.

He snorted. "See? She's fooled you too. She says that if Jesus wasn't God, then He was a maniac or a liar. He made too many claims about Himself to be normal."

I nodded. "I agree."

He scowled, but I refused to let his bad mood affect me. I smiled brightly and watched his scowl deepen in response. "Careful," I muttered. "Your face'll freeze that way."

"Cute," he snarled, but I saw a bit of a smile tug at his mouth.

"Have you always believed differently than your family?" I asked.

"I don't remember a time when I didn't question all the rules and the hairsplitting and the separation from all that's 'worldly.' I decided that if I had to follow the *Ordnung* to be a Christian, then I wouldn't be one."

"Who says you have to follow the *Ordnung* to be a Christian?"

"All my DNA relatives." He looked at me in challenge. "I've known my blood family all my life, Cara, but I've never fit in. I've never really belonged. DNA doesn't guarantee anything. I don't know if Rose is right about Jesus, but I know I'm right about DNA. Don't hold your breath over your new relatives. Blood isn't necessarily thicker than water." He wheeled around and rolled to his apartment. Hawk came running from the field behind the house to join him.

I sat on the steps for several minutes, thinking about Jake and his heritage. I knew he had broken free of the belief system his family held dear, but he hadn't left family. Was that because his disability forced him to stay dependent? Or was it because he loved them in spite of their disagreements? I knew how his mother felt. She loved him dearly even as he broke her heart.

If Jake could leave, would he? Certainly he'd have his own home, but would he break the emotional ties? Somehow I didn't think so. I'd seen the respect he had for his parents and his camaraderie with Elam.

I looked up at the sound of a motor and watched a FedEx truck pull into the drive.

The driver got out and walked toward me.

"Is there a Cara Bentley here?" he asked.

"That's me." I met him halfway up the walk. I loved getting packages. Before technology made it possible to send everything electronically, a large part of my business was transacted through the mail. I got packages containing page proofs or new covers or reviews. I missed the fun of opening something unknown. I looked at the envelope with anticipation as the FedEx guy drove down the road. Maybe this was the new contract?

I rushed to my room and grabbed scissors from the pencil caddy on my desk. I slit the envelope and slid out the contents . . . and felt my heart contract with horror.

Lying on my desk were mutilated pages of *As the Deer.*

Chapter 14

I stared at the carnage in front of me. All the pages of *As the Deer* had been ripped from the binding. Some had been further torn in two, some crumpled into tight balls, some torn into confetti. Some of the tiny pieces floated to the floor, and Rainbow came running, thinking we were going to play a new game. She was quickly disappointed as I could do nothing but stare in shock.

Even the cover had been defaced. The back cover had been cut into tiny pieces the size of my fingernail. The letters on the front cover had been scrawled over with a permanent black marker, obliterating the title. The beautiful forest scene in soft greens and golds had ugly, drooling monsters with lolling tongues, nasty eyes, and spiky horns added to it. And from each letter of my name dripped red drops of blood, forming a large puddle at the bottom of the page. At the edge of the puddle lay two dead chickens.

I don't know how long I stared at the destroyed book. Even if the mailbox hadn't been blown up, my tires slashed, the hens killed, and the note delivered, I'd have felt threatened and incredibly vulnerable by the sheer nastiness of this attack.

The cumulative effect of the hate evidenced in the five occurrences was overwhelming. I didn't know what to do, what to think. The spite made my mouth go dry and my insides clench.

Finally I became aware of coherent thought and realized I had another reason to be convinced that Amos had not done any of these things. The sheer amount of time required to accomplish this literary mutilation as well as the other attacks precluded his involvement. He was a man with things to do and places to go. He didn't have hours to sit around and plot and destroy.

Which left the kids. Angry Mick. Talkative Pip. Lovely Morgan.

With shaking hands I gathered all the pieces into the FedEx envelope. I knew what I had to do. Much as I disliked the idea, I had to go talk with Amos and Jessica. And I had to go this evening. Whoever was committing this petty crime wave had to be stopped before it accelerated into actions that were truly dangerous.

I also wanted the flurry of nastiness to stop for the sake of John and Mary. I disliked intensely having ugliness strike their farm because of me. It wasn't fair. They had enough to deal with due to Mary's fall. They didn't need a vandal with a vendetta against me.

By the time Todd arrived at 5:30, I had calmed down quite a bit. In fact, I felt almost normal, whatever that is. Still I didn't doubt for a moment that my feeling of security was due to his general presence in my life and specific presence here at the farm.

He was truly a gift from God. *Thank You.*

I ran down the stairs with Pop's paper in one hand and the FedEx envelope in the other. I needed to tell Todd about both, but which did I tell him about first?

When I got outside, I stopped abruptly, my eyes drawn to the sky. It had that roiling, boiling look that presaged a monumental storm. To the west the sun was already hidden behind banks of writhing steel gray clouds, and they were moving rapidly in our direction.

Todd looked up too. "Big storm coming." A roll of thunder punctuated his comment. He gave me a quick kiss. "Let's go grab something to eat. I've got to be back at the office by seven. I'm seeing clients all evening."

Disappointed at the brevity of his visit, I decided to hold the slaughtered book until dinner was over. It would undoubtedly be better for our digestion that way. We ate at the Bird-in-Hand Restaurant, and over turkey and filling, I described in great detail my trip to the Archives. Between bites of cranberry sauce, I passed him the copy of Pop's court record, which he read thoroughly.

"And I owe it all to you," I said. "If you hadn't thought of the prothonotary, I wouldn't have said proof that even said Amos can't contest."

He looked up from the document grinning. "They do get a bit carried away by the saids, don't they?"

"*Ad nauseum.* It's a good thing legal documents are so much easier to understand today." I even managed to say it with a straight face.

"Ouch," he said. "It's just that some things are *pro forma.*"

"If scientists accepted that things are just the way they are, there wouldn't be any new discoveries."

"I liked it better when you were grateful for my help."

"Thank you, Todd," I said obediently. "The prothonotary was a brilliant idea."

"Then I can count on your vote for Lawyer of the Year?"

"I'll stuff the ballot box." I ate my shoofly pie with joy. There was something so wonderful about being with this man.

When we left the restaurant, the black clouds had taken up residence overhead, and the wind was whipping like a malevolent fury. It wasn't raining—yet. Gravel, left from cindering the roads in winter, stung as it flew through the air. Gusts buffeted the car as we drove to the farm. When we saw an Amish buggy approaching, horse trotting urgently, I was glad for the sturdiness of our vehicle. A flash of lightning lit the dimness and a crack of thunder sounded as if it were in our backseat. The horse, eyes wide and nostrils flared with fear, shied and tossed his head. The woman driver fought for control, and I was relieved to look back over my shoulder and see her pull into a farm lane.

When we parked in the drive at Zooks', I pulled out the FedEx envelope. "I had another interesting experience today."

"Saving the best for last?"

"Hardly." I held out the envelope. "Someone sent this to me."

He peered inside. "What in the world?"

He dumped the contents in my lap. The pages, half pages, crumpled pages, and confetti looked just as obscene against my tan skirt as they had on my desk.

"Cara! Your book!"

"Someone knows how to stick a knife in a writer's heart without actually committing the crime." I think it was the tremor in my voice that made my attempt at humor miss its mark.

"Oh, honey." He laid his hand against my cheek. "I'm so sorry."

I nodded, his sympathy making tears spring to my eyes.

"You know Amos didn't do this, right?" he said.

"I think it was one of his kids."

"Probably. But which one and how do we prove it?"

"I don't really care which one." And I didn't at this point. I just wanted it all to stop. "I thought I'd go to The Paddock this evening and talk to Amos. I've got my indisputable proof of relationship." I patted my purse which held Pop's records. "And I've got the threatening note and what's left of my book." I began slipping the wreckage back in the envelope.

Todd put his hand over mine. "Don't go over there tonight."

"I want to. I want this settled."

"But I can't go with you. I've got clients coming."

"I know and I feel badly about that. I'd like you with me." I pulled my hand free and returned to putting *As the Deer* in the envelope. "But I've managed on my own for thirty years. I guess I can manage for one more night." I was able to sound confident in spite of my thudding heart. I gave him what I hoped was a convincing smile.

"Don't go, Cara." He leaned toward me, his face intent. "Amos isn't the nicest person in the best of times. Tonight he'll be even more unhappy than usual when he sees your papers."

I gave him a weak smile. "He'd probably be unhappier if you were along."

He blinked.

"You're a threat to him," I explained. "You're an up-and-coming lawyer whom judges congratulate on your work. People respect and like you. I saw that the other night. You're also honest and extremely capable. In other words, you're a threat."

He didn't look convinced, but I was. Amos didn't like competition, and Todd was competition whether he meant to be or not.

"Amos and I faced off in court today," he said. "The judge ruled in my client's favor. Amos isn't used to losing. I think it'd be better if you stayed away from him tonight."

I thought for a moment. He had a point, but I needed to get this thing resolved, to return the farm to its normal peace and myself to my customary unexciting life. "I don't think there's any good time as far as he and I are concerned, so I might as well get it over with as soon as possible." I dropped the last of the confetti in the packet.

"Cara." There was an edge to Todd's voice. "Don't go tonight."

I was touched by his concern. "Don't worry. I'll be fine." I looked up from the packet and saw his face. "Come on. It's not that bad."

"I don't want you to go to Amos's house."

Whether he meant it to or not, his words sounded like an order to me, and in true Bentley fashion, my hackles rose. Still, I forced myself to speak evenly. "Todd, it's my choice to make."

"Not this time," he said slowly and distinctly. "I'm telling you: Don't go."

I felt my jaw tense and my eyes turn flinty. "You can't stand it if someone differs with you, can you?" If my icy tone were any measure of temperature, the coming rain would be snow, June or not.

"And you can't stand to take advice from anyone, can you?" His anger was hot enough to melt the polar ice cap.

I reached for the door handle. "It's 6:50. You're going to be late for your clients."

"Cara!" He grabbed my arm. "Don't. Go. To. Yosts'."

I pulled my arm free. "What gives you the right to tell me what I can or can't do?"

"If you don't know," he said, his voice low and hard, "then I can't explain it to you."

I slid out and slammed the door. He threw the car in reverse. I stalked to my car, and he stormed out of the drive. I jammed my key into the ignition, and he roared down the road. I stared out my windshield and wondered what had just happened.

The Paddock looked as lovely under this evening's threatening skies as it had the beautiful evening Todd and I were there. The tables were gone, the dance floor disassembled, the fairy lights extinguished, but the beauty of the graceful estate was undiminished.

Only I was different. I was alone and remorseful instead of with Todd and full of dreams. I sighed for the millionth time. Gone was my anger; regret filled me instead.

Dear Father, can two highly opinionated people with sinfully strong wills make it? Please tell me they can. I'll even work at becoming a woman of a quiet and gentle spirit. I will! I promise.

I parked outside the garage and walked slowly to the front door. The air was now still and heavy, the quiet before the storm. I shivered in spite of the heat.

Todd was right. I shouldn't have come here alone. Another person would be a witness to what was said, if nothing else. That he might also be comfort, strength, encouragement, support—the list went on—only made me feel more alone.

As I stood hesitantly on the front porch, lightning flashed, and immediately a great crack of thunder ripped the night. I jumped.

I didn't need to talk to Amos tonight, I decided suddenly. I'd face him another time. Solving the crimes didn't have the immediacy I'd thought. No one was in danger beyond the petty war of nerves being conducted, and certainly I was woman enough to stand up to that. I turned to leave.

Before I took a step, the skies opened, releasing a wall of water so dense the air was a river. I wondered there was room left for the necessary oxygen to breathe.

My choices were reduced to facing Amos or drowning. Wondering if this was my don't-go-into-the-basement-in-the-dead-of-night-stupid-woman moment, I took my first step and rang the doorbell.

Pip answered. "Hey, look who's here! Come on in."

Well, at least one person was glad to see me.

Pip ushered me into the front hall. He grinned at me and then leaned his head back and bellowed, "Mom, Dad, company!"

He lowered his voice to a whisper. "I won't tell them who's here. They might not come if they knew." His eyes twinkled and he rocked back and forth on his toes, delighted with himself.

I couldn't help grinning back at him. There was something irresistible and delightful about him. I marveled he'd kept his sense of fun living with Mick and his father.

Pip wasn't as bulky as his father or Mick, and his lean good looks were the kind that appealed to me. He had a wonderful smile, and his brown eyes were guileless and full of wonder, even with the dark circles beneath them.

Heavy footsteps sounded in the hall and Mick appeared. He took one look at me, and his handsome face soured. "Oh, it's you."

"Pleased to see you too, Mick," I said.

"Guess what?" Pip was undeterred by his

brother's ill humor. "Morgan bought one of your books."

"Great! Which one, do you know?"

"There's more than one?" He seemed surprised.

"Several more." I smiled at him. "I'm a writer, remember? To make a living at the profession, you have to keep on producing."

More footsteps sounded in the hall, light and quick, and Jessica and Morgan appeared. Jessica froze when she saw me, but Morgan rushed forward.

"I bought one of your books," she said. "*As the Deer*. If I'm going to be a writer, I thought I should read what a successful author is writing."

As the Deer. I shivered.

"The weird thing is," she continued, "I can't find it anywhere. When I do, will you autograph it? To my favorite cousin or something?"

"Sure. I'd be glad to." But I was afraid the book was right here in the FedEx pouch in my hand. I studied her, trying to determine if she was being clever or just being honest. I couldn't tell.

"Mom!" Pip bounced around the hall with an energy that made me feel weary. "We haven't been very polite to Cara. We need to invite her into the living room."

Jessica looked trapped by Pip's suggestion. "Of course," she said without enthusiasm.

"Please, Cara. Have a seat." She led the way and gestured to a wing chair.

I looked around the living room. At least I wasn't trapped in another paean of praise to Penn State. The greens, blues, and creams were lovely, though the room had the look of a showplace rather than a lived-in space. Jessica and the children sat stiffly, clearly unused to the room.

"So what have you been doing since you were here Saturday?" Pip asked, all excitement. "Anything interesting, especially on the are-we-related scene?"

"When your dad gets here, I'll tell all of you at the same time." I smiled at him so the answer didn't seem too brusque.

He nodded and jumped to his feet. "I'll go get Dad." And he dashed from the room.

I turned to Jessica. "He must wear you out with all his energy."

She offered a courtesy smile, but said nothing. I became aware that Mick was watching her closely. When he felt my eyes on him, he looked at me in anger.

An awkward silence fell over the room, and it was a relief to finally hear two people approaching, even if one of them was Amos.

When he walked into the room and saw me, he froze. It was obvious that Pip hadn't told him I was his guest. Pip giggled at his father's expression.

355

Jessica, Mick, and Morgan all watched Amos nervously. Pip watched me.

Amos finally found his voice. "When I told you to stay away from my mother, I never imagined I'd have to tell you to stay away from us as well."

I tried not to cringe under the lash of his words.

"Dad." Pip laid his hand on Amos's arm. "She's a guest here. We need to be polite." He turned to Jessica. "Right, Mom?"

Jessica opened her mouth, but no sound came out.

"Be quiet, Pip," Amos ordered. "She is not a guest, and I will not be polite."

Praying like crazy, I stood up so I could face Amos on more equal footing. "I won't stay long. I just have three things to give you."

Amos didn't ask what they were, but he didn't walk out of the room either.

"The first is a copy of a legal document I found in the Archives at the courthouse today." I held out a copy of Pop's adoption decree.

Amos made no move to take it, but Pip grabbed it eagerly. He looked it over quickly and said, "She's a Biemsderfer, Dad. It says here that Great-Grandmother Madeleine had a baby boy who was adopted. See?" He held the paper to his father. "Here's Madeleine's name. And here's Cara's grandfather's name."

Amos shut his eyes for a moment, distress and

distrust warring in his expression. He took a deep breath as if to steel himself and reached for the paper. He read it quickly and swore.

"I just wanted you to know that there is proof that my pop was Madeleine and Enos's son," I said.

"How did you know to look in the Archives?" Pip asked, his eyes bright with curiosity. "Dad said adoption records were sealed."

"My lawyer suggested it." I didn't mention Todd's name on purpose. If Amos was upset about the outcome of today's hearing, there was no sense mentioning the man who had bested him, making things worse than they already were.

"Is that Todd Reasoner?" Pip asked innocently. "The guy you were with the other night?"

I nodded while Amos glowered.

"Boy, that was a great idea." Pip nodded as if impressed.

"There will be no money for you." The chill in Amos's voice was enough to make me shiver.

"I don't want any money!" I was appalled.

Amos snorted. "I have power of attorney. I will never let Mother change her will."

"Nor should you," I agreed. "I don't—" I stopped, realizing I could protest all night and he'd never believe me. I scanned the room and saw the others didn't accept my protestations either.

I sighed and reached into my purse. I pulled out the threatening letter and handed it to Amos. "This came in the mail this morning."

He scanned it and went white.

"What's it say, Dad?" Pip wanted to know. The others looked like they were afraid to know.

Amos cleared his throat and read, "You were told not to visit her. You were warned. Now you will suffer. Like the chickens."

"Like the chickens?" Mick asked in a tight voice. "What does that mean?"

"Someone slit the throats of two hens on the farm where I live. They were lying on the front porch this morning."

Pip stared at me, eyes wide. "Someone killed them?"

I nodded. "There's more."

Mick flinched and I thought he was beginning to look scared. But then so was Jessica.

"The mailbox at the farm was blown up last Thursday, and all four tires on my car were slashed Saturday night. I can't prove those incidents are tied to the dead hens, but common sense says the vandalism is connected. And there's this." I upended the FedEx envelope onto the green, blue, and cream Turkish carpet.

The five Yosts watched transfixed as the single pages floated, the crumpled pages tumbled, and the confetti showered until it all rested at my feet.

Morgan was out of her chair and on her knees in the debris in an instant. "Is that my missing book? Is it?" She sounded slightly panicked as she raised fearful eyes to her mother.

Jessica sat white and drawn, hand at her throat. It occurred to me that I'd never considered her as the perpetrator. I thought of all the mystery novels I'd read where it was always the least expected character who was the bad guy.

Just as quickly I thought of M-80's, ruined tires, and slit throats. I looked at the well-manicured hand resting against her neck and knew it wasn't Jessica, who began to cry, silent tears running unchecked down her face.

I studied Mick, my prime suspect, the son who was a problem. He staggered to his feet, took a half step, and then collapsed into his chair again. He put his face in his hands and groaned. Because he was about to be found out?

Amos was scarlet with rage, the threatening note crumpled in his fist.

The only one unmoved was Pip. He grinned and bounced some more.

Amos turned his fury full on me. "How dare you disrupt my family like this? How dare you distress my wife? How dare you!"

I stared at him in disbelief. I didn't expect him to like anything I said, but I didn't expect denial and transference either.

"Amos." Jessica rose timidly from her chair.

She sniffed and dashed a hand at her tears. "You know it's not her fau—"

Amos cut her off. "Get out!" He pointed to me and to the door. Then he turned to his wife. "And you, Jessica, sit down and be quiet." She sat.

With trembling legs I walked across the room. I turned in the doorway. "No more." I gestured to the carnage on the floor. "Or I will tell the police."

"Out!" Amos roared.

I looked at the room full of people who were my blood relatives but far from me in heart. Mick stared at the floor, agony in every line of his face. Morgan, still kneeling among the mutilated pages, watched her parents in uncertainty and fear. Jessica sat in her chair, hopeless and defeated. Amos was rigid with anger and insult. Pip looked from one to the other, excited and strangely happy at the chaos, ready to pop out of his skin.

And suddenly something clicked.

There was more than one way to be a troubled son.

Sorrow filled me as I turned into the front hall. These people were being torn apart by something they couldn't or wouldn't control.

I was reaching for the doorknob when Mick rushed into the hall.

"I'm sorry," he blurted. "I never meant—"

I didn't know what to say in the face of his obvious pain.

He looked at me out of weary eyes. "I never should have—I didn't think—I didn't mean—" His shoulders slumped. "I'm sorry."

"Mick, it's not your fault."

"Yes, it is. I tried to stay awake and watch him, but I fell asleep." He said it as if sleeping were the equivalent of loading the gun for a killer.

"You have to sleep."

"Don't be nice. Please, don't be nice. I should have seen. I should have stopped it."

"You can't see everything or stop everything. It's not your responsibility. And it's too great a burden to put on yourself."

He shook his head. "He's my brother. He is my responsibility. It's for certain no one else around here is looking out for him."

I thought of Ward, imperious, single-minded, kind and loving, as wonderful a brother as I could possibly want. What if he were a Pip? My heart broke for Mick, his hurt, and his noble intentions. A good kid, this one. I felt bad that I had ever suspected him.

"I do have a question," I said. "Since you didn't meet me until Saturday evening, perhaps Pip didn't have anything to do with the mailbox?"

Mick sighed. "He did. He told me about it the next day. That's when I knew I had to watch

361

him every minute. But I fell asleep." He studied the floor. "I'm sorry."

Pip came flying into the hall in time to hear those last words. He punched Mick on the shoulder. "Don't apologize to her! Why should you apologize? She should apologize to us!"

For what? For Pop being born more than ninety years ago?

"How did you know about me before we met, Pip?" I asked.

He grew cagey, his expression sly. "I heard Dad and Aunt Alma talking."

"She came here and told about me?" I was surprised and a bit hurt that she rushed right to the relative she knew would dislike me.

Pip snorted. "Aunt Alma doesn't come here if she can help it. Not that I blame her. I wouldn't come here if I didn't have to either. I listened in on the extension." His smile was full of congratulatory pride, like eavesdropping was something he'd invented.

"How long has he been sick?" I asked Mick while nodding toward Pip.

Pip's perpetual smile and constant movement made so much sense now, as did the dark circles under his eyes. I wondered when his mania had last let him sleep.

"It's been showing about three or four years, and it's getting worse."

"Who's sick?" Pip's voice became strident.

"I'm not sick! *She's* sick! Barging in here and claiming to be family so she can take Dad's money. Well, she can't have it! It's ours!"

"No meds?" I asked Mick.

He shook his head, looking haunted. "I thought when the school authorities got involved, they'd listen." He shrugged. "But Dad's in denial. It would be a blot on the family. No Yost is allowed anything worse than strep throat."

"So you've tried to take care of Pip in lieu of lithium or whatever new pharmaceutical they have now?"

Mick shrugged. "Someone has to."

"No one has to take care of me! There's nothing wrong with me! Dad says!" Gone completely was the charming young man who had welcomed me and conned his family into talking to me. "I'm not bi-polar! I'm not manic-depressive! Do you see a depressed person here? I'm healthier than all the rest of you put together!"

Amos came into the hallway. He hesitated when he heard his younger son ranting, but he turned on me. "Are you still here? I thought I told you to leave."

"You tell her, Dad!" Pip punched Amos in the shoulder hard enough to make him stagger.

"Come on, Pip." Mick threw his arm around his brother. "Let's go back to the living room. Mom's waiting."

"Like I care." But he let Mick lead him away. At the last moment, he looked back at me and grinned. "'Bye, Cousin Cara. So glad you came to visit."

"'Bye, Pip." My eyes teared.

A loud knock sounded just as I turned the doorknob. I opened the door to find a tall, unhappy man with a dripping umbrella furled in his hand.

I ran straight into his arms. "You came!"

"I had to." He rested his cheek against my head.

"Reasoner. Just what I need." Amos slammed the front door in our faces.

We stood on the porch watching the deluge.

"What about your clients?" I asked.

"I finished with one early and left before the other arrived. Mrs. Smiley will just have to keep them happy until I get back."

"Poor Mrs. Smiley."

"Poor clients," Todd said.

I tried to smile, and suddenly the emotions of the night caught up with me. I started to shake. Todd's arms tightened about me, and I hung on for dear life.

"All I wanted was a body-and-bone family," I blubbered into his chest.

"A reasonable thing to want, and a reasonable thing to grieve over when it doesn't work out."

I leaned back and looked up at him. His curls

were a mass of ringlets in the damp. "No wonder you whopped Amos in court today. You know the right things to say."

He smiled wryly and pulled me back against him. "Sometimes."

"You were right when you told me I shouldn't come here alone. I should have listened."

"Yeah, well, I shouldn't have tried to make you do what I wanted, right or not. You're a smart woman. You can make your own decisions."

Two sinfully strong-willed people apologizing? I felt buoyed by hope.

He released me and grabbed my hand. "Come on. I've got clients waiting."

We huddled under his umbrella and ran for our cars. I followed him to his office, and we were both more than a little damp by the time we dashed inside. Mrs. Smiley sniffed disapprovingly at us.

"The Turleys got tired of waiting," she announced with satisfaction.

Todd nodded, unperturbed. "Buzz when the Weisses get here."

He dropped the umbrella in a ceramic stand and guided me into his *sanctum sanctorum*, his hand solicitously resting at the small of my back. He put me in the leather chair opposite his desk as he automatically took his seat behind. He eyed me with concern.

"Are you all right?" he asked.

365

"Sure," I said. "Maybe. Someday. Never."

Amos's hostility and Pip's cruelty slapped me again. Even though I understood that egoism and illness were behind their actions, I felt emotionally bruised.

"I'm too used to people being nice to me." My chin wobbled. "Mom was always so kind, and Pop hugged us all the time. And Ward protected me. Everyone said I love you and meant it. I lived in a warm and wonderful cocoon, and I didn't realize how blessed I was." I clenched my hands in my lap and stared at my fists. "I miss it all so much." I would not cry. I would not. I'd already cried too much. Besides I looked terrible when I cried. I got a red nose and dark circles under my eyes. I swallowed and straightened my shoulders, but it didn't help much . . . or at least not enough.

I dropped my head to my hands and sobbed. "I'm s–s–sorry," I managed and cried harder.

Suddenly Todd was on his knees in front of me, his warm hands covering my cold ones.

"Cara, sweetheart, don't cry." He reached out and pushed my hair back over my shoulder. "They don't matter. You know that. The Yosts don't matter."

I nodded. "I kn–n–ow that here," and lifted my hand to my head. "But—" A fresh season of tears took me. Somehow I managed to get out all that had happened at the Yosts' house.

Todd spread his arms for me, and, desperate, I fell into them. Somehow, as we met, we lost our balance and ended up on the floor in an unexpected but most satisfying attorney–client huddle. We shifted, and soon he sat cross-legged with his back against his desk, and I sat sideways in the well between his knees. His arms were wrapped about me, and he held me and stroked my hair and whispered soothing noises to me as I sobbed against his starched shirt front and silk tie. He didn't even try to move his tie out of harm's way. I had never felt safer in my life.

Eventually my storm of tears wore itself out, and I rested, spent, my head cradled on his shoulder. That's when I realized my arms were clutching him, one across his chest, the other his back. I prepared to force myself to release my death grip, but since I couldn't figure out where else to put my arms and in truth didn't want to put them anywhere else, I left them right where they were.

I felt Todd lower his head. "Feeling better?" he said to my cheek, and I felt the softest of kisses.

I nodded against his shoulder. For a bony surface, it cushioned me with amazing comfort. I gave a great sniff.

He jumped and I realized I had sniffed right in his ear. I sighed. My heroines would never have done such a gauche thing. I needed to take lessons from them.

"Let me get my handkerchief," Todd said and leaned in my direction as he reached into his back pocket.

The physics of our new position was too much for gravity's pull, and we lost our balance. I ended up on my back on the floor and he ended up leaning over me, his weight held on one elbow-stiffened arm. I couldn't tear my eyes from his face.

"Sweetheart," he said in a gruff voice, "don't look at me like that."

I blinked and nodded. I had no idea how I was looking at him, but if my emotions were as obvious on my face as his were, we were in dangerous territory.

Then I couldn't help it. I sniffed. Again. And again.

He grinned and shook his head. "And you're a romance writer."

He took the handkerchief he'd finally retrieved and wiped my eyes. He handed it to me.

I stared at it. "It's ironed. How can I dirty your ironed handkerchief?"

"The cleaners did it once, they can do it again."

"That's a good thing," I said. "I don't do hand-kerchiefs."

With barely a blink or a missed beat, Todd

spoke. "Then we'll have to keep sending them to the cleaners, won't we?"

Nodding, I took the handkerchief and blew my nose, not an easy thing to do on your back.

He reached out his free hand to trace my eyebrows, my nose, my lips. "You are beautiful, absolutely beautiful."

I closed my eyes at his feather touch, knowing nothing I'd ever written came close to the sensation of someone you loved loving you back. I ached all over with the sweetness of it.

Vaguely I heard a buzzer somewhere in the real world, and then a quick knock and an opening of a door. Mrs. Smiley gasped and my eyes flew open.

"I—I knocked," she sputtered.

"I know." Todd didn't move. His fingers were on my mouth. I wanted to nibble them.

Mrs. Smiley swallowed. "Your next client is here."

Todd nodded. "Give me five minutes."

The door closed.

I couldn't help but laugh. "She'll never respect you again." I took his hand and pressed it against my cheek. "Your image is forever tarnished."

"At least I'm not lying on the floor like some people I know." He took both my hands and pulled me back into the circle of his knees. Our faces were so close I couldn't focus. His hand

369

gripped the back of my neck, his thumb caressed my cheek.

"Cara, my beautiful Cara, what are you doing to me? I used to be so organized, so predictable. Now I don't know anything except I'm crazy about you." And he kissed me. That's when I knew that the heart-stopping, toe-curling kiss on his father's porch had been no aberration.

I drew back first, though reluctantly. My nose was still stopped up from crying, and I desperately needed to breathe. While I gasped, Todd kissed away any remaining traces of my tears.

"I'd better go," I said. "Clients."

He nodded, and we picked ourselves up. Arms around each other's waists, we walked toward the door. We saw ourselves in the mirror on the side wall at the same time and gasped.

I had great dark circles from crying, my nose was still red, and my hair flew about my face as if I'd just stuck my finger in an outlet.

"You need glasses," I blurted.

"What?" He ran his hand madly over his curls, seeking order.

"You told me I was beautiful. Attorneys aren't supposed to lie."

His hands dropped from his hair to rest on my shoulders.

"Cara, tonight when you went off to Amos's alone and I was trapped here with clients, I regretted what I'd said so much. Especially how

I'd left you. I knew I had to get there to be with you, to stand by you. My heart broke for you. And I knew I loved you."

He slid his hand beneath my hair, grasping my neck. "I knew I loved your courage, your passion for things that matter to you, even your philosophical discussion of body-and-bone versus heart. I knew I'd love you forever."

I started to cry again.

"Sweetheart?" he asked, concern in his voice.

"Good crying," I said quickly. "Good crying."

He looked at me like I was crazy but he nodded.

"I love you too," I told him. "You are the only sure thing in my life apart from the Lord. And Ward and Marnie and Johnny, but that's way different." I waved them away, my hand almost clipping Todd's strong jaw.

He smiled as he ducked, his brown eyes warm, pleased.

"You are the one who has been here for me, Todd. The one who helped me when everyone else, including my brother, thought I should let well enough alone. You stood by me. You are my rock."

He appeared to like that analogy. I smiled. "And I love you. Always. Forever."

Epilogue

Two years later

I lay in my hospital bed, bruised and broken, but happier than I'd ever been in my life. I looked down at Madeleine Elizabeth Reasoner held snug against my breast. A little knitted cap covered her newborn head, and her red, wrinkled face was beautiful.

Bone of my bone, born of my body, child of my heart . . . our hearts.

I rested against her father, who sat on the bed beside me, my back against his strong side and my head against his shoulder. One of his hands lay gently on my shoulder and the other cupped our baby's head. His look of utter infatuation as he stared at his daughter made me smile.

The last twelve hours had been terrible for him as he watched my pain and couldn't relieve it. His eyes were shadowed by purple and his strong jaw sported dark stubble, but he'd been here the whole time, as he'd always been here for me.

We had married the fall after we met and settled happily if sometimes argumentatively into Todd's house. He continued as a sole practitioner in his office in Bird-in-Hand, supervised by Mrs. Smiley, who forgave him his one evening of unprofessional behavior. I continued writing, and when I felt I had the energy, I was scheduled to begin the third volume in my first trilogy.

While Amos continued to be hostile to us and Jessica followed his lead, Mick and Morgan came to see us periodically. Pip never did. He still fought his medication, and the resulting emotional chaos continued to wrack the family, though he never bothered me again in any way.

From my hospital bed, I looked across the room to the two people who sat in the visitors' chairs. Dad Reasoner and Aunt Lizzie reminded me of the little wobbly headed dolls that people sometimes put in their cars, smiling, smiling, smiling their delight as their heads nodded slightly on their ancient necks. Their pleasure in Madeleine was a joy to me.

"She looks like the Reasoners," Dad said. "Just like Catherine."

"Pshaw," Aunt Lizzie said. "She's all Biemsderfer."

"You always have to disagree with me, don't you, Liz?"

"Only because you always think you're right."

I looked at my husband and smiled. "Do they remind you of anyone?"

Todd grinned as a nurse walked in with a

huge bouquet. Todd reached among the roses, lilies, and iris for the card and passed it to me.

"With all our love, Marnie, Ward, Johnny, and Tess. We'll save all Tess's clothes for Madeleine."

"I can see that having a cousin a year older than Maddy will be a great benefit," I said. I ran a finger gently down Maddy's small cheek. My baby. I started to cry.

Todd leaned over and kissed me.

"I love you, Cara," he whispered. "Heart of my heart."

I fell asleep smiling.

Discussion Questions

1. Is it reasonable that Cara's world is so shaken by her discovery of Pop's adoption? Why or why not? Why do you think some adopted people search for their birth families while others seem content with things as they are?

Why didn't she look for mother's kin?

2. Ward is concerned that a man will take an interest in Cara because of the family money. Does money make a difference in the way people view each other? What does James 2:1-4 say on this subject?

3. Amos Yost gives Cara a very hard time. He is very unlikeable. Do you have someone like that in your family? How do you deal with him or her? How would the Lord want you to handle him or her? Read Ephesians 4:32. What does this mean to you?

4. Alma Stoltzfus is the opposite of Amos. Do you have any Almas in your family? In what ways are you an Alma to those you love?

5. Pip has several behavioral issues. Do you think they are the result of his health or his

family's failure to deal with his issues? Why do you think a God of love allows illnesses like Pip's?

6. When Madeleine gave birth to Pop, unwed pregnancy was cause for great shame. Have circumstances changed? How would you counsel a young woman in this situation today? Is adoption still a viable alternative? Can you think of biblical examples of adoption? What is the great comfort of 1 John 1:9 in situations like this?

7. Cara's family was warm and loving. Todd's was loving but certainly not demonstrative or vocal. What was your growing-up experience? What do you see as possible issues in a marriage between people with such opposite experiences?

8. When Mary runs out of medicine on Sunday, Jake goes for it so Esther won't break the *Ordnung*. Esther uses roller blades, a modern device made with petrochemicals. How do you view these seeming contradictions in the rules that govern Amish living?

9. Cara tells Todd he will know her better if he reads her books. Do you think most authors reveal themselves in their writing? If yes,

give some examples from books you've read. What did you learn about Gayle Roper?

10. Read Galatians 4:4-7. How does this passage speak of adoption? Of *your* adoption?

A Note to Readers

Dear Reader,

I am the daughter of an adopted person and the mother of two adopted sons. Obviously the topic of adoption is one that has long interested me. The discussion in *A Secret Identity* about what makes family—bone and blood, DNA and genes, or affection, acceptance, and heart—are ideas I've long considered.

But beyond these issues, *A Secret Identity* is special to me because it is based on my mother's adoption papers. The document that tilts Cara's world—her pop's adoption certificate—is word-for-word my mother's adoption certificate with the exceptions of changing her name to his and Philadelphia County to Lancaster County. Like Pop, my mother cost six dollars. Like Madeleine requesting a picture of Pop, my birth-grandmother requested a picture of my mother.

Unlike in the book, I don't know whether my grandmother ever sent a picture to my birth-grandmother. I never saw the letter making the request until my mother died. By then it was years too late to ask about the requested picture. I certainly hope Grandmom sent it.

We have never tried to search for Mom's family. Like Pop, she never felt the need to find them. She was content to be part of the family she was raised in, accepting heart and affection as sufficient. I've never felt the need to search either. Sometimes when people tell me I remind them of someone they know, I wonder if it's someone I'm related to, someone I've not met, someone who may not even know there's a half-branch of the family out there. I do, after all, live in the same general geographic area in which my mother was born and raised.

My sons have looked for their birth mothers. We always told the boys we would support this action when they were old enough to handle the emotional ramifications, whatever they might be. We also always refused to put ourselves in competition for the boys' affection with these women for whom I have a great deal of respect. They did not, after all, have to carry my sons to term, yet they were brave enough to do so.

One son has met his birth family—mother, father, half-sister, half-brother, stepbrother. His birthday dinners are very interesting with all of us there and proof that love is an emotion that expands as needed. Our other son has not met his mother at her request. I feel sorry for her because she's missing out on a wonderful man, daughter-in-law, and two great grandchildren. Maybe someday. I hope so for all of them.

Every time I hear people denigrate adoption as an imperfect situation (which it is, but then birth kids can be a handful too), I feel genuine sorrow. I think not only of Mom and my sons, but also of the high view God has of adoption. I think of my position as an adopted child of the King. Where would I be without my Father? Where would I be if He weren't willing to take in a foundling and make her a daughter? It's heart, after all, that makes the difference. The heart of God that loved me enough to accept me—and you—into the Beloved.

About the Author

Gayle Roper is an award-winning author of more than 40 books and has been a Christy Award finalist three times. She enjoys speaking at women's events across the nation and loves sharing the powerful truths of Scripture with humor and practicality. She lives with her husband in southeastern Pennsylvania and enjoys reading, gardening, her family, and eating out as often as she can talk Chuck into it.

Center Point Publishing
600 Brooks Road • PO Box 1
Thorndike ME 04986-0001 USA

(207) 568-3717

**US & Canada:
1 800 929-9108**
www.centerpointlargeprint.com